STOP COCK

JL MERROW

Riptide Publishing
PO Box 1537
Burnsville, NC 28714
www.riptidepublishing.com

This is a work of fiction. Names, characters, places, and incidents are either the product of the author's imagination or are used fictitiously. Any resemblance to actual persons living or dead, business establishments, events, or locales is entirely coincidental. All person(s) depicted on the cover are model(s) used for illustrative purposes only.

Stop Cock
Copyright © 2021 by JL Merrow

Cover art: Christine Coffee
Editor: Carole-ann Galloway
Layout: L.C. Chase, lcchase.com

All rights reserved. No part of this book may be reproduced or transmitted in any form or by any means, electronic or mechanical, including photocopying, recording, or by any information storage and retrieval system without the written permission of the publisher, and where permitted by law. Reviewers may quote brief passages in a review. To request permission and all other inquiries, contact Riptide Publishing at the mailing address above, at Riptidepublishing.com, or at marketing@riptidepublishing.com.

ISBN: 978-1-62649-949-2

First edition
June, 2021

Also available in ebook:
ISBN: 978-1-62649-950-8

STOP COCK

JL MERROW

To the European Union. I miss you.

Lovers, like bees, live a honeyed life — ancient Roman graffiti found on the walls of Casa degli Amanti, Pompeii

I wish! — added by a second writer, directly below the above

TABLE OF CONTENTS

Prologue

It was what you might call a surprise honeymoon.

The first surprise was when I found out my then-fiancé Phil had booked it without consulting me. Which, yeah, initially I was a bit miffed about, but I was later convinced to view it as a romantic gesture. He can be pretty persuasive, my Phil. In the right circumstances.

The second surprise was turning up to find out a deeply loathed figure from mine and Phil's mutual past had got there before us.

The third surprise was the dead body. Although to be honest, given the events of the last few years, running into a corpse on our honeymoon wasn't *that* much of a shock.

It was late in the evening, and I was feeling pleasantly fuzzy from the drinks we'd had after dinner. Not so fuzzy, mind, that I wasn't eager to get to bed with my lawfully wedded husband.

We were leaning on the balcony of our hotel room, watching fireworks over the Bay of Naples and looking forward to setting off some fireworks of our own, when the darkness was pierced by a scream. There was a weird Doppler effect as a blurred form plummeted past only inches from our noses, then the cry cut off with a dull thud.

Me and Phil leaned over the railing, staring in horror at the crumpled form lying on the road, far too many feet below us. Had some poor sod taken a tumble from the hotel roof?

Wait a minute. The light wasn't great, but didn't I recognise that figure, and those clothes? "Hang on, isn't that . . ."

"Yeah. It is," Phil agreed, his tone grim.

I gripped his hand. "Could still be alive—"

A lorry appeared from nowhere, its sides gaily painted with giant lemons, and thundered over the body.

I swallowed. "Okay. Probably not anymore."

Chapter One

Naples was a little on the warm side. By which I mean, blisteringly, arse-roastingly hot. You could have used the pavement to fry your eggs on, not to mention any mad dogs and Englishmen who happened along. Like, for example, yours truly and his newly wedded husband. I couldn't see a handy thermometer on any nearby buildings as we trundled our cases out of the airport, but forty Celsius probably wasn't far off—that's over a hundred in old money.

Rubbing the sweat off my brow, I turned back to Phil. He was looking annoyingly fresh, crisp, and tasty . . . Okay, so the annoyance might have turned into lust somewhere along the route. I sent him an appreciative smile that hopefully didn't come off too soppy. "When they said see Naples and die, they meant from heatstroke, didn't they?"

Phil huffed a laugh. "I thought you liked the sun?"

"I like it better when I'm not hauling heavy weights around." My case was starting to veer off in the wrong direction, so I yanked it to heel.

"Call that a heavy weight? It's half the size of mine."

I gave him a look. "It's not the size. It's how good you are at packing. So to speak."

"Don't worry. I've got no complaints in that department." He sent me a friendly leer, then had to dodge sharpish as a little old lady zoomed past without warning, pulling along a case that was bigger than mine and Phil's combined.

"Think she's got a motor installed on that thing?" Phil muttered.

I grinned. "Either that, or she's heard her hotel's handing out welcome drinks and it's first come, first served."

The coach, when we finally clambered on board, was air-conditioned, which was a blessed relief. "Bagsy the window seat. If you nab it, all I'll see is your big mug."

Phil laughed. "Bagsy? What are you, five? And anyway, I thought you liked my mug. You married it, remember."

I could feel a slushy smile forming on my own face, so I pushed past him before he could notice. And let me tell you, that wasn't easy in the narrow aisle. My beloved husband is the sort of bloke who tends to fill all available space, mostly with his shoulders.

Occasionally with his pig-headedness.

I claimed my seat and settled down to goggle out of the window. The sky was that vivid blue you see in travel brochure photos and always assume they must have used a filter to get. Tiny wisps of cloud floated aimlessly here and there with nothing to do but provide a touch of contrast.

There was the usual hanging about while sundry holiday-makers slogged their way over to the coach, popped their heads in to check it was the right one, and milled around outside until the driver slung their luggage in the hold. The schools back home hadn't broken up yet for the summer, so pretty much everyone on board was old enough to see an X-rated movie. I figured I could grab Phil's hand without anyone getting their knickers in a twist about us corrupting innocent young minds.

He gave a surprised huff and squeezed back, those baby blues of his suspiciously moist. "Didn't think PDAs were your thing."

"Hey, we're on honeymoon." Plus, I didn't reckon we were in any danger of icy stares and/or hostile comments from our fellow travellers. Most of them still had the glazed eyes and haunted expressions of the modern airline passenger. Not to mention, there were only half a dozen or so who could see us from where they were sitting.

A last couple hurried on board—a man and a woman in their midtwenties, good-looking in an expensively groomed way. They'd clearly been together for longer than us, if the constant sniping back and forth was any guide. After a brief but bitter squabble over who got the window seat, they sat down, and the coach gave a jolt and headed off.

We moved swiftly through the back streets of Naples, which were about as scenic as back streets usually are. My mind wandered until I realised I was humming that sixties song about the girl with the cleverly designed topless swimsuit and hurriedly cleared my throat. "Think that's Vesuvius?" I gestured at a mountain out the back of the city. "Is it supposed to be there?"

"I don't think it's been going walkabout," Phil said with the suspicion of a smirk.

I gave him an affectionate dig in the ribs. "Oi, no making fun of me. I never got on with geography in school."

"You did all right as I remember."

"Seriously? You remember how well *I* did at a subject I last took at age sixteen?" It wasn't like I'd been top of the class or anything. I think.

"I always noticed you."

I chanced a glance at Phil. He'd gone all sombre, which, fair dues, the subject of our mutual schooldays wasn't a happy one for either of us. So I didn't say, *Busy thinking of ways you and your mates could duff me in after class, were you?* Instead, I grabbed his hand again, squeezed it tight, and said lightly, "Well, that's where you went wrong, innit? If you'd paid more attention to Mr. Whatshisface instead of mooning over me, you'd have got As across the board in your GCSEs."

Then I rambled on about whether real Neapolitan pizza was going to live up to its reputation, and after a mo he relaxed enough to start dissing my culinary discernment, and we were back on safe ground.

Once we left the city behind us and headed south around the Bay of Naples, the scenery got better and better. There were no blocks of flats or even houses anymore; you'd have to call them villas, all gleaming white against the piercingly blue sky and garnished with exotic plants and flowers us Brits only get to see in reruns of *Death in Paradise*.

"Ah, this is the life." I gestured out the window again. "You know you're abroad when you see real live lemons growing on trees."

Phil smirked.

"What?"

"Oh, nothing."

I didn't get it. Still, whatever it was, there was a fair chance I didn't want it, so I shrugged and soldiered on. "And those trees—see over there? The ones that look like a pine tree got frisky with an umbrella. What are they called, anyway?"

"Umbrella pines."

I sent my beloved a suspicious glare. "Are you yanking my chain?"

"Cross my heart."

"What, and hope to die? You'd better not be planning on making me a widower on my honeymoon." Whoops, that soppy grin was back.

Then again, even Phil was wearing an expression of manly sentiment. "And leave you on your own in a country full of the best-looking blokes in Europe?"

"Hey, short, dark, and handsome is your thing, not mine. Come to think of it, should I be worried? You're the one who booked this holiday."

"There's only one dark, handsome man I want. And don't you forget it." Phil's big, warm mitt came over to grasp my thigh.

I blinked a few times—must be the air-con—and stared out the window before it could all get too mushy. The Italian scenery rolled on by, effortlessly scenic. Big, exuberant bushes were everywhere, covered in blossoms of white, pink, or crimson. Phil probably knew what they were called and all, I thought with a hefty dose of the warm-and-fuzzies as I gazed at the colourful show. It was a world apart from Fleetville, St. Albans. "I can't believe people voted for Brexit. Who'd want to move away from this?"

"You do realise Britain's not actually going anywhere, don't you? They aren't widening the English Channel. This isn't continental drift gone mad."

"You reckon? I wouldn't put it past the Tory government to hitch up a fleet of tugboats and tow Britain out towards Iceland. Ah, I dunno. We're still not going to be part of Europe any longer." I frowned. "Do you think the Italians mind? Like, do they think we think we're too good for them, or something?"

Phil shrugged, which, with us squeezed into two narrow coach seats, was like experiencing a small and very localised earthquake. "I guess we'll find out."

"Huh. I knew I should have brought that T-shirt Gary was banging on about. You know, the one with the EU stars on that said, *Don't blame me, I voted Remain.* Course, with my luck, it'd get me beaten up by a bunch of UKIP supporters here to trash the place on a stag weekend."

"Nobody's getting beaten up on our honeymoon," Phil said with a hefty dollop of calm certainty and just a smidgen of tempting fate.

We were staying in Sorrento, which is the opposite side of the bay from Naples itself. It's set on a peninsula that juts out towards the island of Capri, like one of those old Victorian signs with a pointy finger. Presumably this was a helpful navigational aid to those rich gay blokes who went over to the island to get away from it all early last century.

Not that I'd been buying up every guidebook in Waterstones since I'd found out where we were going or anything. Or googling every marginally related subject under the scorching Italian sun. (The first time, I'd typed *gay men in capris* into the search field by accident and brought up a bunch of images of blokes in calf-length trousers, together with dire warnings that anyone sporting this style was as good as labelling themselves queer. Not something I'd ever thought about before, what with short trousers or "manpris" not being the most flattering for those of less than excessive height. But I was definitely going to keep it in mind for the next time my notoriously unreliable gaydar went on the blink.)

Our hotel was way up on the cliffs, which are about the only kind of scenery Italy doesn't do better than Britain. Not in Sorrento at any rate, although local opinions may vary, of course. Instead of gleaming white chalk, they were craggy grey rock with a few stubborn bushes sprouting out of them like the stubbly bits you end up with after a hasty shave with a worn-out razor. And blimey, that road was steep. You could feel the coach gasping and wheezing as it made its way uphill. I was clearly going to get fit on this holiday, walking up and down between the hotel and the town—if I didn't melt first in the heat. I spared a sympathetic thought for fishermen of yore, trudging up from the harbour with the day's catch—actually, come to think of it, it was probably the womenfolk who had done the trudging, while the lads had sailed gaily off for another bout of messing around on the water.

Or drowning when the ship went down in a storm, as might be. There's downsides to every profession. I sneaked a glance at my beloved, whose profession as private investigator might be said to have more downsides than most, at least of the mortal-peril variety. Then I shook my head. As if anything like that was going to happen on our honeymoon.

Just goes to show you how much I know.

The hotel was bright and cheerful, with the sort of abstract decorative tiles and strong colours I tend to associate with Spain rather than Italy. I hadn't thought the Moors got this far, bringing their art with them, but maybe there had been a few intrepid outliers. It was also blessedly, awesomely cool. The lobby we were set down at even had a trickling water feature to complete the picture of a desert oasis.

I was tempted to throw myself down on one of the comfy chairs and stay there for the duration. "Thank God this place is air-conditioned."

Phil laughed. "Think I'd have booked a place that wasn't? I know what you're like in the heat."

"What, hot?"

"If by 'hot' you mean like a bear with a sore head and a fur coat three sizes too small."

"Am not. I'm fine with hot weather, as long as nobody makes me do stuff in it. Anyway, who doesn't get a bit tetchy when the mercury rises?"

I didn't try to wipe the resulting smirk off Phil's face. You have to work at these things if you want your marriage to last.

We took the lift up to the main reception, which was on the top floor. Maybe the architect had got the plans upside down when the place was built. They welcomed us in with a spot of the old antipasto, served in the adjacent bar. It went down a treat after the airline "food." Mine host—should that be ourn host?—was a portly sort, which boded well for the food here in general. This meal certainly didn't disappoint. The artichokes were delicately flavoured and tender, and the tomatoes a burst of rich sunshine on a plate.

After we'd eaten, we decided to have an early night. Well, that's what honeymoons are for, isn't it? And let me tell you, there were fireworks.

Literally. We were just dropping off into the sleep of the terminally shagged-out when a series of loud bangs coming from outside (as opposed to the quieter bangs that'd been, heh, coming inside) alerted us to a massive fireworks display taking place over the bay. So after pulling on some trousers so as not to offend anyone, we stood out on our balcony and watched the show.

As I said to Phil, it was good of them to lay on all this to celebrate our wedding. It would've been rude not to watch.

So far, so idyllic. I even slept well that night.

Should have known it was the calm before the storm.

Chapter Two

What with one thing and another—this being our honeymoon I'm sure I don't need to spell out to you what said "things" might be—we were a little late getting down to breakfast the next morning. Or rather, up, seeing as the dining room, most of it open-air, was on the top floor, along from reception. This upside-down architecture was taking a bit of getting used to.

The terrace was jam-packed with our fellow tourists stuffing their faces to build up their strength for a hard day's lounging in the sun, and we stood at the entrance for a mo, scanning for a free table.

"Over here!"

I dragged my gaze away from Mr. & Mrs. Snipe from the transfer coach, who were now cooing and canoodling over their coffee as if they were the newlyweds. The shout had come from one of the choicer tables, off to our right—nicely in the shade but still with an unimpeded view of the bay. A man was waving at us. He'd stood up, all the better to attract the attention of us and every other bugger in the restaurant, and was carrying on the semaphore while accessorising it with a smarmy grin, God knew why. I didn't know him from Adam—or did I? There was a faint whiff of familiarity, but maybe he just reminded me of someone I'd met once. He was about Phil's height, but that was where the resemblance ended. Thin, slightly rounded shoulders; a pointy nose; and a weak chin were nicely set off by a receding hairline. Where looks were concerned, the woman seated across from him was definitely his better half, with golden tanned skin, long dark hair scraped up into a doughnut-shaped bun on the top of her head, and doll-like features. She was also about ten years younger than he was. Not that I was judging.

I glanced at Phil, hoping to see equal reluctance to share a table on the first day of our honeymoon with some weird random bloke—and then did a double take. His eyes were narrowed, and his jaw set. Either he was really hangry all of a sudden, or that ferrety face wasn't as unfamiliar to him as it was to me.

Without a word to yours truly, Phil strode over to apparently not-so-random bloke's table, me scuttling suspiciously in his wake. "Wayne. Fancy seeing you here." His tone made it clear that no, he *hadn't* fancied it, which was probably the only thing that saved him from a swift exit via the balcony, and me from self-inflicted widowerhood on my honeymoon.

Because, with the force of an unforeseen hailstorm on an outdoor wedding, it crashed on me who our overfriendly chum was.

Bloody hell.

Wayne Hills: that was his name. We'd been at school together, him and Phil and me. They'd been friends—best friends, even, having bonded over a mutual love of making life as miserable as possible for one Thomas Paretski, Esquire. Because them and me? We hadn't been friends. Not in the slightest. And while these days I'd made my peace with Phil's and my uneasy past and accepted that he'd been going through his own problems back then, I wasn't feeling much like extending the hand of forgiveness to one of his former cronies.

"Phil, you're looking good," Wayne smarmed.

Phil folded his arms with a heartwarming air of menace. At least he was making it crystal clear whose side he'd be on if it kicked off between me and his old mate. It couldn't have been easy. As far as I was aware, Phil and Wayne hadn't seen each other since school. Bloody hell, did Wayne even know Phil was gay?

Heh. Maybe remaking his acquaintance was going to be fun after all. For the few minutes it'd take for him to tell us to sod off before we spread our gayness over his table.

Then I felt bad, because it probably wasn't going to be much fun for Phil. He must have liked the git at some point, mustn't he? Despite the fact Wayne had been a total arse.

Said git's smirk didn't falter. "And, Tom, it's good to see you too. You haven't changed a bit."

He'd never called me *Tom* in his life. *Parrotski* or *Poofski* was more his style. I narrowed my eyes. "You sure about that? Because as far as I remember, the last time you saw me I was lying under a Chelsea tractor with a broken pelvis and a nasty case of road rash." Which, lest we forget, had only happened because Wayne and his mates had chased me down the street with malice aforethought.

And yeah, Phil had been one of them. Like I said, it was water under the bridge, all right? As far as my newly wedded husband was concerned, at any rate.

Wayne didn't miss a beat, the slime. "And it's great to see how well you've recovered. This is Siri, by the way. Siri, this is Tom Paretski, the old schoolmate I was telling you about."

What the hell would he have had to say about me to his girlfriend? I assumed he wasn't introducing me to his iPhone. "Been sharing some cosy little tales about you beating the sh—stuffing out of me?"

He laughed.

I bristled.

Beside me, I swear Phil growled.

Siri giggled. She didn't look like a Siri, which I'd always vaguely thought was an Indian name. She looked like a Chantelle, or a Kourtney, with her plumped-up lips, TK Maxx designer clothes, and a lot heavier makeup than most of the women around here seemed to think worth bothering with at this time in the morning. "Nah, he wouldn't do that, would you, Wayney? He told me about you being psychic and all. I was dead impressed." She smiled prettily, showing perfect white teeth with a smear of lipstick, and held out a nicely manicured hand.

Not being a shit, I took it and said, "Good to meet you," although it came out a bit strangled what with the clenched teeth. What the hell did Wayne think he knew about my so-called gift?

"You too." Siri had a cool but limp grip and a little-girl voice I was ninety percent sure she was putting on for Wayne's benefit. It probably made him feel all big and manly. "You're taller than I thought you'd be."

I smiled back at her. This wasn't her fault, and she was likely a lovely person apart from her bleeding tragic taste in men. "Cheers, love."

"Wayne said you was really short," she went on.

I dropped her hand and the smile.

Siri might not have noticed, as she'd turned to my beloved with another giggle. "He told me *you* were tall. He never said you were so fit, though."

Phil coughed, his cheek a masculine shade of pink. "Wayne? You still haven't explained why you're here." His tone was pointed.

If Wayne felt the jab, he didn't show it. "For a holiday, of course. Spur-of-the-moment decision, wasn't it, Siri?"

Siri looked blank for a moment, as if she needed to reboot, and then nodded so hard I thought the doughnut on the top of her head was going to fall off into her plate of melon slices. "Oh, yeah. Wayne's so impulsive. I love it." She laughed.

I wasn't sure what was supposed to be funny.

"A spur-of-the-moment decision," Phil ground out. "To come and stay at the same hotel Tom and I are honeymooning in."

"Ooh, are you two on honeymoon?" Siri's eyes opened wide. What with the false eyelashes, they were as big and blue as the Bay of Naples. "Oh my God, that's so sweet! Congratulations!"

Phil nodded, tight-lipped.

"Uh, cheers," I said, seeing as someone had to. "You and, uh, Wayne been together long?" And bloody hell, it went against the grain, calling him *Wayne* like we were mates or something.

"Oh, *ages*, haven't we, Wayne? Nearly a year now. We met when I done his nails one time."

A manicure? Wasn't that a bit, well, *gay* for a dyed-in-the-wool bigot like Wayne Hills? I gave him a sharp look. He didn't flinch. Perhaps it was me not being metrosexual enough. If that was still a thing.

"Why don't you join us?" Wayne suggested, pulling out a chair.

Because I'd rather jump in the local volcano? "Uh, cheers, but we wouldn't want to hold you up. I think there's a table free . . ." I scanned furiously through the sea of humanity.

Phil took direct action and grabbed a waiter who'd just off-loaded a tray of coffee nearby. "Table for two?"

"Of course. This way sirs." Our saviour was a tall, young lad, but neither dark nor particularly handsome. If he'd applied for a job at a strip club, they'd probably have taken him on as a pole.

With a hearty *See you later* to Wayne and Siri, followed by a silent *but not if we see you first*, we let the waiter lead us on a winding trail to a table that was half in, half out of the shade. Phil, being a gentleman, let me have the side with the shade.

After Tall, Blond, and Skinny had seated us, explained to us how to eat breakfast in case we'd never stayed at a hotel before, and taken our order for coffee, I leaned in to Phil. "Blimey, what are the odds you and Wayne bloody Hills would randomly choose the same hotel, in the same town in Italy, on the same flippin' week?"

Phil very noticeably didn't meet my eyes, which promptly narrowed.

"What?" I demanded.

He huffed. "Might not have been as random as all that." Then he clammed up.

"Oi. Save the secrets for after the honeymoon." I had a hollow feeling in the pit of my stomach, and it wasn't just me needing my breakfast.

This time, he fixed me directly in the eye. "Don't get mad, all right?"

"Am I likely to?" Bit of a redundant question, seeing as my hackles had already risen at his last remark.

"Remember way back, before we were living together, there was this high school reunion? And you said you'd rather give yourself a ground-glass enema than meet up with that load of gits?"

I nodded slowly. "And?" I said, because I was buggered if I was going to make this easy for him.

"And I went."

"You kept that quiet."

"Didn't want to make a big thing of it."

"You didn't make *anything* of it."

"Because I knew you'd get your knickers in a twist."

"Get my— For Christ's sake, what am I *supposed* to think about you toddling off for an evening of nostalgia about the good old days when you and your homophobic mates made my life a misery?" Damn. I was making angry gestures with a butter knife. I put it down quick before I could take someone's eye out.

"Oh, for— Part of the *reason* I went was so I could set the record straight. Let everyone know I regretted what I'd done. Tell them the truth about myself." Phil folded his arms.

The waiter took his chance to set our coffee down and scuttle off with a nervous air. I glanced around. Several people became intently interested in the contents of their plates.

I leaned across the table and gave my beloved a searching look but kept my voice down this time. "So you're telling me you went to this reunion bash and told everyone that big, bad Phil Morrison is as gay as Tinkerbell and always has been?"

"Tinkerbell's a girl fairy. In love with Peter Pan."

"Stop changing the subject."

"I didn't exactly stand up and make a speech about it. I *did* tell everyone I spoke to that you and me were getting married."

That was . . . big. He went along so he could out himself? That had to have taken balls. Given my social standing back when we'd been at school together, it wasn't like I could accuse him of bragging about having bagged me. "Didn't see any of them throwing confetti on our big day."

"Didn't think you'd want to, so I told them space was limited."

He'd been right there. But I couldn't help feeling curious, despite the lingering sense of betrayal. "How'd they take it, then? You being gay, I mean. Not the wedding brush-off."

"Turned out most of them knew already." He paused. "Several people told me they were sorry you hadn't come along."

"Oh, I bet they were *totally* sincere in that." I snorted. "Like I've become Mr. Popular all of a sudden."

Phil huffed and glanced away. "They can read the papers like anyone else. Wanted to reconnect with the man with the mojo."

Oh. You stumble over a few corpses, save someone from a burning building, and suddenly everyone wants to be your mate. Maybe if I'd have thought of that while I was in school, I wouldn't have had such a crap time. Or was it more of a freak show fascination? *Let's all go and gawk at the bloke with the weird thing.*

Phil poured out the coffee. "Graham Carter was there too," he said after a mo.

Graham Carter, another old school chum of ours—chummier with me than with Phil at the time, although we were anything but close these days—lived in Brock's Hollow, which was only down the road from St. Albans. I hadn't so much as bumped into him in the last year or two. Not since Phil and me had saved him from a murder charge when his girlfriend got clobbered. I had a strong feeling it was to our mutual satisfaction. Not much of an ally to the LGBT community, our Graham. He'd been honestly dismayed to learn my old school nickname of "Poofski" hadn't been baseless slander.

"How's he doing now?" I asked out of... I dunno. Guilt? Regret? Nostalgia for what might have been? But also a heartfelt desire to stop thinking about my unwanted notoriety.

"He's still off the drugs, or so he says." Phil passed me the milk with a wary air, and I remembered he still had some explaining to do.

"Oi. You changed the subject. What's not so random?"

Phil's expression was so shifty it was in danger of hopping off the hotel balcony and plummeting to a messy death on the road below. "We got talking about the honeymoon, me and Wayne."

I blinked. "You mean you'd already booked it way back then?"

"No, but I was thinking about it. And when I told him you wanted to see Pompeii, he started going on about Sorrento, how it was a great base for exploring." Phil paused, as if steeling himself. "And he mentioned this hotel. Said he'd stayed here before and the food was great. I thought, 'That's one less thing to worry about.' You know how fussy you are about what you put in your mouth."

The smile he ended on was oceans away from his usual smirk, and yeah, I could tell he was feeling bad—but for Christ's sake. I put my coffee cup down very, very gently. "This is my bloody honeymoon, and you're telling me it was all planned by Wayne sodding Hills?"

CHAPTER THREE

I tried to keep my voice low, honest, but I swear the ears of the family on the next table all swivelled in our direction.

"He gave me a hotel recommendation. That was all."

"Uh-huh. Did he give you a list of dates he'd be free for the honeymoon too?"

Phil rolled his eyes. "You honestly think I had the faintest idea he'd be here?"

"I don't know, do I? You're the one who's matey with him. You always were." Yeah, okay. I knew it was a low blow even as I said it.

Phil sighed. "Tom . . . I'm sorry."

He looked so genuinely miserable it took the wind out of my sails. "It's all right," I ground out. "He's just not a bloke I wanted to bump into unexpectedly."

"Believe me, if I'd had any idea Wayne Hills was going to turn up here . . ." He growled. The earwigging family next door flinched. Then he took a deep breath. "It's okay. We can change hotels. Resorts, if you want."

What? "No way. This is our honeymoon. Why should we be the ones to move?"

"Good luck getting Wayne to vacate the premises. He always was a stubborn sod."

"Yeah, remind me again why you and him were ever friends?" Guiltily, because somehow Phil suggesting a solution made me feel like I was making a fuss about nothing, I hurtled on, "It's okay. We're all grown-ups, here. Water under the bridge. Lava over the ancient Roman villas. Whatever."

If I could forgive Phil for his part in making my schooldays the worst time of my life, to the extent of actually marrying the bloke, surely I could be civil to his one-time partner in crime for a fortnight? I took a gulp of coffee, feeling in need of fortifying.

Phil was still frowning. "I wanted this to be perfect for you."

Now I felt like a bastard. "It is. You, me, sunshine, and sea. Hey, this place is even bringing out the poet in me."

It was obvious Phil still felt he was on shaky ground, as he didn't make the practically obligatory quip about shoving my inner poet back in the one place around here where the sun wasn't shining. "You're sure?" he asked gruffly. "I'm serious. If you want to move, we will."

"Nah, this place is great. And if what we had last night is any guide, Wayne was right about the food here." The coffee was all right too, I realised, tasting it for the first time since I'd started the cup. "Maybe he's not all bad."

Phil's eyes narrowed. "Your jaw twitched when you said that."

"No, it didn't. It moved. Because I was *talking*. And you'll get a headache if you keep squinting. Now, are we going to go raid the buffet, or just live on coffee and sunshine? Because *some* of us worked up an appetite last night. Not to mention this morning." I sent him an affectionate leer.

Phil's face relaxed at last. "Enough of that. Or I won't be able to get up to go to the buffet."

It was probably coincidence that the Earwig family (mum, dad, and a couple of preteen Earwigs who ought to have been in school) decided it was time to leave that minute. For a mo I worried we'd been too gay in public—then I thought, *Sod it.*

This was our bloody honeymoon.

Breakfast successfully consumed and Wayne Hills equally successfully avoided—I'm sure he kept looking our way, but Phil had his back to the bloke and I made a point of not meeting his eye—we returned to our room. Not for what you're thinking, because even on honeymoon there are limits. We just needed to get ready to head out.

We'd decided to take the first day easy and have a wander around Sorrento, rather than going further afield—me, because I'm firmly of the belief that holidays are not for wearing yourself out on, and Phil, because he seemed to think we should save Pompeii itself for later in the trip. Actually, I pretty much agreed on that point. It was funny—me saying we should go and see Pompeii had been a throwaway remark at the time, but once I'd found out we were really going to do it, I'd been getting into the idea big-time.

I'd even brought along the T-shirt Gary had got me, the one that said, *"The floor is lava" —everyone, Pompeii 79AD.* I wasn't sure I was going to wear it, mind. I didn't want to offend anyone.

Was two thousand years after the disaster still too soon?

I'd searched out a couple of programmes about the place on iPlayer, so was fully equipped to identify cart ruts and store frontages. Although I'd have to confess I'd paid closer attention to the section on Pompeii's unfeasibly large amount of penis art, which had been narrated with disturbing relish by a grey-haired, motherly historian. That's art depicting penises (some of them also unfeasibly large), not eye-wateringly intimate tattoos. It made me feel a weird connection to those ancient Romans, somehow. People haven't changed much over the millennia, have they? Most schoolboys' first urge when they see a nice blank surface just gagging for a bit of graffiti is still to draw a cock and balls on it.

Not that I'm, you know, speaking from experience here.

The walk down to Sorrento proper from our hotel was great—beautiful views over the sun-speckled waters of the bay, with a gentle breeze wafting away the fumes of the road. It was pleasantly hot this time of the morning and there was nary a cloud in the sky. Everything shone brightly, all the colours so much more intense than you see at home. Well, than I see at home, at any rate. Your mileage may vary. Trees were greener and flowers pinker. Even the people we passed were gaudier than usual, all decked out in their holiday gear. Tourist stalls and little shops were selling bags, caps and T-shirts, souvenirs of places we hadn't got to yet, like the islands of Capri and the other one I could never work out how to pronounce.

"Do you say that Ishia, or Iskia? Or even I*shee*ya?" I asked my beloved as we ambled past a display of navy-and-white–striped bags embroidered with the name *Ischia*.

He smirked. "I don't. I let you do all the getting-words-wrong stuff. Nobody minds when it's you. It's all part of the Paretski charm."

"Cheers, mate. So helpful." I gave him the side-eye. "Of course, if I had an iPhone, I could ask Siri."

Phil's smirk died a swift, unhappy death at this unsubtle reference to our breakfast companions, and I felt like a bastard.

"Hey, I wasn't having a dig. Not much, anyhow. We've gotta laugh, haven't we?"

He huffed, which was good as.

"So what d'you reckon is their deal? All right, I know I'm biased in Wayne's disfavour, but going on looks alone she's an eight at least and he's a two at best. And don't get me started on personality."

Phil laughed properly then. "He's not that bad looking. A five at worst."

I could feel my forehead furrowing. I'd have to watch that in this weather or I'd get a corrugated tan line. "You honestly think so? I mean, would you sleep with him?" We dodged around a slow-moving old couple. A hideous thought struck me right in the solar plexus, and I stumbled and almost fell in front of a Vespa. Phil grabbed my arm, eyes wide. "I'm fine. But, uh, you *didn't*, did you?"

He stopped dead in his tracks, which when you're built like him is a lot of inertia. The old couple pulled up behind us, tutting. Phil's expression was equal parts gobsmacked and nauseated. "Christ, what do *you* think?"

"I'd hope not, but what do I know? You and me weren't exactly best mates back then. Maybe it was all some big double bluff." I shivered despite the heat, and grabbed his arm to encourage him to get moving again. There was a pointed *Grazie* from behind as we resumed our pace.

I didn't pay a lot of attention to where we were going. It was bad enough he'd bullied me because he'd struggled to come to terms with being gay back when we were all at school together. It'd have been a bloody sight worse if he'd done it as a cynical bid to divert attention from him and his boyfriend.

Ugh. Imagining Wayne Hills as Phil's boyfriend left me with a nasty taste in my mouth.

"It wasn't, and we didn't, okay?" Phil choked out at last. "Wayne's straight. And he's really not my type."

Thank God. "Coffee?" I suggested as a peace offering, seeing as we were coming up to a pavement café.

Phil shook himself. "In a bit. Come on. We should keep moving."

Why? In case Wayne Hills had followed us? I didn't say it. And to be honest, it was probably just a sound instinct that facing each other across a coffee table right now would lead to silences of the awkward variety.

True enough, after we'd had a wander and worked up a sweat under the relentlessly blue skies, tensions seemed to have eased for both of us. I managed to talk Phil into sampling a couple of café freddos in a local establishment. They were ice-cold and refreshing, but I was gutted to discover they didn't, in fact, come with a chocolate frog. I was even more gutted five minutes later when guess who marched into the place?

Bloody hell. *Had* he followed us? I grabbed a menu to hide behind. "Trouble's here," I stage-whispered.

Chapter Four

My beloved, of course, made no attempt at concealment as he turned to gaze at our honeymoon nemesis, Wayne "Mr. Unwelcome" Hills. He made a noncommittal grunt and returned to his cold coffee, but I noticed the direction of his eyes hadn't wavered.

"Do you think he's seen us?" I hissed.

"No."

There was something in Phil's tone that caught my attention. "What's up?"

"Looks like he's here for a meeting."

I tried to peer over the menu without making it flippin' obvious. "Huh. I didn't realise he was with them." Wayne had walked in, sans Siri, on the heels of a trio of Italian men—at least, I assumed they were Italian, seeing as we were in Italy and they were in business suits. No ties, but in this heat that was a matter of self-preservation. Heavy gold chains showed at the open necks of their shirts, and they had the sort of tan an Englishman can only dream of, or alternatively purchase at high expense. Two of them now sat at a table in an open-legged, macho sprawl Wayne had aped with little success—he came off more like a sullen teenager—while the third flirted with the waitress.

From the frowns around the table, a serious subject was under discussion. Business, maybe? Come to think of it, what *did* Wayne do for a living? Was this a working holiday?

If so, had he bothered to mention that to Siri?

"What do you think that's all about?" I asked in a low voice.

"Not sure. Something about them, though . . ." Phil frowned, as though checking Wayne's companions against a mental rogues' gallery of miscreants and ne'er-do-wells.

"I thought you liked dark, handsome European men," I teased.

Phil huffed a laugh and turned back to me. "Just the one. Finished your coffee?"

I downed the last mouthful. "Have now. Are we sneaking out before Wayne and his mates can spot us? Or do you want to keep an eye on them until you can work out what that *something* is?"

He shook his head and placed a couple of Euro notes under his saucer. "It's nothing. And we're on holiday. Let's go. We can head to the station and check out the trains."

We went.

I wasn't sure if the Circumvesuviana (that's "round the volcano" to you and me) train line had been planned with tourists in mind, or if it was simply a happy accident that it connected up most of the places your average visitor would be likely to want to go to. It runs from Naples to Sorrento, taking in Pompeii and Herculaneum, or Pompeii-on-sea as I like to think of it. The good news was that it made getting to the sights logistically painless. The bad news was that we'd probably end up bumping into Wayne at the station all the time.

I tried to push that thought out of my head as we wandered on, and gradually relaxed as the old stones and the bright sunshine worked their magic. I'd been worried that Phil, who's all for holidays being so active that it's a relief to get back to your desk—not that I have a desk—would have our itinerary planned down to the minute. But he seemed happy enough to go with the flow for today at any rate. Heh, maybe we were actually suited to one another. Who knew?

We ambled around a few tourist shops to check out the tat we'd be lugging home to our nearest and dearest at the end of the fortnight. Lemons seemed to be a common motif: lemon soaps, lemon candles, lemon liqueurs and a whole wedding gift list's worth of lemon pottery. Proof that I wasn't the only one intrigued by the Penises of Pompeii—should that be the Penii of Pompeii?—was found in the form of souvenir calendars with a different piece of, *ahem*, artwork for each month. "Now we know what to get for Gary and Darren," I mused.

In fact, my big sister, Cherry, would appreciate one too, but seeing as she was now married to a man of the cloth, it probably wasn't the sort of thing she could hang up in the downstairs loo these days. It was a shame the master bedroom at her new abode, the Old Deanery, didn't have an en suite, but when the place had been built having an inside loo at all must have been regarded as dangerously avant-garde and probably immoral to boot.

You could catch boats to loads of places from the harbour at Sorrento, including Unpronounceable Island, but first you had to walk down a steep road with hairpin bends—something of a feature in this part of the world—in single file to leave room for more wheezing buses. And not a few wheezing tourists struggling up the other way.

"If your hip's bothering you, we can get the bus back," Phil said out of the blue after the first few bends.

"My hip's fine," I only half lied. The old injury didn't usually act up unless it was cold, so I was putting the odd twinge I'd been getting down to seeing Wayne bloody Hills. I wasn't about to start taking buses for something that was all in the mind. It'd only encourage it.

I made a point of not limping as Phil eyed me suspiciously. Then he smiled, shook his head, and went back to looking where he was going, so I could relax and walk normally.

Not long afterwards, we were rewarded for our efforts with the sight of blue sea, blinding white boats, and a thing of true beauty: a stall selling iced lemon drinks. The dark, pretty lady behind it gave me a smile and greeted me with a torrent of Italian, which left me pleased that I wasn't too obviously British.

"Sorry, love. English? Uh, two, *per favore*?" Always learn your pleases and thank-yous in the local language when you go abroad. You can get a long way with those. I held up two fingers to get the rest of the message across. Not that I needed to, it turned out—her English was probably better than mine. We had a natter about the weather and the footie and stuff, and then I took the drinks back to Phil.

He smirked. "No breaking hearts on our honeymoon."

"Who, me?" I took a sip of the iced lemon and groaned. "God, this stuff is gorgeous. Really hits the spot on a hot day."

Phil had stalled with his cup halfway to his lips, looking a bit more hot and bothered than he had a minute ago. Covering a smirk, I took another sip and groaned again, on purpose this time.

I got an eye roll for my trouble. "Enough of the bad porno soundtrack. Or do I need to throw my drink in your lap?"

"Not that I'm not tempted, but I can think of better ways to get all sticky." I leered to make sure he got the point, innuendo very definitely intended.

He laughed. "Cool down, Casanova. Plenty of time for that."

We strolled around the harbour, taking snaps on our phones of the various boat timetables posted up next to ticket offices. While I had my phone out, I tried to check my notifications, but the signal was struggling to reach half a bar. Still, that was probably just as well. I was on honeymoon, for God's sake. The emails and social media could wait.

I shoved my phone back into my pocket. "We're going to Capri, right? And the Iss-place, if only to find out how to pronounce it."

"Anywhere you want."

"Hey, it's your honeymoon too."

"And I want to spend it making you happy."

Bloody hell, the sun was fierce, glinting off the waves like that. The glare was making my eyes water.

Shut up.

The walk back up the hill to the hotel was a sweaty slog. We had our backs to the views and the breeze seemed to have buggered off all of a sudden. Stepping inside our air-conditioned hotel at the end of the trek was an almost religious experience.

"God, that's better." I lingered by the water feature in the lobby, fighting the urge to dunk my hands in. Or the rest of me, come to that. "Look, I'm gonna suggest something, and you can say no if you want, and it's no big deal."

Phil raised both eyebrows, then cast an unsubtle glance around. "Sure you want to talk about spicing things up in the bedroom where anyone could walk in?"

"Spicing— Oi, get your mind out of the gutter, Morrison." I glared at him, and he laughed, the bastard. I folded my arms. "I was talking about, uh, maybe going for a swim?"

"Sounds good to me. If you're up for it." He frowned, like he reckoned it should have been obvious.

Had he got what I was getting at? "Yeah, but . . . in the pool? The one on the roof here, I mean."

He cocked his head. "You're the one who's got the problem with pools, not me. 'Too much dead water,' you always said."

"Yeah." I grimaced. "Probably time I got over it, right? But you're sure you're okay with it?"

"Why wouldn't I be?"

"Uh, a little matter of being almost killed in one a while ago?" He'd been shoved into one and bopped on the head by a murderer, before being tied up and bundled into the boot of a car to await disposal. And it hadn't been in high-thirties temperatures, either. Not unless you were talking Fahrenheit.

"That was ages ago. I've been swimming since then."

"You have?"

"There's a pool at the gym."

There was? "I thought you spent all your time there chucking heavy weights around."

"And then I go and chill in the pool. Although not so much lately, seeing as I've had someone to get home to." He stepped closer, a tender smile on his face doing all kinds of things to my insides. "You honestly thought I had a problem with swimming pools?"

"Well, yeah." The same incident had definitely left him leery of enclosed spaces. He probably wouldn't thank me for pointing that out, though.

He reached a hand to my face—then jerked back as an elderly lady barrelled in from the street. "*Scusi*," she snapped in a distinctly British accent, barging right between us.

It was the old dear I'd seen with the monster case yesterday. What'd got her goat? Maybe it was us. You know, engaging in homosexual acts of affection in a public place. Or at any rate, trying to.

Or maybe I was being unfair. From the way she jabbed at the lift buttons, you'd be forgiven for thinking they were the ones who'd offended her. I turned my attention back to Phil. "So, pool?"

"If you're sure you're up for it."

"Course," I said confidently.

Phil narrowed his eyes, and I knew he'd seen right through me.

Chapter Five

The hotel pool wasn't one of those infinity ones—the place wasn't that posh—but it was a decent size. And, yeah, dead. Standing by the edge, I suppressed a shudder. It's just not natural, dosing water up with that amount of chemicals and trapping it in a box.

My so-called gift for sensing water (and hidden things, but we don't need to go into that right now) isn't exactly *on* all the time. I can't turn it off entirely—it's not like I've got a switch—but . . . Look, think about it like standing in a spotlight with your eyes shut. Some of the light still gets through, but it's way dimmer than when they're open. That's what it's like with me. When I'm not actively listening for the vibes, I can pretty much ignore them.

Trouble is, when I'm next to a body of dead water, it's kind of hard *not* to listen. Like not looking at a car crash, I guess. You want to know the worst and get it over with.

It was pretty quiet up here—only half a dozen sun-worshippers on loungers, and nobody in the pool at the moment. The rest of our fellow guests must still have been out and about, or maybe they were a few storeys down sipping Aperol Spritzers on the terrace. So there weren't too many witnesses as I braced myself to *listen*.

"Want to soak up the sun for a bit before we get in the water?" Phil asked, totally breaking my concentration. "You don't have to swim at all if you don't want to."

"I know that." Well, sort of. It wasn't like I reckoned he'd think any less of me if I chickened out now. Probably. It was just that now I'd screwed myself up to it, *I'd* think less of me if I backed out.

It was only a flippin' swimming pool. Babies get in them all the time. Some are even born in them.

"You go ahead and catch some rays," I told him. "I'll do a couple of lengths first."

He hesitated, then nodded about a millimetre and bagged the nearest lounger.

Right. Here goes. I sat on the edge of the pool, took a deep breath, and slipped into the water, trying not to think about cold, corpse-like hands caressing my naked skin.

After a mo, I realised it wasn't that bad. Pretty refreshing, actually. Had I just been making things harder for myself all this time?

Maybe I was the one with the lingering trauma from Phil's near-death experience. I struck out into a vigorous front crawl to focus my thoughts on the here and now.

The irony of a rooftop pool is that although there might be a great view from up there, you can't usually see a thing from in the water.

Unless you count the sight of my other half lounging around looking muscular and gorgeous in swimming shorts, which I certainly did. I was pretty sure at least sixty percent of our fellow guests did too. I slowed down after a few lengths of the pool to better appreciate the sights. One couple in particular—Mr. and Mrs. Snipe, I realised when I'd adjusted to seeing them without their clothes on—looked as though they'd like to order my Phil delivered to their room for a midafternoon snack. And then wrestle for him. Or maybe with him.

I swam up to the foot of Phil's lounger. "Room for two on there?"

"What, and scandalise the natives?" He budged up as he said it, though.

I heaved my dripping self up out of the water and nabbed a towel. "There aren't any natives around. Everyone around the pool is on holiday, and most of the hotel staff aren't Italian. You know, I wish I'd thought of working a summer job abroad when I was fresh out of school. Travel the world, stay in swish hotels, and get paid for it."

"Says the bloke who hates doing stuff on holidays. You do realise they have to work, right?"

"Yeah, but they must get days off too." No longer dripping, I considered lying down next to him on the lounger. But I regretfully decided that discretion was the better part of not collapsing the flipping thing, and perched on the edge instead. Ready to leap off at the first hint of catastrophic failure.

"They probably don't even live in." He smirked. "Actually, I can see you as a waiter. You'd be charming the pants off all the female guests—"

"They can keep their pants on, ta very much."

"—and telling the chef where he's gone wrong with his risotto."

"You ever see a professional chef when he's working? Trust me, they're in no mood to hear anyone dissing their dishes." *Sod it.* I lay gingerly on one side, all the better to ogle my husband from close quarters.

"And how would you know? Admit it, you got all that from watching Gordon Ramsay on the telly."

"Oh my God!" A female voice burst in on us. "You two are so adorable!"

I looked round so quick I got a crick in the neck. It was Siri in a bikini with, I swear, more frills than there was room for on those tiny scraps of fabric tied together with string.

And Wayne, his figure pallid and unappetising in swimming trunks that showed off his paunch. I returned my gaze to his better half, sharpish. "Uh, thanks. Nice tan," I added, rubbing my neck.

She beamed. "Aw, thank you! I got it last week, before we came here."

Exactly how spur-of-the-moment had this trip been?

"I tried to persuade Wayne to get one too," Siri gushed on, parking her bum on the next lounger. "But he reckoned it's too g—girly."

I deliberately didn't narrow my eyes, although it'd probably just have looked like I was squinting in the sun anyway. But I was pretty sure she'd almost said *gay* instead of *girly*. Huh. So Wayne felt getting a manicure cast no doubt on his hetero credentials, but a fake tan was up there with rainbow flags and booty shorts? You live and learn. If by *learn* you mean *chuck straight in the bin labelled* toxic masculinity.

The man himself coughed. "Drinks? There must be some staff around here somewhere. Siri, find a waiter."

For a moment I expected Siri to say, in a faintly robotic voice, *The nearest waiter is fifty metres away.* Or, as might be, *Get off your arse and find one yourself, you lazy sod.* Instead, she hopped straight back off that lounger. "You want the usual, babe?" Wayne nodded, and she turned to us. "What about you two lovebirds?"

"Diet Coke, ta," I told her with a smile. Phil indicated his willingness to down a sparkling mineral water.

There was an awkward silence after she left. I coughed. "Uh, when did you and Siri get here? I don't remember seeing you on our flight."

Wayne smirked. "We've been here since Wednesday. I never travel at the weekend." His tone managed to imply that Saturday flights were for plebs.

"Just staying a week?" I asked hopefully.

"Three, actually."

Great. Not only would he be here for the whole of our honeymoon, but he'd got here first and would be staying longer.

"Surprised you can leave the business all that time," Phil chipped in.

"The secret is to employ people you can trust. There's no point skimping on staff. Pay peanuts, you get monkeys. I always go for the best."

"Got a lot of people working for you, then?" I pitied them, whoever they were.

"Enough. And as I said, good people. You're a tradesman, aren't you?" He shot me a fake-sympathetic glance, the turd. "Mind you, there can be money in that too."

Cheers, mate. "Plumber. What's your business?" I didn't add, *and why don't you bloody well mind it?*

"Property. In Spain, chiefly."

Huh, that'd explain why he felt so at home in this hotel. Moorish must be moreish.

"It's easy to make a killing out there if you know what you're doing," he went on. "And if you know the right people, of course."

Christ. I couldn't remember which A levels Wayne had taken, but he'd clearly got an "A" in Being Smug. And an A-star in Patronising.

"I could put you two in line for a little home away from home, you know," Wayne offered.

"We'll pass, thanks," Phil said shortly.

"Are you sure? You won't get a better deal."

Didn't he ever give it a rest? "We're sure, thanks." I tried to make it sound final.

I was heartily relieved when Siri got back, bringing with her a tray-bearing waiter, one I hadn't seen before. He was a good-looking bloke with dark blond hair, pale English skin that argued against my days-off-in-the-sun theory and, if I wasn't mistaken, starry-eyed admiration as he gazed at Siri. She was bouncing along beside him talking nineteen to the dozen, although apparently she had allowed him to get a word in edgewise at some point since she introduced him with, "This is Will. He's from London, working here for the summer. He's studying economics—ain't he clever?"

Will ducked his head, smiling.

Wayne scowled. "Let the boy serve the drinks and get back to work, for God's sake."

Siri deflated down onto the lounger with a wounded expression.

Young Will, his face now smoothed out into a professional mask, handed over the largesse.

I gratefully accepted my Diet Coke. "Ta, mate. Room 206 for this one and the mineral water. Sorry I can't tip you but, uh . . ." I gestured at my general lack of anywhere suitable to keep my wallet and/or loose change.

"Don't be ridiculous," Wayne butted in. "Room 227 for all of them. I'll sign the chit. I can afford to buy a couple of old friends a drink, after all."

"Thanks," Phil grunted, possibly to forestall me from coming out with anything along the lines of *Couple of old friends? Who are they, then?*

Wayne didn't tip, and he didn't apologise for it, either.

"Seen much of the sights yet?" I asked a glum-faced Siri.

She brightened. "We've been to Herculaneum, haven't we, Wayne? And Pompeii, and the museum in Naples where they put all the stuff they dug up. There's only, like, walls of houses left in Pompeii, and dead people and that, but there's these amazing statues in the museum. Some of them are really rude." She giggled.

Blimey, these two didn't hang around. Also—"Dead people?" The past few years had made me a mite paranoid on the subject.

"Yeah, but they're only made of plaster," Siri reassured me. "There's one of a dog and all, poor little thing. It was chained up and trying to get away when it got buried in, like, boiling hot ash. It's so sad."

Wayne rolled his eyes and patted her thigh. "It was rather hotter than *boiling*. They estimate air temperatures were around three hundred Celsius."

"Pyroclastic flow," I said to show I could remember stuff I'd seen on the telly too.

The gentlest of huffs came from my beloved. I ignored it.

"It's dead scary, isn't it?" Siri shuddered. "You think, there they were, going about their lives like we are, and then they got roasted alive."

We all glanced at the pool, gauging how quick we could jump in if Vesuvius abruptly threw another epic wobbly and whether that would save us or simply prolong the agony. Or maybe that was just me.

"It could go off again at any time, you know," Wayne put in with frankly unnecessary relish. "It's overdue, in fact, and the next eruption could be cataclysmic." He smirked at me, as if to say, *Yes, I know big words too*. I wondered who he was trying to impress. Siri? *Phil*?

"Don't!" Siri squealed and batted at him with one little paw. "I don't want to end up like one of those skeletons we saw."

"Fake. The guide said so." Wayne's tone was dismissive.

Seriously, fake skeletons? Like there wasn't enough doom and destruction about these places anyhow?

Wayne leaned forward, his elbows on his knees. "The most interesting thing is, there's a huge amount of Pompeii that's never been excavated. It's still buried. There's even more at Herculaneum. God knows what treasures are lying hidden." Avarice glinted in his eyes, unless it was simply a reflection from the pool.

"Never knew you were into archaeology," Phil said mildly.

Wayne's smirk made a reappearance. "People change. You should know that."

There was an awkward silence. Then Siri gave an overloud giggle. "So how did you two get together? Was you like childhood sweethearts?"

Phil and me exchanged rabbit-in-the-spotlight glances. "Uh, not so much," I managed, at the same time as Phil came out with, "Something like that."

Wayne laughed. "Babe, they hated each other at school. They got together over a case."

"A case?"

"I *told* you. Phil's a private investigator."

"I know *that*, but Tom's just a plumber." She turned her lush eyelashes in my direction a moment too late to catch my wince at that *just*. "Aren't you? Ooh, did you hire him? Like, to see if your ex was cheating on you, and he was, so you and Phil got together instead?"

I blinked. She had it so fully worked out I hated to disappoint her. "Something like that," I said, at the exact same moment Phil decided to speak over me again with, "No."

Siri burst into peals of laughter. "You're so funny, you two! Right, who's up for a swim?" She hopped off her lounger and bounced on the balls of her feet.

"Already been, ta," I said, but Phil was already standing. I enjoyed an all-too-brief view of his finely muscled arse in his swimming trunks before he was sliding into the water, Siri dropping in a moment later with a splash.

Only me and Wayne were left on the loungers. Wasn't that cosy?

Wayne cleared his throat. "I'm glad we bumped into you again."

I was glad one of us was glad. Okay, no, I wasn't.

"I wanted to talk to you." Wayne leaned over towards me, his pallid face coming unnervingly close to mine. Back in our mutual schooldays, he'd always been *very* careful to maintain a safe distance in the changing rooms. Was he planning to nut me for old times' sake? But, instead, he said the last thing I would have expected: "I want to apologise."

Chapter Six

Where the hell had this come from? I shot a wide-eyed glance over to my better half in the pool. Or rather, I tried. Where the hell was he? Panic surged—and then so did Phil, the bastard, coming out of a fancy underwater turn.

Wayne went on, clearly oblivious. "I think you know what I'm talking about. The way I treated you at school. And, well . . ." He gestured at my side.

My bad side. The one with the scars. I'd been doing a bloody good job of not being self-conscious about them until then too.

I mean, they're not actually hideous. But they are there. I shoved down the urge to shift around so they weren't in his line of sight, and took a swig of my Diet Coke to hide any pesky emotions that might be leaking out.

Wayne fixed me in the eye. "You've no idea how bad I've felt about it all since then. Not only the accident. All the insults . . . everything about how I behaved towards you when we were at school together. I was using you to cover up my own inadequacies, and what I did was unforgiveable." He turned away then and shook his head.

Words. I'd known how to use them once, I was sure of it.

The thing was . . . back in school, I'd have given my right arm to have him, or Phil, or any of their gang stand up and say what they'd done to me was wrong and they regretted it. I'd maybe fantasised about it once or twice. Imagined what I'd say if they did. Would I be the bigger man, shake their hand, and lie through my teeth that there were no hard feelings? Or would I just tell them to eff off?

Turned out I'd sit there gaping like a gobsmacked goldfish.

Wayne scrubbed his face with his hands. "I don't have any right to ask you to forgive me, and I'm not going to, but I wanted you to know how very sorry I am for all I put you through."

See, what got me, what *really* got me, was that he wasn't trying to make excuses or tell me he'd been egged on by someone else. Like, for instance, someone I might happen to be married to. Wayne was shouldering all the blame. And he seemed sincere about it, for all that the words were maybe a bit stilted. It couldn't have been easy.

Him and me, we were never going to be mates—Christ, no—but I could respect him having what it took to come out and say all that. For having made the effort to understand what he'd done.

"It's, uh. It's nothing. Water under the bridge. Bygone . . . bygones. Hardly think about it these days. Not even sure I remember what you're talking about." I gave a hideous laugh and turned away, blinking. Coke bubble must have popped in my eye. Or something.

A shower of pool water announced Phil's return. "Everything all right here?" he asked in that carefully neutral tone they teach them in police training.

I nodded, a warm surge of affection flooding through me at him (a) cutting short his swim to rescue me and (b) paying enough attention to notice I might need rescuing in the first place. "Yeah." It only came out a little hoarse.

He sent me a long look, then grabbed his towel. "Probably about time we headed back to the room. Don't want to be late down for dinner."

"Uh, yeah. Dinner." I got up.

"We'll see you later, then," Wayne said.

"Oh, you off?" A dripping Siri pouted briefly, then smiled. "Course. You want your couple time, don't you? Bless."

Right. Couple time.

I'd managed to get my head in gear by the time we got back to the room, so when a grim-faced Phil turned to me and said, "Talk," I was ready for it.

"It's not what you think. At least, I don't think it's what you think." I took a deep breath. "He apologised. For all that stuff when we were at school."

Phil was silent a moment. Then he nodded. "Good. Are you okay?"

"Yeah, just . . . you know. For a bit."

Phil, bless him, nodded again like I'd been perfectly clear.

Then he sat down heavily on the bed. "Christ, sometimes I wonder why you're even with me."

Chapter Seven

"*What*?" Where the hell had that come from?

Phil looked up at me from his seat on our bed. His expression was bleak. "Wayne apologised. I never even did that, did I?"

"Yeah, you did—didn't you?" I tried to think back to when we'd first got reacquainted with each other. Had he?

To be honest, what I could remember best was him telling me he'd hated me in school because he'd fancied me. My stomach felt hollow.

"Tom, you do know I'd do anything to change the past, right?" Phil's tone was rough and pleading.

My head cleared. Because yeah, I *did* know that. I knew it from the concern he showed about my dodgy hip. I knew it from his zero tolerance to bullies. I knew it because I knew him, and I knew how much he was still beating himself up about the whole thing. I grabbed hold of him and slung myself onto his lap, managing not to wince at a sharp twinge from my bastard hip. "Course I do, you muppet."

There might have been some kissing at that point.

Eventually we realised (a) it had got late, (b) our stomachs were rumbling so loud people in Naples probably thought it was thunder setting in, and (c) we had a soggy duvet from sitting on it in wet trunks. So we quickly slung the duvet out on the balcony—God knew what the neighbours were going to think—and bunged our clothes on to go to dinner.

We sidled into the bar en route. Call me a coward, but I wasn't sure I could take Wayne Hills calling us over to share a table for dinner. Now he'd apologised, I'd look like a total git if I refused, but the old nerve endings were still a bit on the raw side for any more of his company today. So I reckoned if we dawdled a little and grabbed a couple of drinks, there was a good chance him and Siri would've finished eating by the time we went in.

Case-lady was sitting alone at the bar, her body language a lot more relaxed than when we'd seen her on the way to the coach from the airport. It might have been due to the large glass of red she'd all but drained, but seeing as I was feeling charitable, I put it down to the air-con and the fact she wasn't currently hauling heavy luggage around. Although come to think of it, she'd been pretty brusque when she barged into us in the lobby, too. Wine it was, then.

I leaned on the bar and ordered a couple of Aperol Spritzers. When in the Italian city of your choosing, and all that. Then I turned to give Case-lady a smile. Drinking alone's no fun. "On your own tonight?"

She seemed startled. "Yes. I was *supposed* to have met my sister here this afternoon, but she was delayed." Case-lady frowned as if tardiness was only one step up from beastliness.

I soldiered on. "Yeah? That's a shame. Hope she makes it here soon. I'm Tom Paretski, by the way." I held out a hand.

She took it gingerly, as though it might do something lewd if she didn't keep an eye on it. "Jane Higginbottom. That's *Mrs.* My dear husband passed away last year."

"Sorry to hear that. You must miss him a lot."

"Dreadfully. Although I wouldn't have wished his suffering to continue."

Every cloud, I guessed. "Oh, and this is—" I looked back over my shoulder, only to find Phil had wandered off and was peering at the notice board. "Uh, that's Phil. We're here on honeymoon."

He pricked his ears up when he heard his name, and sauntered over.

"Both of you?" Mrs. Higginbottom's—Jane's? Were we on first-name terms now?—face cracked in the first proper smile I'd seen from her. "Oh, how lovely. I do enjoy a good wedding. And well done you for doing things the proper way. So many young couples these days don't." She glanced around the room, a faint line appearing on her freckled brow. "The girls are powdering their noses, are they?"

"Girls?" And while we were at it, *powdering their noses*? Did women still do that, outside of 1940s films? Did they even still make powder compacts? I imagined some family-owned factory in the Midlands still cranking them out, along with dance cards and bullet bras. Actually, come to think of it, I wouldn't be that surprised if my sister owned one. A powder compact, that was, not a bullet bra, her not having been over-endowed by nature with, er, ammunition.

Jane tittered. "Your *wives.* Don't tell me you've forgotten them already!"

Phil coughed, holding up a flyer advertising a local restaurant to hide his face and being no help whatsoever.

I sent him a brief but heartfelt glare. "Nah, there's no wives. *We're* married. To each other. Me and Phil."

"Oh." She didn't add *how lovely* this time. "I'll . . . I'll leave you to it, then. Wouldn't want to get between a married, um . . ."

I never got to hear a married *what.* Dear old Jane didn't quite shake the dust off her feet as she left, but it was clearly a close-run thing.

Phil smirked. "Looks like the old Paretski charm's wearing thin."

"Must be married life grinding me down."

"That or too much grinding of a different kind." He leaned in so close I could feel his breath on my neck.

I backed away hastily. "Oi, none of that. Come on, let's go eat before we offend any more sensibilities."

We'd timed it perfectly—Wayne and Siri were on their way out of the dining room as we went in. Siri giggled when she saw us. "Enjoy your couple time, did you?"

Wayne frowned. "Siri, don't embarrass them."

"What? They're on their honeymoon. When Mason and Emma got married you was all over them with jokes about what they'd be getting up to on Kos."

The frown deepened. "Yes, but . . . This is different. There might be children here." Wayne's gaze jittered across the surroundings, failed to alight on anyone under twenty-five, and eventually settled on Phil's left shoulder.

Colour me unsurprised that Wayne's regret for being a homophobic bully only extended to the latter part of the equation.

Siri looked blank, bless her.

"We're not embarrassed, are we?" I said heartily. "But we don't want to keep you. Catch you later, maybe?"

Wayne gave a curt nod, and they toddled off.

After all that, it was a bit of a relief to get to our table on the balcony and find ourselves roundly ignored by everyone. Except, thankfully, the waiter.

Once we'd scoffed our way through a passable chicken Alfredo and a frankly sinful chocolate-ganache thing for dessert, we ambled out through the bar again.

Jane was still perched on her stool, but she wasn't drinking alone anymore. I'd have assumed her sister had finally turned up, but the lady standing next to her was as different from her as chalk from cheese. More so, in fact—I mean, you could mistake a properly shaped lump of chalk for, say, a nice bit of Wensleydale from a certain distance, couldn't you? Where Jane was ramrod straight and skinny as a rail, this new lady was all curves—even her hair was curly, like the sort of old-lady perm you see in telly shows from the seventies and which I thought had gone out of fashion before I was born. Where Jane's hair was wispy, wishy-washy white, the other lady's could have been made from coiled steel. She must have been at least ten years younger.

Phil excused himself, and I headed to the bar to order us some coffees.

Jane glanced up as I approached, and her pale cheeks coloured faintly. "Mr. Paretski."

"Hey, call me Tom." I turned to the new lady, about to say hi to her too, but she beat me to it.

"A fellow Brit? I'm Cassie." She thrust out a tanned, heavily be-ringed hand, and I took it automatically. Her grip was firm, and the eye-contact piercing.

Jane gave a gentle cough. "My sister, Cassandra Austin."

"But neither of us writes," Cassie/andra butted in with a roguish smile. "Not even Jane."

My lack of comprehension must have shown on my face.

Jane tutted. "Jane Austen? Surely you've heard of her. And her sister was called Cassandra. Our father was *such* a fan."

"Just like a man." Cassie snorted. "All those virginal heroines and no sex. I always preferred the Brontës myself. Life's not all dainty dances and fine words."

Jane changed the subject with an air of disapproval that was starting to become familiar. "Tom is here with his *husband*. They're on honeymoon."

Cassie snorted again. If she ever went to Pamplona, she'd have to watch out for crowds of young men chasing her down the street. Although I strongly suspected she'd enjoy that. "What are you doing with *us*, then? Still, I suppose you have to have a break every now and then."

"*Cassandra*!"

"You had a honeymoon once, as I recall." Cassie sent her sister a knowing look. "And I don't think you and Ralph spent *all* of it visiting churches. It certainly wasn't what Brian and I did on ours."

"That's . . ." Jane coloured, but at least she'd stopped herself saying *that's different*. She rallied. "That's quite inappropriate as a subject of conversation."

"You're, uh, married, then?" I asked Cassie, feeling some sympathy for her big sis. "Husband not travelling with you this time, is he?"

"I should bloody well hope not. He's been dead for the last fifteen years."

Oops. "I'm sorry."

"Oh, don't be. He turned out to be a bit of a shit, in the end. Good thing I never bothered to take his name." Cassie grinned. "I hope yours is more of a keeper. Where is he, anyway?"

Good question. The loos weren't *that* far away. "Uh, he's . . ." I glanced around, and saw Phil bearing down on us from three o'clock. "Here," I finished.

"So he is." Cassie gave my beloved a thorough once-over. "I'll never complain about the youth of today again."

Phil was clearly bemused, which wasn't surprising. It'd been a long time since anyone had used the word *youth* to refer to me, either. Not that we're in our dotage or anything, I hasten to add. Isn't thirty the new twenty?

"Phil, this is Cassie," I said quickly. "She's Jane's sister, imagine that."

Then I shut up even quicker.

"We had different mothers," Jane said frostily. "Cassandra's mother was my father's second wife."

"Widowhood runs in the family," Cassie said breezily, as if it didn't run in every family. "So what do you do, Phil? I'm guessing something physical, from that magnificent physique."

"Private investigator."

"How thrilling." Her eyes went comically wide, then she lowered her voice and darted her gaze around, presumably to check for ne'er-do-wells, rascals, and other assorted miscreants. "You're not on the case now, are you?"

"Nope," I answered for him. "He really did marry me, and we are genuinely on honeymoon."

"Oh, that's a shame. Not for you, of course, but I've always rather fancied being in a real-life detective story in exotic climes. Like *Death on the Nile*. Or *Murder in Mesopotamia*."

I grinned. "*Scandal in Sorrento*? *Violence on Vesuvius*?"

She laughed. "*Bullets in the Bay of Naples*?"

"*Crime in Campania*?" Phil suggested.

Me and Cassie looked blank.

He sighed.

Jane harrumphed. "Sorrento is in the Campania region. I'm *quite* certain your guidebook must have mentioned it."

While I was kicking myself, there was the suspicion of an eye roll from Cassie. "Oh, well. Phil dear, you'll have to regale us with stories of your most exciting cases of the past. But not right now. I've only just got here and I haven't had my dinner. Come on, Jane, we haven't got all night." She grabbed her sister's arm with a grip that looked like it wouldn't be dislodged by anything short of dynamite, and hustled her into the dining room.

Phil and me took our coffees out onto the terrace (all right, we let a waiter follow us with a tiny tray, because apparently carrying drinks wasn't something they let any old Tom, Phil, or Siri do around here.) It was nicely set up out there for lounging around in the evening. Small wrought iron tables and chairs with comfy cushions were scattered on the terracotta-and-cream chequerboard flagstones, and the low balcony wall was topped with bright red railings to match the chair cushions. The air was mild after the heat of the day, and a gentle breeze wafted the scent of salt mingled with a faintly floral aroma towards us.

We grabbed a free table next to a planter filled with an exuberance of greenery and blossom—red, to match the décor—and relaxed into the chair cushions. There were a few low lamps amongst the tables, but they weren't doing a lot to compete with the twilight, so it took a mo for me to realise that Wayne and Siri were only two tables away. He was sipping from a brandy glass while she pursed her lips around a straw stuck into something tall and colourful. She must have felt my gaze, as she looked up and gave us a cheery wave.

"Uh-oh," I murmured. "Could be incoming at any moment."

Phil huffed. "Paretski charm or not, they probably aren't after your company 24-7."

"No? Then how come they're heading our way right now?" They were and all, bringing their drinks with them. The waiting staff must be having conniptions. When they got near enough, our dynamic duo grabbed a chair each and pulled them up to our table like they'd been choreographed.

So much for couple time.

"Good meal?" Wayne opened with. "I thought the chicken Alfredo was passable."

"Could have used a heavier hand with the chilli," I lied, annoyed to find myself sharing an opinion with the git. Then I felt bad about it. Petty, much? The bloke had apologised. What else did I want?

Oh, yeah. To spend my time on honeymoon cosying up to my lawfully wedded husband, not assorted ex-hangers-on.

Siri made a sympathetic pout. "Yeah, Wayne can't have spicy food. It upsets his tummy. Me, I love the stuff." Fortunately she missed the death glare Wayne sent her, presumably for impugning the manliness of his digestion.

"Pud was nice, though," I said to avoid stilted pauses. "Did you have that chocolate thing?"

She giggled. "No way. I just have to look at that stuff and my bum gets two sizes bigger."

"You don't need to worry about anything like that," I said gallantly. Not that I'm any kind of expert on women's bums, but the junk in her trunk wouldn't have made much of a dent in your average wheelie bin.

Siri squealed and gave my shoulder a shove. Fortunately I'd put my coffee down or mine and Phil's honeymoon activities might have been seriously impaired. "Aw, you're such a sweetie! Isn't he a total sweetie, Wayne?"

Wayne cracked an awkward smile. "Totally."

I winced.

"I had a fruit salad," Siri added, clearly oblivious to any undercurrents.

"Good for you," I said, trying to edge my chair away from her before any further assaults on my person ensued. "Keep up your vitamins."

Wayne cleared his throat. "Have you made plans for tomorrow?"

"Haven't thought about it yet," I said quickly. The last thing I wanted was him inviting himself along for the day. "Hey, you can see the whole bay from here. Wonder if you can see where the boats come in."

I jumped up and nipped over to the balcony, where I peered intently at the town below, probably fooling no one. But at least the view here was better. After a mo, I sensed someone joining me, and tensed.

Nope, not due to any forebodings of future events. I've only got one unwanted psychic gift, thank God. I was just worried it might be Wayne.

Siri bent low to lean her elbows on the railing next to me, her folded arms pushing her boobs up so far that every time she turned her head, a dangly earring narrowly escaped being gobbled up by her cleavage. Her (as already noted, moderately sized) bum stuck out behind her, a hazard to passing waiters, not to mention elderly gentlemen with strong imaginations and weak hearts. "Innit lovely?" she breathed.

I relaxed, seeing she hadn't followed me up here to carry on the interrogation. The sun was setting over the bay, and salmon-pink light dappled the surface of the water far below us. Shoals of white boats bobbed up and down like toys in a kiddie's bathtub.

"Could be worse," I admitted. I glanced back over my shoulder. "Your other half seen it all before, has he?"

"Wayne? He doesn't like to come too close to the edge. Says it makes him come over funny." She sighed. "It's, like, an inner-ear thing? He's had it since he was a kid." She brightened. "You knew him back then, yeah? When you was at school together? What was he like?"

A vicious little shit . . . "Tell you what, why don't I get you a drink first? Another of those tall ones with the straw?"

"Better not. I'll be toppling off the roof if I have any more of them things." She laughed and gave me another shove.

For a moment I wondered if her game was to get *me* toppling off the roof. *Nah, lighten up.* She must have weighed all of three pounds, and I couldn't imagine her doing anyone in with malice aforethought. "Aperol Spritzer, then?" I asked.

"Ooh, yeah, ta, that'd be lovely. But it's Aperol Spritz. There's no *er*."

That told me. I went to get the drinks. Halfway to the bar I remembered I could have stayed put and flagged down a waiter, but as I said, I was halfway there. Might as well go and prop the bar up like an Englishman who didn't know they did things differently here.

I wasn't the only one. Mr. & Mrs. Snipe were perched on barstools—or rather, Mr. Snipe was; Mrs. Snipe was perched on him, with a hand disappearing up his shirt.

"Nice night for it," I said to be sociable.

"Yeah. Nice," Mr. Snipe agreed, not bothering to glance my way. Mrs. Snipe giggled as he shoved a hand down the back of her shorts.

I exchanged a long-suffering grimace with the barman and ordered our Spritzers. Sorry, Spritzes. Spritzi? Spritzalotti? Nah, I was making it up now. He politely but firmly refused to let me hang around for them—maybe the waiter was his nephew and desperate for the work?—leaving me no choice but to go straight back out there. Siri had sat at the table again, so I more or less had to as well.

"I've been talking to Phil about your psychic abilities, Tom," Wayne said, again with the awkward smile. "We never thought you had such *hidden* depths at school."

I suppressed a groan while sending an annoyed glare in Phil's direction. Couldn't he have found something better to talk about? "It's just a thing, you know?"

"Don't be so modest. You've saved lives."

Yeah, and there were the ones I hadn't saved too—the bodies I'd only managed to discover after it was too late for the poor souls who'd once inhabited them. "I was in the right place at the right time, that's all."

He leaned forward. "How does it work?"

I wished our drinks would hurry up and come.

"Well . . . I can find hidden things." My so-called gift isn't as useful as people might think. I'm as badly off as the next bloke when the TV remote does a lemming-leap into the sofa cushions. I can find water, which occasionally comes in handy in my work as a plumber—but nine times out of ten, the customer's already located the leak.

I didn't get to explain any of this to Wayne, as he was already cutting me off. "Yes, yes, I know that. But how does it *work*?"

"I just . . . hear the vibes, that's all. If I'm listening for them."

"What do they sound like?"

"Uh . . . Bright? Or, you know, dim? It's, uh, hard to explain."

Wayne nodded, looking thoughtful, which was a new one on him. "Have you ever been wrong?"

"Wrong like how?"

"Have you ever thought you were going to find something, heard your 'vibes,' but there was nothing there?" His gaze didn't leave my face for a second, even when he was doing air-quotey gestures for *vibes*.

"No, but—"

"That's amazing! And you've tested this thoroughly?"

"Not really. It's just . . . this thing I do, that's all."

"You should test it out. Find your limitations. Work to go beyond them. It's all very well having a natural talent, but it's what you do with it that counts."

I glanced at my beloved, half for help and half-suspecting I'd find him nodding along. It wouldn't have been the first time Phil had been on at me to push the boundaries.

Weirdly, he had a pinched frown on his face. "This isn't the time or place for that though, is it?" Phil rumbled.

Wayne turned his gimlet glare in the direction of his ex-mate. Or possibly current mate, seeing as they apparently still had so much in common. "Why not? He could use his leisure time to properly get to grips with his abilities. Stop wasting his talents—"

"He isn't wasting anything," Phil snapped back.

"*He's* sitting right here, ta, and he can speak for himself," I pointed out a little testily.

Siri jumped up. "You know what, I think I will have one of them chocolate things. They looked lush. Phil, can you come and give me a hand?" She grabbed Phil's arm, but stopped short of attempting to pull him out of his chair, which was probably wise, given the weight difference. Oh, and the minor detail that he was my husband, not hers.

Why hadn't she grabbed Wayne? He was the one causing all the trouble. And the only one around here who'd actually signed up for any manhandling coming from her direction.

I stared at her. Everything went quiet.

She flushed.

Wayne coughed and stood. "I'll take you, Siri. We'll see you later, Tom. Phil."

I gazed at their retreating backs, baffled. Then I shook my head. "Saved by a chocolate ganache. Who'd have thought it?"

Phil was still frowning after them as the drinks I'd ordered arrived. I took one Spritz and handed him the other. "You might as well have Siri's. It'd only taste funny with the chocolate stuff. I'll get her another one later."

He stood, glass in hand. "She can get her own drink. How about we take these to the room instead of waiting for them to come back?"

Heh. I guessed we were on the same page after all. We escaped, and I stopped myself worrying about Wayne being weird. I had a much better bloke to concentrate on.

Chapter Eight

I didn't sleep too well that night, and my dreams were of the *nought-out-of-ten, would-not-recommend* variety. Me, Phil, Wayne, and Siri were out on the terrace, but for some reason we were all in our swimming cossies. Except me—I'd forgotten to bring mine, so I was standing around with my hands over my bits hoping no one would notice. I was starting to think I'd got away with it when Jane Higginbottom stomped up with Will the waiter in tow and pointed a classic *Invasion of the Body Snatchers* finger at me, saying, "That's the one—positively indecent!"

I froze, as Wayne muttered something to Phil and they both laughed.

Then they came towards me, shoulder to shoulder, fists clenched, and I bolted.

Straight into the road—because somehow we were no longer six floors up from street level—and into the path of an oncoming car, which bore a suspicious resemblance to the four-by-four that'd flattened me back in my teens. *The bang's always louder than you expect,* I remembered—and then the car hit me, and I woke up, thank God.

"All right?" Phil asked, presumably tipped off by me sitting bolt upright in bed and gasping like I'd just run a marathon. He looked like he'd been awake already—either that or he'd mastered the knack of checking his phone in his sleep.

"Fine," I gasped. "Bad dream. Nothing to worry about." No way was I admitting my traitorous bloody subconscious had invited an unpleasant incident from our mutual past, not to mention Wayne Hills, into our honeymoon bed.

Phil put down his phone and raised an eyebrow. "If you're sure . . . Breakfast? Or . . ." He lowered his voice suggestively.

I leapt out of bed. "Breakfast. I'm starving, aren't you? Don't think I ate enough last night." In fact I was feeling a bit queasy, but I reckoned I could face food more easily than I could stomach anything amorous with visions of Wayne Hills and Jane flippin' Higginbottom ganging up on me still dancing in my head.

Luckily the real Wayne was nowhere in evidence when we got up to the dining room, and we had a peaceful meal, for once. My appetite even returned in enough force for Phil to tease me about the amount of parma ham I was scarfing down.

After breakfast we walked into town, the heat rising as we descended. We got to the station in plenty of time for the train, and wandered down to the end of the platform in the hope of getting a less crowded carriage. Like a lot of places in Sorrento, the station had clearly been set up with tourists in mind, and non-Italian-speaking ones at that. Big boards advertised which trains were going where and when, presumably to save station staff dealing with daft enquiries in mangled accents. Plus, with Sorrento being the literal end of the line, you couldn't exactly get on a train going the wrong way.

"We're going to Ercolano Scavi, right?" *Ercolano* being modern for *Herculaneum*. I squinted in the bright sunlight. It was about ten degrees hotter down this end, compared to the shady bits nearer the station house. "What do you reckon *scavi* means? Caves?"

"Close. Excavations."

"Yeah? Since when do you speak Italian?"

Phil held up his phone. "Got an app."

Huh. Why hadn't I thought of that? I pulled out my own phone—never too late, and all that—but the signal was weak to nonexistent. Typical. I'd gone to all the bother of sorting out data roaming before we came too.

By the time the train got there, so had a lot more tourists, but thankfully there was room for all of us to get on. There was none of the sort of packed-in-like-sardines, enforced armpit sniffing you get on the London Underground if you're unwise enough to venture on it at rush hour. Given the heat here, it was just as well. Me and Phil parked ourselves on a too-narrow wooden bench facing an elderly

Italian couple. At any rate, they looked Italian, her in her neat floral frock and him in his baggy trousers and proper shirt. I couldn't tell for certain as they didn't say a word, simply smiled and nodded at us as we sat down, then carried on silent and serene.

It was like they'd said all they had to say to one another years ago, but were still content in each other's company. Would me and Phil be like that one day?

Nah. Catch me shutting my gob that long.

I dug out a guidebook and flicked through to the right page as we jolted along the tracks. "Says here Herculaneum was where all the posh people lived. Think they'll let us in the door?"

Phil smirked. "Why not? Even the Romans had drains that needed seeing to."

"Hah. I bet plumbing was a respected profession in those days. All those viaducts and hyper-wotsits. You know the word itself has Latin roots, right? Plumber comes from their word for lead." My turn to smirk. "And here was you thinking I wouldn't know a Latin root if I dug one up in the garden."

"When have I ever doubted your professional knowledge?"

"There's always a first time. Especially with you spending so much time with Darren." Okay, so Darren generally confined himself to digs at my height, but give it time, give it time. "Speaking of which, have you heard from him and Gary lately?"

"We're barely three days into our honeymoon. Why would they be getting in touch?"

"I don't know. Maybe to make sure it's going okay?"

"Why wouldn't it be?" He looked hurt.

Oops. "Well, obviously *we* know it's going okay. Always knew it would. But you know how Gary's got, uh, a bit of a thing about you and me. Not that he thinks we're doomed to failure or anything. He just might want reassuring."

I mean, it's not that *I* was hurt that Gary hadn't checked in. I was . . . surprised, that was all.

Phil was still frowning. I wished I hadn't mentioned it.

"Want this?" I shoved the guidebook in his direction and when he took it, pulled my phone out of my pocket. I composed a quick text to Gary—*Having a really hot time in Italy, bet you wish you were here*—and queued it up for sending whenever I managed to get a connection. Probably in a week and a half's time as I stepped onto the tarmac at Heathrow.

The train emptied out when we got to Pompeii, over half of the passengers in our carriage opting for the big-name ruins. It made a noticeable difference to the amount of air flowing through, and the remaining dozen or so stops before we reached Ercolano passed in relative comfort. Emphasis on the word *relative*. The bench seats got harder the further we went, and except for a couple of tunnels, the sun streamed in nonstop. I was glad to stretch my legs when we finally disembarked.

It was a short walk down the street from the station to the ruins. Modern Ercolano buzzed around us, literally in the case of the lads (and it was mostly lads, not lasses) on Vespas. Much of the town seemed geared up to cater to tourists, although it wasn't quite as in-your-face as Sorrento. The main street led us towards the sea, and I fancied I could catch a whiff of brine over fumes from the traffic and the savoury aromas coming from the many restaurants we passed.

We got to the historical site via a wide, tree-lined walkway that definitely fitted in with Herculaneum being on the upmarket side. Halfway across, I ambled to the side to lean over the railings. The old Roman town lay at my feet—or more precisely, about sixty feet below them. "Blimey, that's a long way down. That volcano wasn't messing around, was it?"

Phil's solid forearms rested on the railing next to mine. Even in the rising heat of the day, I could feel the warmth coming off him. "Scary thought," he murmured. "Being buried under all that ash."

"I'm pretty sure they were dead already." As consolations went, it wasn't much.

He nodded, as if it was something to be grateful for, after all. "Come on—there's a queue for tickets."

We got a shift on and joined the queue, which was orderly and reasonably fast-moving, giving the lie to the old adage that only Brits know how to queue properly. At the ticket booth, they tried to sell us on the museum with its 3D film, but like pretty much everyone else, we were there to see the actual ruins so we said a firm *No, grazie.* By the time we made it out the other side and onto the site, the sun was high in a cloudless sky, and I was wishing I hadn't decided I'd look daft in a sun hat.

I made the mistake of mentioning that to Phil, who promptly doffed his own straw trilby and plonked it on my head. "There you go. Can't have you baking your brains out."

"What about your brains?"

Phil smirked. "Larger. Takes longer to cook."

"Up yours." I whipped the hat off and held it out to him. "Come on. You're fairer than me. You'll burn."

"Aw, you guys are *so sweet*!"

Chapter Nine

At that familiar squeal, I spun. Siri was all of three feet away, hanging off Wayne's arm and beaming at me. When had they snuck up on us?

"Surprise!" she went on cheerfully.

"Uh, yeah." I tried, honest to God, but I'm pretty sure my tone still said loud and clear that it wasn't exactly a *nice* surprise.

Wayne gave a thin-lipped smile, so maybe I'd pulled it off better than I thought. "Not so astonishing. Herculaneum is one of the major sights, after all."

"Thought you'd already been?" Phil, who'd put the hat back on, narrowed his eyes at them, looking like a PI from the thirties who'd brought the mean streets with him on his summer hols.

Funny that, in the light of future events. And by *funny* I mean *not amusing in the slightest.*

He got an airy shrug from his old mate for his trouble. "Oh, you can't see it all in one trip. Siri and I always intended to come again, didn't we, Siri?"

"Oh, yeah. It's really good." She made a face. "Hasn't got the naughty bits like Pompeii, though. Just to warn you."

That was thoughtful of her. For all she knew, mine and Phil's enjoyment could have been totally ruined by a surprise lack of penis art. "I'm sure we'll cope," I told her. "A little culture never hurt anyone, right? Speaking of which, we were planning to do one of the guided tours, so I guess we'll—"

Wayne cut me off with a smarm. "Oh, you don't need to pay for a guide. We've done the tour. We can tell you all about it."

Me and Phil exchanged glances. "Uh, cheers, but we wouldn't want to put you out like that."

Wayne stepped closer. "It's no trouble."

"Yeah, we don't mind," Siri put in earnestly.

Phil's expression was stonier than the ruins. "Kind of you. But no." He put a hand around my waist and gently but firmly steered me away from them.

"Get you, coming over all masterful," I murmured out of the corner of my mouth as we made tracks.

He huffed. "Enjoying it, are you?"

"Maybe." Although I did feel bad for Siri. I nodded towards a petite woman standing alone under an enormous faded red umbrella with an air of endless patience about her. "Hey, she looks like she might be a guide."

We ambled over, and I gave her a smile, at which she beamed and rattled off some Italian.

I winced. "Uh, English? Sorry. I'm crap at languages."

Her smile didn't waver. "Ah, I did not realise. But English is fine."

"He's half-Polish," Phil told her for no reason I could see.

"I'm sorry. I know English, French, and German. But I don't know Polish."

Seeing as neither did I, I accepted her apology graciously. We introduced ourselves, confirmed the lady—Giulia—was, in fact, a guide and not just waiting for a companion who'd gone to the lav, and haggled over the price of the tour. By which I mean, winced and handed over one arm, one leg, and a couple of internal organs, metaphorically speaking. Giulia stashed the cash and beamed at us, as well she might. "It's your first time in Italy?"

"First time together," I said, and couldn't help casting a soppy smile in the direction of my beloved.

Giulia's eyes crinkled. "You're British, yes? I lived in London for a year, but the skies there . . ." She threw up the hand not holding the umbrella. "So grey! They made me sad."

"Not a problem around here," I agreed, squinting up at the unbroken blue above us.

Maybe if you lived here full-time, you got used to the heat? Grew to enjoy sweating buckets every time you so much as breathed hard? I'm all for blue skies and sunshine on holiday, but if I've got to work, I'd prefer to do it in subtropical temperatures. But maybe that's just me.

"Now," Giulia was saying, "we wait a few more minutes to see if anyone else comes to join us, and then we start."

Phil and me made a tactical move into what was probably the last bit of shade we'd see for a while, under a spindly tree that bordered the path. We were still high above the ruins, at modern-day street level, looking down at what was left of the town. There was both more and less than you'd think. In terms of square footage, or streetage, or however you measure the size of a town, it was barely bigger than your average housing estate, but on top of the expected crumbling walls, there were roofs. Some of the buildings seemed to have more than one storey.

It wasn't like when you see a ruined castle or monastery, where you can see where the rooms used to be but can't properly picture them. I could imagine people living in these buildings. Walking down these streets. The streets themselves were straight and square—well, that's Romans for you. None of that shoddy meandering around natural features you get in medieval-era towns and villages back home. Someone had sat down and planned this place with a ruler and a sharp pencil. Or whatever the Roman equivalents were.

"Did Romans have pencils?" I asked idly, still gazing down at the town.

"No." Phil's tone was curt, and I glanced back up at him, about to ask what had got his knickers in a twist, when the source of said emotional wedgie became annoyingly clear.

Wayne and Siri had not only snuck up on us again, but they were busy handing over wodges of Euro notes to our guide, Giulia.

Spotting me staring, they wandered over to join us without a shred of shame, Wayne pocketing his wallet. "We decided to come round with you after all."

My eyes narrowed, but knowing Wayne, he probably put it down to the bright sunlight. "I thought you said you'd already had the tour?"

He shrugged. "Different guide."

Must be nice to have cash to throw around like that. I guessed the European property business was booming.

Siri nodded. "Yeah, we had a bloke last time. He was good, wasn't he, Wayne? Showed us all the fancy parts."

Wayne took her arm. "And he pointed out where they're tunnelling into the unexcavated parts of the city. You know—"

"Think the tour's about to start," Phil interrupted, taking my arm and practically frog-marching me over to Giulia.

"You're keen to get your money's worth, aren't you?" I muttered.

He gave me the side-eye. "Are you telling me you *want* to be joined at the hip with Wayne for the entire honeymoon?"

I made a face. "When you put it like that . . ."

Half a dozen other people were now clustered around our guide. There was a couple—a man and woman, both middle-aged and European looking—and a family of four. Mum was talking to a twelve-year-old boy who clearly thought he was above all this, while dad held a squirming little girl of around three or so. Of course, they might have been two single parents, but the matching blond hair and backpacks were something of a giveaway. I wondered what the deal was though, with ten years between the kids. Second marriage? Problems conceiving the second time?

Or the wife having an affair during a marital slump, with resultant cuckoo in the nest? Nah, that was probably just me projecting.

Ms. Quadrilingual raised her umbrella and addressed the group. "Is English good for everyone?"

Our multinational companions confirmed that yes, it was only Brits who were too lazy and/or thick to learn other people's languages. I amused myself by guessing Spanish for the middle-aged couple, and some variety of Scandinavian for the family, based on what I'd seen and heard of them.

"So first of all, a little introduction. I am Giulia, and I have been a guide here for three years. Now, it is very hot here, and so we will be in the shade as much as possible. Do you all have water? Good. Now, we start with a look over at the archways down below us . . ."

We all crowded over to the side and leaned on the railings to stare down at what looked a lot like railway arches. With jumbled heaps of skeletons in them. What the hell?

Scandigirl, lifted up by daddy to see over the railings, stared with ghoulish delight, while her brother took a brief glance and turned away again. He was probably trying to convey what a yawn all this was, but I reckoned he had more of an imagination than he liked to let on.

"Seems a bit, I dunno, disrespectful, leaving them lying around like that," I muttered to Phil.

"Oh, don't worry," Siri's voice chirped in my ear, like one of those unnecessarily cheerful birds you get on summer mornings when you're trying to sleep in. She mercifully dropped it to a whisper. "They're not real. The other guide told us."

If Giulia was also privy to this reassuring bit of info, she didn't bother imparting it to us. "Most of the bodies found sheltering under the arches were women and children, with men found a little further out, by the shore. In Roman times the sea came much closer to the city, nearly up to these arches. Perhaps the men were readying boats to take their families to safety?"

I swallowed. It really brought home what had happened here. Lovers waking up together to find the world was ending. Parents, frantic to save their kiddies when the sky was literally falling in. They were all real people who'd had plans and dreams. Maybe some were on their summer hols, like the family with the kiddies on the tour with us. Maybe some of them were even on their honeymoon. Christ, what must that have been like?

I wanted to grab Phil's hand, but it didn't seem the time or place. So I gazed at him instead—solid, reassuring, *alive*. He caught my eye, and something in his face softened.

Bit of a moment, there.

Wayne, I noticed, hadn't bothered to join the crowd at the railings. Still, he had seen it all before.

"You see," Giulia continued, "Herculaneum was buried very deep. It was discovered only by accident in 1709, when a worker was digging a well and found the marble steps of the theatre. We will not see the theatre today, as it is still buried and there is much water underground. But come, we will go now into the town."

Giulia led us down into the ruins, and then we were treading the streets that had echoed with the footsteps of ancient Romans. And a shedload of tourists since then, obviously. We goggled at cart ruts, peered at decorative bits made more vivid by Giulia splashing water on them, and were invited to guess the purpose of a broad counter set with round, open-topped pots about a foot across.

"It is for the toilet?" Scandidad hazarded, as his daughter stuck her head in one of the pots.

Siri nearly pissed herself laughing. "They're for food, not . . . that! Aw, bless."

I gave the now red-faced bloke a commiserating smile, glad he'd said it, not me, because at first glance they *had* looked an awful lot like a communal lav. I'd never have lived it down if I'd got it wrong about the flippin' plumbing.

"They are for hot food," Giulia confirmed—not laughing, so presumably it wasn't the first time someone had leapt to the wrong conclusion. "This place was a thermopolium. Like a fast-food restaurant. The poor people might not have cooking facilities in their homes, and so they would come to eat here."

"Ah, like McDonald's?" Scandidad was obviously keen to make up for his earlier blunder. This proved to be a mistake, as the kiddie's eyes lit up like fireworks and she started tugging on her dad's sleeve, chirping away in one of the many, many languages I don't speak.

I had to smile. Kids: they're the same the world over.

Giulia led us further on while he was still—I guessed—gently explaining that no, there weren't going to be burgers or fries in the immediate future, and trying to buy her off with a carrot stick. Poor kid.

We stopped between a couple of buildings, right on the edge of the ruins. There were a couple of archways opening into the sixty-foot stone walls that surrounded the site. "And here you see a tunnel entrance. This leads to the unexcavated part of the city."

"How much of Herculaneum would you say remains to be uncovered?" Wayne asked loudly.

I shot him a glance—it was the first time he'd shown any interest in the tour.

Giulia smiled at him and swept a hand around at the ruins behind us. "You see the site behind us? This is only one fifth of Herculaneum. Many important buildings are still buried, including all of the forum and the theatre. And if you look up, you see what is the problem."

We dutifully raised our eyes, and were met with a view of modern buildings that came up almost to the edge of the sheer drop.

"Ercolano." Giulia pronounced with relish. "How do you excavate a site when people are living on top of it? But the tunnels, they go a short way underneath. And the archaeologists have found many interesting things."

"Valuable things?" Wayne stepped forward to peer into the gloom of the tunnel entrance nearest to us, as if he expected to see some kind of Aladdin's cave of gold and jewels just gagging to be looted.

Giulia gave Wayne a tolerant smile. "Of course. All these discoveries are of immense value in reconstructing the lives of our ancestors."

Yeah, no, I didn't reckon that was what he'd meant, either. His mouth turned down at the corners. That and the balding head giving him a strong resemblance to a grumpy baby.

Siri linked her arm in his. "Ooh, innit exciting? Like, *literally* buried treasure."

"Indeed." Wayne wasn't looking at her, though. For some reason, he was staring at me. Uncomfortable under the weight of his beady gaze, I turned and surveyed the street behind us, squinting into the sun.

Why was he being weird again? And why the hell was he so determined to crash my and Phil's party at every opportunity?

Chapter Ten

Giulia moved us on then, to treasure of the unburied kind. When we stopped again, outside an open-fronted two-storey building, Phil murmured into my shell-like, "Funny how some people don't change."

I wasn't sure what he meant, and I didn't get a chance to ask because Giulia was explaining, with appropriate gestures at the things in front of us, how in a few cases, wooden stuff had survived because it'd instantly carbonised in the heat. Which . . . I didn't think she was telling us porkies, but it sounded incredible. I've been in a fire. Wood burns, and stuff starts collapsing all over the shop. Yet here she was, showing me an honest-to-Jupiter ancient Roman shelf unit.

It somehow made everything more real, that kind of stuff. The people who'd lived here were people like us, with stuff they needed shelves for. You could imagine them putting them up on a day off, then having arguments about whether they were straight or not and whose turn it was to dust them. Despite the heat, I shivered.

"Someone walk over your grave?" Siri skipped up to ask cheerfully.

"What, like we're doing right now? To the Romans, that is," I added in the face of her puzzled frown.

"Oh . . . Yeah, but it's not like it's their *actual* grave, though, is it?"

I shrugged. "They were dead. They got buried. Seems pretty grave-like to me."

Her pretty face twisted. "When you put it like that, it's not very nice."

"That's sudden death for you. Not generally nice, no."

Siri pouted and went to hang on Wayne's arm again.

Phil huffed and leaned in close. "Watch it. You're taking all the fun out of the mass fatalities for her."

"In fact," Giulia said loudly, "most of the inhabitants were evacuated before the city was destroyed. Only around four hundred skeletons have been found."

Which would have been more reassuring if she hadn't already told us eighty percent of Herculaneum was still buried underground.

"Come, now, I take you to the bathhouse." Giulia swept her umbrella into the street.

I nudged Phil. "Bathhouse? Things are looking up."

He huffed. "Don't start getting your kit off in anticipation. I'm pretty sure there aren't any ancient Romans still hanging around hoping for a threesome."

"No? How about a modern Briton hoping for a twosome?" I leered at him, in case he was in any doubt precisely which modern Brit I had in mind.

Then I felt a small, sticky hand slip into mine and nearly had a heart attack at the cognitive dissonance.

"Kaija!" Scandigirl's dad bounded over as I stared at the pink-sun-hatted head toddling along beside me. "I'm sorry," he said, scooping her up. "I think maybe she thought you were me."

"Uh, yeah. I guess when you're that height we're all just legs anyhow." And we were wearing fairly similar stone-coloured trousers. "Nice to meet you though, love," I added to little Kaija, who was staring at me solemnly from her dad's arms. "I'm Tom."

I gave her a wave, feeling a bit embarrassed, and she took her thumb out of her mouth long enough to wave back.

Scandidad smiled. "You have children?" His gaze included Phil.

"Uh, no. Not yet, anyhow. We've only been married three days." I couldn't help a soppy grin as I said it.

"Ah, congratulations." We had a brief chat about how we were enjoying our holidays while getting a shift on to catch up with the rest of the group, and made it in the nick of time to slip into the bathhouse behind Giulia, who'd left her umbrella propped up by the entrance.

"Think that's a signal to other tour guides that our group's in here?" I murmured to Phil. "Like a sock on the door handle, but, uh, not quite?"

"Maybe." He paused. "You were getting on well with the kid."

"She's cute."

"Yeah. She is." He had a faint smile on his lips. Was he getting broody?

I wasn't sure whether to tease him about it, but we had to stop nattering then anyway and listen as Giulia told us all about the Romans and their bathing habits—with especial glee when pointing out the lack of a plug hole. Apparently these so-called clean-living ancients had basically sat around marinating in each other's filth, and visiting the baths with an open wound had often been the first stop on a one-way trip to Hades.

Then again, to them it had probably been just one more item on a long, long list of premature deaths in their ancient Roman world. "Makes you feel grateful for living in the modern era, despite all the crap," I muttered to Phil, with yet again an impressive lack of foresight.

Soon after that, Giulia seemed to think we'd had enough banter for our buck and left us to toddle round the rest of the site on our own. I thought we'd have to duck into doorways to give Wayne and Siri the slip, but as it happened, they seemed to have had their fill of dogging our heels and were heading for the exit.

I frowned after them. "Huh. Think they finally got the hint?"

Phil raised an eyebrow, then gave me a knowing look. "You're feeling guilty now, aren't you?"

"No. Maybe."

"Don't bother. Wayne's got a hide like a rhinoceros. Always did have."

"Yeah, but Siri hasn't. Probably. And she's okay, leaving aside her poor taste in men."

Phil stared at their retreating figures. "She means well."

"Ouch."

"What?"

"That's like saying someone has a nice personality, that is."

He smirked. "Don't worry. I'd never say that about you."

"Yeah, and *no one* would say it about you."

"I'm wounded. I thought you loved me for my personality."

"Maybe I do. Doesn't mean it's *nice*. After all, there's a lot to be said for being naughty." I grinned, and we almost had a moment on the streets of Herculaneum, but then Kaija and her dad trotted around the corner, closely followed by another tour group, so we had to save it for later.

After a late lunch in a nearby café followed by a mooch around modern Ercolano looking for any more tourist must-sees (if there were any, we didn't find them), we took the train back to Sorrento. It was the hottest part of the day now, and by the time we got to the end of the line I felt like I'd been lightly sautéed in my own sweat. Phil, who apparently had his own internal air-con, was raring to go ambling around the town searching out interesting and/or historical stuff. I was raring to do bugger all. Being grown-ups, we compromised: I made my way down to the postage-stamp-sized patch of beach by the harbour to wait for him while he got his cultural fix.

Not having brought my cossie—did people ever swim from this beach anyway?—I sprawled on the sand and watched the boats come in and go out again until I'd been thoroughly baked by the sun, which still had its hat firmly on and was, presumably, still keeping Giulia smiling. There was enough of a breeze to keep me from spontaneously combusting, and the air tasted fresh and clean after the close confines of the railway carriage. Lovely.

I had another go at getting a signal on my phone, but it was pants as usual. Clearly, though, I'd been within range at some point today, as my message had sent itself and there was a reply from Gary. Expecting a dirty joke to pay me back for all the ones I'd sent him and Darren when they were on their honeymoon, I was gobsmacked to read, *Tiny footsteps on horizon—so excited!!!*

I blinked and read it again, but it still said what I'd thought it said.

They were going to have a kid? Well, adopt a kid, presumably. Unless they were using a surrogate? I wondered whose DNA would be going into the melting pot, if it's not disrespectful to refer to a uterus in those terms. Gary's, perhaps, seeing as Darren already had a kid? If me and Phil were right about him being Lorelei's dad, that was. Maybe he wasn't.

Maybe he didn't even know himself, which must be well weird.

But . . . Gary? Having a baby? I wouldn't say the foundations of my world were rocked, but they were definitely lightly shaken. Was it the whole Lorelei thing that'd prompted this? Given him the urge to pass on his genes, or if not that, to have a hand in rearing the next generation?

Of course, kids could be dead cute. Little Kaija at the ruins today had been a case in point. And for a lot of people, once they'd been married a while, having kids would be the logical next step. Me and Phil were planning to have kids one day—that is, *planning* in the sense of having both said we wouldn't mind some at some point in the unspecified future.

Maybe that future was creeping up on me faster than I knew. I wasn't sure how I felt about that. Was I ready to swap pints at the pub for evenings in with a bottle of formula?

I was still musing about it when Phil joined me a while later, frowny and red in the face. Score one for lazing on the beach instead of traipsing around town.

"Miss me?" I asked with a grin.

He shook himself and plopped down on the sand beside me. "Might have."

Aw. "So what stunning sights of Sorrento did you see without me?"

Phil huffed. "Popped my head in a gallery."

From the shortness of his tone and the scowl on his face, I guessed the pictures hadn't impressed. "No penis art?"

He broke into a smile and lay back on his elbows. "No penis art. You'd have hated it. How's the beach been? Not a lot of it, is there?"

"Oi, don't be a size queen. It's got sun, sea, and sand—what more could a man ask for?"

"How about one of those lemon drinks?"

I grinned. "I knew I'd married the right bloke. You stay here, I'll get them." I jumped up—he was looking a little on the weary side.

The drinks went down a treat. I couldn't say the same for the sweaty slog up the hill to our hotel that followed, though. And okay, we could have got the bus, but we were a couple of blokes in the prime of life so there was honour at stake.

"Shower?" I suggested when we got back to the room.

"You go first," Phil said absently. He'd been quieter than usual on the way up here for some reason. Not quite himself.

I wasn't having that. Not on our honeymoon. I stepped up to him and ran a sweaty hand down his equally sweaty chest. "I was thinking we could share. You know—do our bit for the environment and all that."

He smirked. "'And all that'?"

I leered. "Actually that was the part I was most interested in, yeah."

Spoilers: neither time nor water was saved. But Phil had definitely cheered up by the end.

Chapter Eleven

Refreshed, sated, and bloody ravenous, I suggested we head to dinner. Phil raised an eyebrow. "Clothes first, maybe?"

I gave him a long, slow look up and down. Yep, the view was still bloody amazing. "Nope, can't see any need for that kind of thing."

He laughed properly that time. "Get your kit on."

I did, then sat on the bed, drumming my fingers impatiently on the bedside table while he faffed around with hair products. Still, mind you, completely starkers. Most of me was fine with that, but my stomach had a different opinion and wasn't shy about making its views known. After a mo, Phil turned and rolled his eyes at me. "I'll be *five minutes.* Go and get us a couple of drinks at the bar if you can't wait that long."

I jumped up and saluted. "*Si, Barone.*" Then I legged it downstairs to grab a Spritz and see if I could scare up an olive or two to stave off the impending starvation.

Hey, I'd had a salad for lunch. I wouldn't be making that mistake again.

Cassie was sitting at the bar next to a middle-aged bloke in a stripy shirt the 1980s had inexplicably failed to claim back, with honest-to-God red braces holding up his wide-boy trousers to complete the image. Despite the air-con, Eighties Geezer was mopping his brow with a folded pocket handkerchief, and I wasn't sure if it was gel slicking up his side-parted hair or plain old-fashioned sweat and grease. He leaned in closer to Cassie, put a hand on her arm, and said something that made her throw back her head and bray with laughter.

Jane, on Cassie's other side, sniffed and took a hefty swallow from her wine glass.

About to wander over and say hi, I jumped as an arm slipped into mine. "Tom!" Siri giggled. "Where's your other half? Not worn him out already, have you?"

"He'll be down in a mo. Where's yours, for that matter?" I tried not to picture Siri wearing Wayne out.

She pouted. "He's not feeling too well. Something he ate, poor love. He told me to come down on my own."

"Oh, that's a shame," I lied through my teeth. "You'll have to join me and Phil for dinner," I added, because it seemed rude not to. Who likes dining alone?

"You sure?" She bit her lip. "We probably ought to ask Phil first. I don't want to butt in where I'm not wanted."

Oops. Maybe my lack of enthusiasm was showing. I patted her hand. "Course you're wanted. Why wouldn't you be?"

She gave me an unreadable look, then broke into a sunny smile. "Oh, no reason. We gonna get a drink first? I could murder a Coke."

We'd carried on walking as we talked, and when we reached the bar, Cassie and her companion turned on their stools.

"Oh, excellent," Cassie pronounced. "Martin, some fellow Brits for you to meet. This is Tom and Siri."

Eighties Geezer—Martin—gave us a smile as oily as his hair. Close up, he wasn't as old as he dressed and there was more muscle than fat on his stocky figure. I revised my estimate of his age down to midthirties at most. "Well, well," he said in a slow, public-school drawl that made me think of Tory politicians and hand gestures designed to ward off the evil eye. "I must say you two lovebirds make a charming couple."

Me and Siri turned startled looks on each other, and Cassie split the air with her laughter. Jane sniffed again. Bit rude of Martin not to offer her his hanky.

Cassie calmed down enough to say, "Oh dear. Barking up the wrong tree there, I'm afraid. Tom's a fairy," she added helpfully, leaning in towards Martin and patting his leg. "On honeymoon. His husband's *very* handsome."

She had a point there, but what was I—fegato alla veneziana?

"And I'm here with my bloke," Siri put in.

Martin pantomimed looking around, his eyes wide. "He must be rather small, then."

Siri's peals of laughter were a sight more musical than Cassie's bark. "Oh, bless. He's in our room. Got a dicky tum-tum tonight. But his head's much better now," she added earnestly.

It was probably all to the good that Wayne wasn't around to hear her talk about him like he was a toddler. Had he been coming down with it at Herculaneum? Was that why they'd left early?

"Leaving such a beautiful young lady to dine alone?" Martin slid down from his barstool and crooked his elbow. "Never. You must allow me to escort you."

Siri took it with a smile and a hint of pink, while you could colour Cassie miffed.

I didn't get it. Luckily for me, I didn't need to. As Martin and Siri promenaded foodwards, Phil turned up, fresh and crisp as an iceberg lettuce but much tastier, in a dark blue, fitted shirt I hadn't seen before and a pair of pale grey trousers that looked almost as good on as they would off. "Finally ready to chow down?" I asked, and offered him my elbow.

He gave it a raised eyebrow but took it anyway.

Behind us, Jane sniffed again. "Oh, hang on a mo," I said and rummaged in Phil's trouser pocket. If I knew my lawfully wedded . . . Yes. I pulled out a neatly ironed handkerchief, turned around and offered it to Jane. "Here you are, love. Have a good blow."

She declined, frostily. Cassie snorted, noisily. My beloved whispered in my ear, "Do I want to know?" and escorted me into the dining room.

It wasn't until we'd been seated at a prime balcony table (had Phil been late because he'd been busy bribing the waiters?) that I realised what we'd done. Scratch that, what *I'd* done, because Phil had simply been following my lead.

He frowned at me over his water glass. "Something worrying you?"

"Nah . . . Just realised we've outed ourselves to the whole place."

He huffed. "If they haven't noticed by now we're a couple, they haven't been paying attention. Does it bother you, everyone knowing?"

"I dunno. A bit, maybe? I mean, it's one thing telling people when we're talking to them, but there could be all sorts on their hols here. Religious fundamentalists and what have you. Could do without people having a dig while we're on our honeymoon."

"Hasn't happened yet."

I had a nasty little urge to ask him if it'd happened on his *previous* honeymoon, but managed to squish it. Course, I had no idea where him and the mysterious Mark had whisked themselves off to after celebrating their nuptials. Could have been a gay resort for all I knew, with everyone and his dog wearing booty shorts to breakfast and nothing at all in the pool. I could have asked, I guess. But I didn't want to.

"So who's Siri with tonight?" Phil asked as we perused the menu. "And where's Wayne?"

"Wayne's been put to bed early with a dicky tum-tum. Siri's words, not mine. Maybe he ate too many sweeties. And the refugee from the eighties is a smarmy git—I mean Brit—called Martin. He was cosying up to Cassie until Siri turned up."

"They're friends?"

"I reckon they are now, but no, didn't seem like she'd met him before." I grinned. "He thought me and her were an item."

Phil smirked. "Hope you told him you go for brains as well as looks."

"Oi, no being rude about Siri. Maybe she isn't the sharpest nail file in the salon, but she's a lovely girl. Now, are you going to choose, or are we going on a starvation diet tonight?"

Predictably, despite my best efforts, Phil's dinner choices were red meat all the way, but I had spinach cannelloni, followed by a marinated mixed fish dish. When you're staying by the sea, you have to sample the old *frutti di mare*, don't you? I almost didn't go for the seafood—what with Wayne's dicky tum-tum, it made you wonder—then I told myself not to be daft. He hadn't even eaten here tonight, had he? Most likely it was something he'd had for lunch God knew where that had upset his delicate digestion. My innards definitely approved of the lush mix of flavours on my plate, and I eased the taste buds down with a delicate panna cotta for dessert. Nice.

I put my spoon on my empty plate with a happy sigh, and glanced up to see Phil with a resigned expression. "Planning to leave me for the chef here?"

"Nah, now we're married, I thought I'd murder you for the life insurance. Me and him could start up our own restaurant on that." I grinned. Then I started to second-guess myself—Phil's first husband (civil partner, whatever) had died. Was I being insensitive?

"Wouldn't advise it. You'd hate the hours," was all Phil said, before suggesting, "Coffee on the terrace?"

We had an oddly peaceful hour or so out there, with Siri still fully monopolised by Martin. They were sitting by the balcony at a cosy table for two, and her laughter rang out every other minute at something he'd said. There were a fair few empty glasses on their table too.

"Think Wayne needs to worry?" I muttered to Phil, wondering if *someone* ought to be worrying about her. Yeah, she was a grown woman, but she'd struck me as liable to be a little too trusting of the wrong sort.

"She'll be fine. She's drinking sparkling water." My Phil: mind reader. Also, scarily observant, but that presumably went with the profession.

"Yeah? Guess it's only Wayne who drives her to drink, then."

Phil's answer, whatever it might have been, was interrupted by a loud bang, followed by a concerted *Ooh!* From our fellow terrace-sitters.

"Blimey, fireworks again already? And here I thought they'd only laid them on to celebrate our first night here. I don't feel special anymore." I gave Phil a significant look, which he ignored, so I prodded him. "Oi. You're supposed to say I'll always be special to you."

He smirked. "You're special, all right."

"Back in school, are we?" It just slipped out, honest. "Oh, hey, that was a good one," I added, moving on quickly. The lights on the balcony dimmed, presumably so we could all focus on the light show. I watched for a few minutes, then realised Phil's focus was on something else entirely. Namely, yours truly.

I turned. "What? Have I got sauce on my face?"

Phil's smile was eerie in the near-darkness, all the shadows falling wrong and giving him faint serial-killer vibes, but I worked out after a mo it was simply an expression of unusual mushiness. He cleared his throat. "You will be, you know."

"Uh?" I said, in a stunning display of my effortless wit and charm.

Phil's voice was low as he took my hand. "Special. Always." His thumb made rhythmic caressing motions that set off their own fireworks all through me.

It was a real honeymoon moment—until, out of the corner of my eye, I spied a dimly lit Wayne striding onto the balcony, apparently now no longer poorly and on a mission to harsh our buzz. "Uh-oh, we've got incoming."

Phil followed my gaze—then stood up so quick his chair skittered over the tiles with a nasty rasp. "Come on. We can watch the fireworks from our room."

"Good plan." I wasn't going to argue with a spot of Wayne-avoiding. I stood up with equal haste, and we scarpered. Circuitously, so as to avoid bumping into the git and defeating the object. Luckily everyone else was apparently too busy *ooh*ing and *aah*ing at the fireworks to notice our unseemly haste.

A couple of Italian-looking guys were waiting in the corridor as we got out of the lift on our floor. Phil stepped aside to let them get in. He seemed to pay them more attention than was strictly warranted by their flashy clothes, dark good looks, and . . . Okay, so it might have been *warranted*, but I couldn't help feeling it wasn't exactly polite while in the company of his newly wedded husband, aka me. Especially as at least one of the blokes was returning the attention with interest. "See something you like?" I asked a bit sharply after the lift door had slid shut.

Phil raised a mocking brow. "Jealous?"

"What? Me? Never." I fixed him straight in the eye as I lied through my teeth.

Phil huffed a laugh, so clearly I needed to practise in the mirror. "Course not. And you don't need to worry. I wasn't eyeing them up. Didn't you recognise them?"

Well, no. "From where?"

"From that meeting with Wayne at the café."

Huh. "Do you think they were here to see him tonight?"

He shrugged. "They're on the wrong floor for any of the public rooms."

"Good of them to be concerned about his dicky tum-tum. Wonder if Siri knew they were coming?"

"Shouldn't think he involves her in a lot of his business decisions."

"Shouldn't think he involves her in the decision about what to have for dinner."

"No. He always did like to think he knew best." Phil's steps slowed, presumably bogged down by whatever the opposite of nostalgia is. Nostrophobia, aka a fear of being trapped in the past?

At any rate, I hoped that was how he was feeling. It wasn't like *I* had a lot in the way of fond memories of our mutual schooldays. Reaching our door, I pulled out my key card. "Ready for those fireworks?" I asked with a flirtatious glance. "And then an early night after the, uh, banging stops?"

Phil smirked. "Who says it'll still be early by then?" He grabbed me around the waist as he followed me into the room, and there was a very real danger we were going to forget all about taking in the view from the balcony. Until, that was, a particularly loud explosion in the sky outside reminded us.

"Come on," I chivvied. "Light show first. Sex later."

"Sure about that?" Phil did his best—with both hands—to shake my resolve, but I wasn't having it.

"Hey, I want your full attention on me when we're in bed. Can't have you getting distracted by loud noises at a crucial moment." I pulled him by the hand onto our little balcony, where outside, the firework display was still in full swing.

Phil settled in behind me as I leaned on the railing, his big arms around me and one part of him clearly giving me its full attention already as it pressed into my lower back. I watched the fireworks glitter through the sky, shooting to the heavens and falling in a shower of multicoloured sparks over the picturesque bay. Tiny boats far below appeared like pale ghosts in the bright flashes, then drifted back into darkness, while my arguably better half kissed the back of my neck and whispered promises in my ear.

Just like on the terrace earlier, it was a perfect honeymoon moment.

Until some bugger ruined it by sailing past our window and going splat on the tarmac below.

Of course, the fireworks didn't end just because some poor sod had gone off to meet his maker. But their continued celebration of whatever-it-was took on a macabre air—*Ding dong, the witch is dead.*

Okay, so maybe my perceptions were coloured a touch by my strong suspicions as to who was currently rapping on those pearly gates.

I couldn't turn away from the grisly sight on the road below, although the street lighting was doing a mercifully poor job of illuminating its details. The lemon truck that had decisively extinguished any lingering hope of life screeched to a stop. The driver hopped out and walked back to the bump in the road—quickly at first, but then slowing, as if he'd realised that he really didn't want to see what he'd run over. I couldn't blame the guy.

Other drivers swerved around the obstructions, and horns blared, their outraged honks interspersed with the bangs of the fireworks. There was a more immediate *bang* as two cars tried to occupy the same space at the same time, and angry shouts were added to the mix.

It didn't sound like the dearly departed would be resting in peace anytime soon. "It is him, innit?" I said, my throat dry.

"Wayne? Yeah." Phil's voice was clipped, and his arms had stiffened around me.

"Christ, that's . . . But we were just with him." Avoiding him, to be strictly accurate. I swallowed around a hard lump of guilt.

"Yeah."

He'd sounded as shaken as I felt, and I squeezed his arms in an attempt at comfort. "Think we ought to call 999? Or whatever number it is here?"

"It's 112," Phil murmured. "Pretty sure someone who speaks Italian will have taken care of that by now."

He was almost certainly right. "What the hell do you think happened?" I cleared my throat. "I mean, it's obvious what's happened, but, you know, *how*?"

There was a pause. "The railings on the terrace aren't that high."

"So you think, what, he tripped or had a dizzy spell or something and toppled over?"

It couldn't be that simple.

Could it?

My stomach lurched. "Bloody hell, Siri. She was on the terrace. She probably saw the whole thing."

Even as I spoke, Phil's warm arms released me and he stepped back. "We should go up there."

Good thing we hadn't managed to get our kit off yet. I checked myself to make sure nothing needed tucking back in and then followed Phil's determined stride out of the room.

Halfway down the corridor I had a thought. "Are we going to the right place? Maybe they went back to their room after we left, and he fell from there?"

"No. That's down the far end of the corridor. This floor. He wouldn't have fallen past our window. And we're directly below the end of the terrace."

I was equal parts impressed by his observational skills—I'd had no clue where these places were in relation to each other—and queasy from picturing it all again.

And God, if I felt that way, how was Phil coping?

"Are you okay?" We'd reached the lift now, but it was taking its sweet bloody time coming. "He was a mate of yours."

The lift arrived—empty—and we got in, Phil jabbing the button for the top floor. "I'm okay."

"Good," I said, because I couldn't think of anything else to say and, well, it was good, wasn't it?

Or it would have been, if I'd believed him.

The top floor, when we got there, was bedlam. The lights had been turned up brighter than I'd ever seen them, shrill voices filled the air, and everyone—guests and staff alike—had crowded over to the balcony railings. I hoped Wayne wasn't about to have some company down there on the tarmac. Okay, not everyone was rubbernecking at the railings. The guy behind the reception desk was stage-whispering down the phone in rapid-fire Italian, his face ashen, and a few of the guests were sneaking off with nothing-to-do-with-us expressions. I spotted a reluctant Cassie being hustled away by her tight-lipped sister, while Mr. and Mrs. Snipe were at the back of the queue to have a good gawp, looking disgruntled. Presumably they'd been busy either fighting or fondling each other at the fatal moment.

And off to one side, Siri was in Martin's arms, her head on his shoulder. I legged it over to them, Phil behind me.

What did you say to someone who'd just watched her bloke die? She didn't raise her head, so I spoke to Martin instead. "How's she doing?"

"Not well. Not well at all," he said severely, patting her bare shoulder as she sobbed. "I take it you're aware of what happened?"

I grimaced. "We saw. From our balcony."

"What exactly did happen?" Phil's low rumble was calm but steely. He sounded more in control of himself now. Police training had kicked in, I reckoned.

Martin rolled his eyes. "I thought you said you'd seen it? He *fell.*" There was a louder sob from Siri. "And would you mind keeping your ghoulish curiosity to yourselves? We have a grieving widow here."

"Yeah, and Phil here and Wayne were mates from way back." I was rapidly going off this bloke.

"I'm fine," Phil barked out before Martin could reply to that.

Martin gave us both a hard stare instead. "Indeed. You got back from your room remarkably quickly."

And what the bloody hell was that supposed to mean? Sod it. Arguing with the bastard wasn't going to help anyone. Least of all Siri. I put a hand on Phil's arm. "Uh, right. Siri, if you need anything, you let us know, yeah?" The shoulder I'd addressed quivered, but she didn't reply.

We shuffled away as the *polizia* arrived. A matched pair of uniforms, one occupied by a dark-skinned young jack-the-lad and the other by a white bloke who was grizzled and thickset but still fit. The older officer greeted the guy at the reception desk with a hearty handshake and shoulder clasp, like they were old mates, then sauntered onto the terrace with a visible air of command.

It's times like these you realise how much difference the choice of uniform makes. Think of the UK boys and girls in blue, and you're immediately hit with words like *solid*, *dependable*, and *Dixon of Dock Green*, even if, like me, you're way too young to have seen the show. It's like a cultural memory or something. Bobbies on bikes, and *If you want to know the time, ask a policeman*. What your average British uniformed copper is not, however, is sexy. Maybe it's the helmets, and those daft hats the women wear.

Italian cops—and they're definitely cops, not coppers—are a whole different kettle of *pesce del giorno*. Maybe it's not just their short-sleeved shirts that show off tanned and/or toned forearms, or the cut of their dark uniform trousers with the nifty go-faster red stripes down the legs. Maybe they get the swagger from the motorbikes they ride, the guns they carry—or maybe it comes from being Italian. Who knows? All I knew was, despite my fairly extensive experience with the lads and lasses colloquially known as the filth (although not in Phil's hearing if you knew what was good for you), I felt well out of my depth here. All right, these guys seemed to be doing the same sort of thing my mate DCI Dave Southgate now has minions to do—taking names, asking questions, marching around like they owned the place—but I still felt off-kilter. Like any minute they might round the lot of us up and charge us with conspiracy.

Were you innocent until proven guilty in Italy?

I had a hot, prickly sensation inside, as if my conscience was tugging on my sleeve and shouting *Oi* in my ear. But that was daft. What did I have to feel guilty about?

I needn't have worried we'd be up all night answering official questions. The younger and fitter officer of the law didn't take long to establish that me and Phil hadn't been anywhere near poor old Wayne when he'd taken his tumble—at least, not for more than half a second or so when he hurtled past our window. He quickly told me and Phil to shove off and stop wasting their time, although he put it a little less rudely than that.

"Do you feel like a spare part?" I asked Phil as we made our way back to our room. "I feel like a spare part. Hope Siri's okay. I'm not sure I like leaving her with that Martin bloke. She only met him this evening."

"She only met you and me two days ago."

"Huh. Is that all it's been? Feels longer." My head was reeling. "Poor kid. Not what she expected when she signed up for this. But anyhow, I trust me and you with her. I don't trust him not to take advantage."

"She's a grown woman. If she wants us, she knows how to get hold of us." Phil slung an arm around my waist. "There's not a lot anyone can do for her right now."

Probably not. God, what must it be like for her to lose the bloke she'd perhaps been hoping to spend her life with?

I shivered as we walked into our room. Maybe we needed to turn the air-con down a notch.

Of course, after a shock like that, there was no going to sleep for a while, and neither of us was up for anything else associated with going to bed. I sprawled on top of the duvet, while Phil stood and stared out of the window, gazing into the darkness.

I hoped that was what he was looking at. Rather than, say, watching Wayne fall again and again in his mind's eye.

I don't know how long he stayed there. I must have dozed off at some point, and when Phil finally came to bed, I barely woke up enough to shove my kit off and creep under the duvet to join him.

When I drifted off again, he was still awake.

Chapter Thirteen

It probably wasn't surprising I had weird dreams again that night. I was back on that rooftop terrace, with Wayne leaning on the railings with me. He was explaining earnestly to me that he'd never hated me back when we were in school together; in fact he'd been in love with me, although he had plenty of arguments why that didn't in any way, shape, or form make him less than one hundred percent straight.

"So you see," he was saying, "it'll break my heart. But it has to be done." Then he pushed me over the railing. I woke up with a lurch as I was about to hit the ground, my heart heavy with an inexplicable sense of loss.

I must have gasped or flailed, as when I blinked open bleary eyes, Phil was staring at me. "You all right?"

"Yeah. Course. Uh, time to get up?"

He paused, searching me with his gaze, and then nodded.

Breakfast was a little on the subdued side, for me and Phil at any rate. We'd slept later than usual, but I was still feeling tired and raw. Even Phil's eyes had a hint of circles under them.

Everyone else seemed to be chatting away happily enough, although I noticed the tables nearest to the balcony weren't as popular as they normally were. Was it really only a couple of days since Wayne had stood up and hailed us from his breakfast table? The clash of cutlery against china and the scraping of chairs on tiles sounded excessively loud this morning. Disrespectful, even. Whatever happened to stopping all the flippin' clocks?

"We should hit Pompeii today," Phil said as he passed the butter.

I took the little dish of silver packets, grumpily wondered what people in Europe had against salt, and frowned at him. "Are you sure?

I mean, it seems a bit, well, *off*, somehow, us going gadding about while Wayne's barely cold in his . . ." I wasn't sure how to finish. *Grave* wasn't exactly accurate, but specifying *mortuary drawer* seemed more unfeeling than I was already accusing Phil of being.

Phil gave me a look. "You didn't even like him."

"That's . . . not the point. And anyway, *you* did. Once, anyway."

"It's complicated." He frowned at the generous serving of prosciutto crudo, salami, and cheese on his plate, then fixed me in the eye. "I told you I wasn't going to let him ruin our honeymoon, and I meant it. Alive or dead."

I leaned on the table, bringing our heads closer. "And there's the stubborn git I know and love. It doesn't matter, okay? So this holiday hasn't turned out as planned. So what?"

I swear I heard his teeth grind together. I made a mental note to remind him to go for a dentist's checkup when we got back home.

"*So*, this is our honeymoon," Phil insisted. "We only get one, remember."

"Technically, this is your second," some bastard evil spirit made me quip.

Phil froze.

I winced. "Shit. Ignore me."

He swallowed and took my hand. "You think it means less to me because I've been married before?"

Did I? I hadn't *thought* that was what I thought, but maybe it'd been in the back of my mind somewhere. Round about the place I was hiding the old, old insecurity Wayne's being here had stirred up.

I didn't say that, obviously. I said, "Course I don't. It was a bad joke, that's all," gave his hand a squeeze, and told him to eat up before I got my hands on his meat, innuendo definitely intended.

Phil didn't smile. But he did start munching on his prosciutto crudo, so I counted that as a win.

We wandered out onto the terrace after we'd eaten. I'd wondered if there'd be a morning-after feel to the place, a sudden death being bound to mess up the usual routine. But glasses had been cleared from tables, and all the chair cushions were freshly fluffed. In the light of what'd happened last night, the blood-red colour scheme didn't look quite as cheery as it used to, but that was possibly just me.

The only sign of Wayne's passing was a pathetic bit of police tape stretched across a yard or two of balcony rail. Some of the plant pots had been shifted over in an equally half-hearted attempt to block the awful site from view.

I nodded in that direction. "Guess that's where he went over."

Phil had been dead right about the positioning; at the end of the balcony farthest from the bar and the lights. I sidled around the plant pots and took a peek down over the railing, then wished I hadn't. There were some darker patches on the tarmac below that hadn't been made by burning rubber.

"Steady," Phil murmured, and I stepped back from the railing to find myself the object of several gazes. Expressions on the faces of the onlookers ranged from concerned (Will the waiter, who'd served us all drinks at the pool around a millennium ago) to disapproving (Jane Higginbottom, who seemed to have mislaid her sister again and was either annoyed about that or, more likely, about my rubbernecking.)

Phil's face was mostly unreadable, although there might have been a touch of wry amusement in there at me making a spectacle of myself.

"Rather ghoulish, don't you think?" Jane snapped.

Had she been talking to Martin? I opened my mouth to defend myself, but Phil beat me to the punch. "Did you see what happened?"

"I hardly think that's a suitable topic of conversation in the circumstances."

Sensing Phil about to come over all *Just trying to get the facts, ma'am*, I shoved an ingratiating oar in. "Must have been pretty traumatic for you and Cassie."

"A dreadful business. Dreadful. We didn't sleep a wink last night. Poor Cassie couldn't even come to breakfast this morning. She can be very sensitive."

From what I'd seen of her, Cassie was about as sensitive as a Chieftain tank, but Jane probably knew her own sister best. I gave her a sympathetic grimace. "Yeah, had trouble sleeping myself last night. He went right past our window, you know."

Jane looked like she wasn't sure what to make of that nugget of extra colour. "Dreadful," she said at last, clearly feeling safe with that one.

"Yeah. You see something like that, and there's nothing you can do to stop it . . . It's tough, innit?"

Her mouth pursed. "I suppose it must be upsetting for you, having been on friendly terms with him. Although . . ." She frowned again and turned away.

I was still wondering what she'd been about to say when Phil stepped in. "We were at school with him. Long time ago, of course."

Jane glanced back sharply. "You were? Both of you? I didn't realise you'd been together for so many years."

I put an arm around my husband's waist and gave her a smile. "Yep. Childhood sweethearts, that's us." I'm pretty sure Phil's snort was too faint for her to hear.

One way or another, we'd rendered her speechless, so I pushed the advantage. If Phil needed to learn the full story of how his ex–best mate kicked it—and it certainly seemed like he did—then he was bloody well going to, if I had any say in the matter. "Yeah, we've known Wayne a long time, so obviously, what happened . . . Well, it shakes you up, doesn't it? We just thought it might help, knowing how he'd fallen. Give us some closure, you know?" Okay, so I couldn't actually see inside Phil's head, but *I* was sort of feeling that way, and I hadn't even been friends with Wayne.

She nodded, her face pained. "I can see that. Yes, that makes sense. But it was very dark out here last night, and we were all watching the fireworks."

"So you didn't see him go over the railings?" Phil asked gently.

"If I *had* seen anything, don't you think I'd have told the police? Although whether one can really trust these Italian police is another matter. From what I hear, corruption is rife in this country. *Rife*. Now, if you'll excuse me, I must see to my sister." She stalked off like an angry peacock, her sharp nose leading the way. Apparently she'd reached her daily limit for suffering ghouls gladly.

I turned back to Phil with a rueful smile. "Talking of family, I s'pose the police will have notified Wayne's next of kin, right? Would you still have a number for his mum and dad, in case they haven't?"

Phil shook his head. "You know his mum died, right? Just after we started in the sixth form."

She did? That was young. "I didn't spend a lot of time in sixth form, if you recall." I'd been in hospital for a large part of it, recovering from an argument with a four-by-four, and had never bothered going back for the rest.

Phil coloured a smidge. Probably because I'd never have been in harm's way if I hadn't been running away from him and dear old Wayne at the time. Still, forgive and forget, and all that. "Wayne and his dad didn't get on after she was gone," he said. "Not sure he kept in touch with him."

Would that make it better or worse for the old bloke, hearing his kid had died? My money was on worse, but families can be tricky things. Not all still waters run deep. "I guess Siri would know. Gotta be hard on her, though, if she's the one who has to break the news. Think we should go check on her? Find out how she's bearing up?"

Phil nodded, and we set off. I snuck a glance his way, to check on how *he* was bearing up, but it was a toss-up as to whether the faint crease in his forehead was down to Wayne's death, or the imminent prospect of speaking to a grief-stricken Siri.

"'Spect she'll be heading home soon as she can get a flight," I mused as we got in the lift. "Not exactly the holiday of a lifetime she was expecting."

"If the police haven't asked her to stick around," he murmured.

"What, to deal with the body and stuff?" I shivered and quickened my steps. "Poor kid. She's all on her own in a foreign country."

Phil nodded and matched my stride.

When we knocked on Siri's door, though, it was Martin who answered. He looked—as far as I could see through the three-inch crack in the door—tired, dishevelled, and not very chuffed to see us. "Oh. It's you."

"Been here all night? Don't hang around, do you?" I said before I could stop myself.

His eyes narrowed. "Are you insinuating something? That's absurd."

Nothing absurd about it. I could just see him doing the whole *You shouldn't be alone right now* routine. "Taking care of Siri, I mean. In a totally platonic way. Obviously. How's she doing?"

"How do you think she's doing?"

Phil cleared his throat. "Is she up to seeing us?"

"Not now. She's sleeping." He ran a hand through his hair, messing it up even worse. Oddly, it made me feel a little more sympathetic towards him. "She had a dreadful night. Come back this evening."

"You're staying in her room?" It came out a bit sharp, but then I *was* suspicious of his motives, not to mention his morals.

Martin didn't seem to notice. He nodded. "She shouldn't be alone."

Hah. I'd *known* it.

"There's a chair I can get some rest in," he added, so maybe my face had given away my suspicious little mind. "Come back tonight."

I looked at Phil. He looked back.

What could we do, apart from barge our way in, wake up Siri, and cause a scene? From what we'd seen last night, she trusted the bloke. Setting ourselves against him on no evidence but our lack of faith in human nature would only make it less likely she'd come to us for help if she needed it.

"Tonight," Phil said with a nod, and we slunk back down the corridor with our tails between our legs.

Having bugger all useful to do, we did what Phil had suggested in the first place and went to Pompeii. The train was crowded, proving that life went on, except, obviously, when it didn't. It was only half as far to Pompeii as to Ercolano, but I was still sweating enough for the leading role in *porchetta alla romana* by the time we finally squeezed off the train and straight into the queue for the historical site.

Had I thought Naples was hot? Pompeii was something else again. A blinding expanse of one-storey, white stone buildings reflected the heat of the sun directly at the hordes of unwary tourists as we sweltered our way from street to dusty street. Probably, back in Ye Olde Roman Tymes, the town had been full of cool porticoes, with maybe even a hint of greenery here and there, but now there was barely a whisper of shade to be seen. I'd have tried to muscle into Phil's shadow for a bit of relief, but with the sun so high in the sky, his normally tall, bulky shade had shrunk as if he'd somehow picked up Darren's dwarf-sized one by mistake.

Only five minutes in the sun, and I was dripping like a burst pipe. Even Phil, who could generally be relied on to make a cucumber look as though it'd run a marathon in a heatwave by comparison, was mopping his brow with a well-pressed handkerchief.

"Which way first?" I squinted at the guidebook, its pages dazzlingly white. We'd decided to forgo a guided tour here, which probably saved us at least a liver and a kidney apiece. "Forum? Or do you want to hit up the brothel before it gets too busy?"

Phil huffed. "Pretty sure the brothel's always busy. Let's do the forum."

I peered at the site map. Pompeii, bless those straight-line-loving Romans, had been laid out on a grid system, so it was dead easy to work out our route. Particularly as the forum turned out to be only a couple of streets distant from where we'd entered the site. "This way."

We set off. It seemed weird to think of these parched streets being trod by the sandalled feet of long-dead Romans, two thousand years in the past. It seemed even weirder to think of them being trod by the not-so-long-dead Wayne, only a few days ago.

I still felt guilty, going out and enjoying myself so soon after Wayne had been whisked off to the great tourist destination in the sky, but sod it. Phil was right. This was our honeymoon. And it wasn't like moping around would help anyone.

The forum, the city's main square, was bigger than it'd looked on the map. It was a wide, open space bordered by the remains of pillars and archways, built of a lot more red brick than I'd been expecting. I guessed they'd been part of temples and government offices, back in the day. A couple of nude statues stood around on plinths with a vaguely embarrassed air, and at one end was an enormous disembodied face, its style way too modern for the rest of the site. From where we were standing, there was a spectacular view of the agent of the city's destruction, Vesuvius, sitting deceptively serene under achingly blue skies.

Even the hordes of tourists that'd swarmed up with us from the train station couldn't make the place feel crowded.

"Bit, well, desolate, innit?" I muttered, turning slowly on the spot to take it all in.

And that was before we took a proper gander at the plaster casts housed in a series of open-faced sheds to one side. There were quite a few of them—men, women, children; even Siri's poor chained-up dog, its body contorted in its final agonies. I wasn't sure how I felt about all those re-creations of the dead caught in their last moments.

No, scratch that. I knew how I felt, and what I felt was *Bloody hell, what happened to Rest in Peace?* I gawped at all the tourists taking holiday snaps of contorted—okay, not actual corpses, but they might as well have been—and couldn't help thinking about paparazzi chasing Princess Di to her death back when I'd been a nipper. It wasn't right.

Some of them were taking *selfies* in front of the dearly departed, for Christ's sake.

Beside me, Phil huffed. "So much for 'The grave's a fine and private place,'" he muttered.

He had that right. Then I gave him a sharp look. "Was that a quote?"

"A poem. By some bloke called Marvell." He went pink, and I was fairly sure it wasn't the world's quickest sunburn.

I took a step back, the better to stare at him in amazement. "Since when are you into poetry?"

"I used to travel on the underground in London, didn't I? And they had poems up on the trains."

"Huh." In fact, that did ring a bell, not that I'd ever gone into London all that often. "So what's the rest of that one? Was this Marvell bloke some sort of goth, into all the death and decay stuff?"

"Don't remember the rest." He gave me a sly smile. "But it was about sex, not death."

"Seriously? What, the advantages of having it off with someone in their tomb? If you ask me, they ought to be sending the boys in blue round to see this Marvell bloke, not bunging his dirty limericks up on trains. There's laws against that kind of stuff." I frowned. "There *are* laws against necrowhatsit, right? You ever arrest anyone for it?"

"No, thank God. But yes, there are laws against it."

"Yeah, and that's got to be a fun job, right? Making the laws in the first place, that is. Did some legal geezer sit in a room on his own thinking of all the deviant practices he could come up with so he could make them illegal?" I made a face. "I suppose they've got to have some compensation for all those years of studying law."

"Far as I know, the authorities used to wait for issues to arise and then legislate. No point making laws about it if nobody's doing it."

Ye gods. "Guess it'd be a shame to have a shiny new law on your books and never get to prosecute any poor sod with it. But you can put me down for cremation when I kick the bucket. You know, just in case. At least that's one thing the people who lived here didn't have to worry about. Okay, where to next?"

I let my gaze drift around idly, and I swear I'd never have noticed the bloke if he hadn't been staring at me. For a second our eyes met, and icy fingers ran down my spine at that cold gaze.

The bloke giving me the hairy eyeball was over the other side of the forum, so a fair distance away, but he seemed familiar, somehow. Too smartly dressed for a tourist, for one thing, and wasn't that a flash of bling around his neck catching the sun and throwing it back at me? I frowned. "Okay, my last brain cell's probably melted and dribbled out my ears, so I may be seeing things, but do you reckon that's one of Wayne's local mafia mates? Over there, by the stumpy pillar."

Phil glanced round sharply—but not sharply enough; the guy must have clocked my interest, and he'd turned his back. "Are you sure?"

"Well, no, or I wouldn't have asked."

"Let's get a closer look." Phil strode off. Even as he did so, Mr. Maybe Mafia loped away, his step apparently unhurried but still too quick for us, unless we wanted to break into a run. Which would have (a) caused a scene and (b) led to a swift and sweaty death from heat exhaustion. By the time we made it to where he'd disappeared around a corner, there was no telling which way he'd gone.

Phil's brow furrowed as he stood in the cobbled street, hands on hips, glowering into the heat haze.

"Sod it, I was probably imagining it anyway," I said, feeling like I was making Vesuvius out of a verruca. Chances were he'd been staring because he was a bigot and me and Phil had been acting too couple-y or something. Or on the less homophobic hand, maybe he'd thought we were fit? "Why would one of Wayne's mates be stalking us?

And anyway, we're in Italy. Dark-haired blokes with a flashy dress sense are ten a sesterce around here. Did you know there were four sesterces to the denarius? Or possibly the other way around. But the brothel prices were in asses, and I swear I'm not making that up. Amazing what you can learn from guidebooks."

Phil huffed and turned around. "You're probably right about the bloke. Neither of us slept well last night. Come on—let's go and see that brothel you're so obsessed with."

"Obsessed? No. Nosy, yeah. And we have to watch out for a penis in the street. Apparently it points the way."

We managed to miss the penis en route—Gary was never going to let me live that down when he heard about it—but found the brothel anyway, chiefly by the large queue of people outside waiting for their turn to go in and ogle at the frisky frescoes.

For a place so popular, it was surprisingly poky. Pun not intended. The single-bedded rooms might have been adequate for a quick bit of how's-your-paterfamilias, but there really wasn't room to swing a cat, if that happened to be the fetish of your choosing. I left the place untitillated by the heterosexual erotic art but with a new respect for the ancient Roman prostitutes, forced to ply their trade on beds made out of stone. "Hope they had cushions on top of those," I murmured as we made our way down the street afterwards. "Or handed out kneepads."

Phil didn't answer, and he didn't look at me either, so I elbowed him in the ribs. "Oi, am I boring you?"

He blinked and turned to me. "Thought I saw that bloke again."

Great. Now I'd made him jumpy too. "Where?"

"On the corner. He's gone now."

"Was it definitely him?"

Phil shook his head. "Didn't see his face this time either. But the clothes were right."

I sighed. "We could head over that way to check. You know, if you're worried." In other words, if I'd totally bollocksed up our day out with my infectious paranoia.

"No. It's fine." It didn't sound fine. Then his face changed. "Unless you're worried . . . ?"

"Me? No." I forced a laugh. "Wish I'd never mentioned the bloke. But I don't mind if you want to—"

"It's fine." Phil folded his arms. "So what are the other must-sees in that book of yours?"

I gave in, and we set off for a nose around the houses and civic amenities of the place. To be honest, halfway through it all I started to forget what we'd seen and what we hadn't—there was a staggering number of streets and buildings that'd been excavated and were open to view. One thing that struck me was how much colour those old Romans had liked in their interior decorating—there was a wealth of rich reds, greens, and ambers, in stark contrast to the white stone of the exteriors. Although maybe they'd been painted too, once upon a time? I couldn't remember anything in the guidebooks about that, but to be fair I hadn't read every word.

Several hours later, we'd still only seen a fraction of the place, but my head was ready to explode from an overdose of ancient artwork. I was fairly sure I'd seen more tits than penises too. Talk about your false advertising. Apparently all the best phallic art had been carted off to the museum in Naples, where it couldn't frighten the horses.

We eventually admitted defeat and traipsed back to the station. I had a feeling Phil was keeping half a weary eye out for Mr. Maybe Mafia en route, but he'd clearly buggered off to stalk someone else.

Or, you know, gone home for his tea because he was a completely innocent member of the ruins-visiting public who'd simply happened to glance in my direction at the wrong moment.

Yeah. That was probably it.

So what if the back of my neck prickled as we made our way through the crowds? It was just a scratchy shirt label, right?

Chapter Fourteen

By the time we'd got back to Sorrento and slogged up the hill to the hotel, there was barely time to shower and change before heading to the restaurant for dinner. I scanned the crowd as we made our way to our table. "Can't see Siri. Or her knight in stripy shirts."

"Are you surprised?"

"Not particularly." If it'd been me, I wouldn't have much fancied going to dinner to be gawked at. Then I frowned. "Hey, you don't think she's gone home already, do you? I feel a bit . . . I dunno. Like we should have made more of an effort to see her off."

"Martin said we'd see her this evening," Phil reminded me, taking his seat.

"Yeah, but he's not the boss of her."

"After what happened, she might be glad to have someone else making the decisions for a while. Anyway, we'll find out soon enough. We'll go by her room after we've eaten."

I nodded, and we chowed down on food that was probably every bit as tasty as all the other nights. I just wasn't in a mood to appreciate it. Ever since we'd got back to the hotel, I'd felt the weight of . . . reality, I guess. Mortality, even. Which was weird—after all, I'd spent pretty much the entire day thinking about death. But this was different. I'd known Wayne. I'd been speaking to him only a short while before he'd died. No offence to all the dearly departed Pompeiians, but their deaths didn't hit me in the gut like Wayne's did. It wasn't that I exactly missed the bloke—but I did feel desperately sorry for Siri. And the father Wayne had left behind, who presumably must have loved him once.

"Did he have any brothers or sisters?" I asked, chasing my dessert around the plate with a half-hearted fork.

Phil raised an eyebrow. "Wayne? No. Only child."

"Huh. No surprise there. Uh, not that I'm saying he was spoilt or anything."

"He was, a bit. His mum could be smothering." Phil gave a half smile. "He used to complain about it, but I think he liked it really. His dad used to say she was turning him soft."

And there was an insight into the Hills family dynamics I'd never have expected to get. "I s'pose you used to go round his house a lot," I mused, pushing my plate away. "You and him being mates, and all. Did you keep in touch after you left school?"

Phil put down his fork. "No. You ready to go and see Siri?"

I took the hint, nodded, and we stood.

We were walking back through the bar when blow me if I didn't see Siri heading towards us. All on her lonesome, moreover. Not a pair of red braces in sight.

She was a mess, bless her. Yeah, she'd always been slender, but she'd never seemed so fragile to me before. Hunched in on herself, her arms wrapped around her middle as if to hold herself together, she even appeared shorter than she'd been only a day ago. Her sleeveless cotton top hung on her slumped shoulders like yesterday's dishcloth.

If Martin had been with her, he'd have been getting dagger glares from me. Had he forgotten she needed food as well as sympathy?

Her face looked odd, somehow, and it wasn't all down to the puffy eyelids and red tint to her eyes. I realised after a mo that it was the first time I'd seen her without makeup. Her eyebrows had all but disappeared and her full lips were pale as death.

Not a good thought, that.

"Oi, come here," I said, my voice gruff as I opened my arms.

Siri flung herself at me, and the floodgates opened. Her face burrowed into my neck, and stifled sobs wracked her sparrowlike frame. Something inside me twisted at the sheer pain I could feel coming off her in waves.

Maybe Wayne had been a tit—and not of the feathered variety—but she'd loved him.

I held her, and Phil patted her shoulder, until the heaving subsided a little. Then I pulled back to look her in the face. "Let's get you a cup of tea, all right?"

She gave a hefty sniff, visibly pulling herself together, and nodded. Phil produced his trusty handkerchief, and she gave a good blow, then absentmindedly shoved it in her bra for safekeeping. Which I'd have thought wouldn't be very comfortable, but what did I know?

Pockets. They're a feminist issue.

"What are you doing here on your own?" I asked, as Phil strode over to the bar. "I thought Martin was taking care of you."

Siri glanced over her shoulder. "He's been great, yeah. But I wanted to find you and Phil."

"We were just on our way to see you, as it happens. How've you been?"

She managed a wobbly half smile. "Been better. But it's so sweet you were thinking of me. You been out and about?"

"Yeah. Pompeii." A smidge of free-floating guilt made me add, "Martin reckoned there wasn't anything we could do for you, so . . ."

"It's dead good there, innit? W-Wayne loved it." She sniffled loudly but managed not to break down into sobs again.

I was still desperately trying to think of what to say to her when Phil came back with Will the waiter bearing a tea tray. I wasn't sure how much he must have tipped the bloke to get it that quick, but it had been worth it. "Let's sit inside," I suggested, leading the way to a low table that was partially shielded from casual view by a large potted plant.

I didn't reckon it'd do Siri any good to go out for fresh air on the balcony, in the circs.

We could have done with a proper builder's brew, but this being Italy where coffee is king, had to settle for watery English Breakfast. Siri had hers with a shedload of milk and sugar, which ought to do her some good even though the taste would've made me gag. I got the waiter to bring us some biscotti as well, seeing as she obviously needed fortifying.

"I could kill for a chocolate HobNob," Siri sniffed bravely, taking a biscotti. Biscotta? Luckily, she didn't seem to notice her somewhat unfortunate wording.

"Have you had dinner?" Phil asked.

Siri shook her head. "Couldn't eat a thing." She grabbed another biscotto, though, and gave me a hint of a smile when I pushed the plate nearer to her.

"S'pose you'll be wanting to get back home soon," I said. "Need any help changing your flight?"

"No. I'm not going." Her tone was high but defiant.

I stared at her in surprise, and even Phil, over on the other side of the table, had raised an eyebrow. "You're going to stay the whole three weeks? On your own?"

"As long as it takes."

"As long as what takes?" Phil asked gently.

"I want justice for Wayne."

"Justice?" I frowned. "You mean you want to sue the hotel? For not having higher railings?"

"No. It's not the railings' fault. Wayne was pushed."

Phil's ears pricked up. "You saw someone push him?"

"Who?" I blurted.

Siri glared at us like *we* were the ones who'd shoved Wayne off that balcony. "I didn't *see*, but Wayne would never of leaned over like that. Not even after a few drinks. He hated heights. They used to make him dizzy."

Which, not to be the devil's advocate or anything, seemed to be a point in favour of him having toppled over by accident. Despite what Siri seemed to think. "Maybe he was trying to conquer his fear?"

She gazed at me with earnest, reddened eyes. "That's what that policeman said. But Wayne wasn't *scared.* It was, like, an inner-ear thing. He told me all about it."

It would have been pretty insensitive to call bullshit, so I didn't.

A few of our fellow guests wandered through the bar, fat and full after their dinner, and cast curious glances at our little huddle. I glared at them until they went away.

Phil bent forward, keeping his voice low. "So the police believe it was an accident? You're sure of that?"

Siri leaned over the table so far they nearly bumped heads. "I *told* them. I kept saying it couldn't have been. But they kept telling me to calm down, like . . . like I was hysterical or something. And I *wasn't*. I mean, I was upset, yeah, but they still should have listened."

Phil gave a minute nod. "Can you think of any reason why someone would want to harm Wayne?"

She shook her head, unkempt locks flying. "No. Everyone loved him, didn't they? Even you and him was mates now, wasn't you, Tom?"

"Uh, yeah." I resisted the urge to cross my fingers behind my back. "But if it wasn't an accident . . ."

"Someone must have been responsible," Phil finished for me.

"Maybe it was a, you know, mistaken-identity thing? Like, they were aiming for someone else? It was really dark." Her lip wobbled. "He was just in the wrong place at the wrong time, maybe?"

"It's possible," Phil said noncommittally. "But I think we also need to consider whether he might have been deliberately targeted. If you're sure it wasn't an accident."

She reached over the table to clutch his hand with both of hers, narrowly avoiding sending his teacup flying. "Then you'll do it, yeah? Investigate? That's what you do, isn't it?"

"It's . . . part of what I do," Phil said cautiously. He glanced at me. "But I'm on my honeymoon here—"

"You and Wayne was best mates, yeah? All them years ago in school. He looked up to you, I know he did. You can't . . . You've got to do right by him." Siri's knuckles had turned white, and I winced on Phil's behalf.

Phil, of course, was like a granite statue. Or maybe one of those plaster casts of the eruption victims . . . on second thoughts, best not to go there. "It's not just me I need to consider," he said with another glance at yours truly.

I wasn't prepared for what happened then, which was me getting an armful of Siri. Or to be accurate, her getting two handfuls of my upper arms, the awkward angle meaning she was practically in my lap. "You'll help me, won't you, Tom?" she begged, her pincerlike grasp presumably her way of making sure I paid proper attention while she was talking. "You will, won't you? Wayne was dead chuffed you and him was getting on now. He tried so hard to make you like him."

Her red-rimmed brown eyes blinked moistly in my face, and I caved. "Course we'll do it," I told her, patting her gingerly on the back.

Then I really did have an armful of Siri, as she flung herself around my neck and buried her face in my shoulder again. The ache in my upper arms had eased, but I was pretty sure the renewed sobbing was worse.

Not to mention the pain in my neck, as Siri's surprising weight all but dragged me out of my chair. We were drawing stares now too, so after I'd patted her back some more and murmured useful stuff like *there, there*, I gently prised her grip away. "How about we get you back to your room, now, hey? Not here to be the entertainment, are we?"

She did her best to blink back her tears, while I tried not to be too obvious about unkinking my spine. "You won't leave me alone, will you? I don't want to be on my own."

Phil coughed. "Is there someone who could come out here to be with you? Your mum, maybe?"

"She won't come. She'd have to shut the salon with me off too, and we can't risk losing the business. And she never liked Wayne." Siri's face crumpled. "She always said it'd end badly."

Chalk one up for mother's intuition. "Dad, then?" I suggested. "Brothers or sisters? Uh, friends?"

"I'll be fine," she said with a brave tilt of her chin. "I'm not a kid. And I've got you. And Martin, of course."

"Yeah . . ." I glanced at Phil. "Listen, about him. It's great he's been looking after you, but you've got to remember you've only just met him. I mean, what do you really know about the bloke? Do you even know his full name?"

Siri was frowning. "Yeah. It's Martin Kingsman. He told me. What are you trying to say?"

"You should be careful, okay? For all we know, he could be—"

"Hello, Martin," Phil interrupted. Loudly.

Chapter Fifteen

Me and Siri twisted in our seats. Yep, here Martin was, looking harassed but not quite as knackered as he had this morning. Blue braces and a shirt with a thinner stripe, so he'd clearly been back to his own room for a quick wash and brush up.

"*There* you are," he said to Siri, like she was a small child who'd run off in the shops. "I've been searching everywhere for you."

"I wanted to find Phil and Tom." Her voice held a hint of defiance. Had he been trying to tell her what she could and couldn't do?

Then again, if he had, her doing it anyway was a good sign—and hopefully meant the warning I'd been prevented from giving her wasn't needed, after all.

Martin gave a tight smile. "And what do Phil and Tom think about your theory?"

"We're looking into it," Phil said curtly. "Anything you can tell us about the incident?"

I'm pretty sure I didn't imagine the glare of intense loathing Martin shot him. But it was gone in an instant. "I didn't see what happened. I wasn't with him at the time he fell. Or was pushed," he amended after a small but significant pause.

"So where were you?" I prompted.

"Hmm. I'd escorted Siri over to the balcony to watch the fireworks. He'd . . . wandered off, I think. To be honest I wasn't paying him much attention."

Yeah, I could believe that, with fireworks going off overhead and, more to the point, an attractive young lady hanging off his arm.

The young lady in question nodded eagerly. "I wanted to see the boats below being all lit up. And I knew Wayne wouldn't want to.

So it was best for everyone, wasn't it? Me going with Martin." Her face crumpled again. "I wish I'd stayed with him now."

Martin put a hand on her shoulder. "Hush. You couldn't have known what would happen."

"Can you take us through the scene? From the start," Phil asked her.

Siri cringed, and Martin gave an exasperated growl. "Haven't we just done that? As I said, we were watching the fireworks until we heard a scream. That was when Wayne fell," he explained, in case we were too thick to make the connection.

"How far away were you from him when he fell?" Phil directed his question firmly at Siri.

She gazed up at Martin. "Where was we standing? It was close to the bar, wasn't it? I remember, cos—"

"Yes." Martin nodded emphatically. "And he fell from the other end of the balcony."

Phil's expression didn't flicker, even as he conceded defeat and addressed the annoying git directly, although he had to be getting a crick in his neck from craning up at him. "Do you remember who was near you at the time?"

"Hardly." Martin made a helpless gesture. "People were milling around all over the place, and as I said, we were watching the fireworks. Not the people. For God's sake, I've been over all this with the police, and if I'd been able to give them any evidence that it might not have been an accident, don't you think they'd have been acting on it?"

"So you think it *was* accidental?" Phil asked.

Siri gasped and turned a look of betrayal on her tarnished knight. "You said you believed me!"

"He's twisting my words. Of course I believe you." Martin patted her shoulder, then glared at Phil. "All I said was that I didn't *see* anything untoward. Now come along. You've had enough upset for one evening. I'm sure Phil and Tom can get on with their investigation without our help."

He took her hand, and she let him pull her up and lead her away.

"We need to get her on her own," Phil muttered as we watched them toddle off, arm in arm.

I nodded. "Yeah. Think it's deliberate, him not letting her get a word in edgewise? It's the sort of thing you'd do if you had something to hide, innit? And it's definitely suspicious how Martin turns up out of the blue, and then a few hours later, Wayne's dead."

"But if Martin was with Siri when Wayne fell . . ." Phil didn't bother finishing the thought.

"Shame, that," I mused. "If someone's got to go down for murder, it couldn't happen to a more irritating bloke."

Phil huffed. "No argument there. What do you reckon his deal is? Odd, him being here on his own."

"Maybe he came here hoping for a bit of the old holiday romance? I've been on hols on my own. It doesn't mean you're weird or anything." I grinned. "Course, I didn't *stay* on my own."

"I'm pretty sure I don't want to hear the details," Phil muttered.

"Could act some of it out for you instead," I said with a pointed leer. "If you fancy getting an early night."

Phil made a face. Unfortunately, it wasn't a sexy one. "We should probably hang around here for a while first. Talk to the other hotel guests. See if anyone remembers any useful information." He paused. "Sorry. Not what you wanted to be doing on your honeymoon."

"Oi, no apologies. It was me that told Siri we'd look into it for her, wasn't it?"

"But she wouldn't have asked if it hadn't been for me."

"No, and I wouldn't be married if it wasn't for you, so stop feeling guilty." I paused. "Do you think she's right? It wasn't an accident?"

He shrugged, the movement tight and jerky. "Don't know, do we?"

"Yeah, but . . . who'd want to kill Wayne? He was a bit of a . . ." I winced and managed to stop myself from calling the recently deceased a dick. "Well, you know, but he was just an ordinary bloke. We were at school with him."

Phil huffed, an unhappy sound. "Should think most murder victims went to school with someone."

"S'pose so." Maybe this was how people whose neighbours turned out to be serial killers felt. Like stuff shouldn't happen so close to home.

After all I'd seen in the last couple of years, you'd think I'd be over it by now.

"Right," I said briskly. "How are we going to do this? United front, or divide and conquer?"

"Bit of both, I'd say. Pretty much everyone here is in couples, so we go over and get chatting, then I'll deal with the men and you can take the women." Phil smirked. "Give them some of the old Paretski charm."

I rolled my eyes. "Got it. You talk about manly things with the manly men, and I'll swap makeup tips with the girlies."

Phil made an affectionate two-fingered gesture in my direction, and we stood up and got to work.

Phil's theory was that the people most likely to have seen something were the ones who'd be least comfortable having a cosy after-dinner drink right next to the crime scene, so we'd started with the ones sitting closest to the bar. Also, that happened to be where we were right then. Of course, it didn't quite work because people were coming and going all the time. Some of the families with kiddies were already heading off to get them into bed before the last of the couples had even tasted their starters.

Then again, they'd probably only had eyes for the fireworks and their offspring on the night in question, so they were probably no great loss to the investigation.

The first couple we latched on to were a middle-aged man and woman from Yorkshire. After a good quarter hour of chatting them up, we found out they'd gone to bed early last night and missed the whole show.

The next table along turned out to be occupied by our favourite happy couple, the Snipes. For once they were neither all over each other, nor apparently one well-chosen insult away from someone getting a fork in the eye. In fact, they weren't interacting at all—merely sipping their drinks and gazing coolly out across the bay.

I was tempted to give them a miss but had the bad luck to catch Mrs. Snipe's eye before I could suggest it to Phil. "Enjoying the evening?" I raised my glass to her, making the best of a bad job.

Mrs. S. arched a perfectly groomed eyebrow. She had the straightest, smoothest hair I'd ever seen outside a L'Oréal ad, and it cascaded over her tanned shoulders like a waterfall of chestnut silk.

"The honeymooners getting tired of their own company already? That doesn't bode well for the marriage."

"The honeymooners are doing fine, ta," I said shortly, thinking this didn't bode well for the coming conversation. "We're just the friendly sort."

She smirked. "Mm. I've heard a lot of gay couples are into open relationships. Tell me, how does that work?" Her gaze left mine to rake slowly and thoroughly over my husband's admittedly gaze-worthy body.

"Wouldn't know," Phil told her affably before I could get a word out of my thoroughly smacked gob. He even sent her a smile and pulled out a chair to join them at the table.

Great. Now I'd have to make nice too.

"How long have you two been together?" Phil asked as I sat my reluctant arse down in the chair next to his. "Or are you also on honeymoon?"

That surprised a sharp laugh out of her. "Oh, years."

Mr. S. curled his lip. "Decades."

Given neither of them could be long past the big three-oh, I doubted that. Still, I pasted on a smile. "Well done you for staying together so long. Not all couples get to do that," I added, thinking it'd be a lead-in to talking about Wayne's sad demise.

"No." Mrs. S.'s tone was mocking. "But then, not all couples would want to, would they?"

Mr. S. tossed back his drink and made an arrogant gesture to Will the waiter, who was setting down some drinks for our friends from the north. "Same again. And whatever these two are drinking."

"Cheers," I said, instead of *Oi, it's polite to offer, not assume.*

I turned back to Mrs. S. When had her chair got so close to Phil's? She was leaning towards him, her hand almost on his arm. "So how long have you two known each other?" she purred.

Phil, bless him, looked amused. "We were at school together."

"How precious," Mrs. S. said archly. "Of course, most people grow out of their childhood romances."

Me-owch.

"Doesn't it get a little . . . stale, after all this time?" she continued. Now she was actually stroking Phil's arm.

Paretski charm: nil; Morrison muscles: one.

Floored, I snuck a glance at Mr. S., who was glaring at something over the edge of the balcony, his jaw tense.

An awkward silence fell until Will the waiter popped up to save us with a tray of four Spritzes, which he set nervously down on our table. That had been quick. Either the Snipes were good tippers or bad complainers. I knew what my money was on. "Anything else for you?" he asked with the barest hint of a stutter.

"No." Mr. S.'s voice was curt, and I got an uneasy premonition that things might be about to kick off.

"You two were out here last night, weren't you?" I blurted.

"You mean when that man fell to his death?" Mr. S. turned his harsh gaze on me. "Why do you care if we were here or not?"

I felt, rather than saw, Phil stiffen beside me, and I shifted in my seat. "Just, you know. Trying to make sense of it all."

Mrs. S. spoke up, sounding miffed. "Do we have to talk about that? We're supposed to be here to have some fun."

Her bloke rounded on her. "And exactly what about *this*"—he jerked his head in mine and Phil's direction—"is supposed to be fun for *me*?"

He didn't mean . . . did he?

Mrs. S. shot him a glare, and if looks were daggers, he'd be doing pincushion impersonations right now. "If you weren't so bloody close-minded—"

"I've told you before, I'm not gay, bi, or bloody pan. I'm not *curious*, either."

Oh. He *did* mean.

Phil stood up abruptly and put a hand on my shoulder. "It's been good talking to you. Enjoy the rest of your holiday."

"Uh, yeah. Have fun. Don't do anything I wouldn't do," I babbled weakly as I stood, grabbing my drink. "Cheers."

We found a nice, empty corner to retreat to, and I took a hefty swig of my Spritz. "Was she really trying to get us into bed with them? I know some people are into that sort of thing, but bloody hell, we're on our honeymoon. Is nothing sacred?" I took another gulp, choked, and spluttered as Phil patted me gently on the back.

"Not sure," he said thoughtfully. "Could be. But it made a pretty good conversation stopper."

I blinked and ran the last few minutes over in my head again. "You mean it was just to avoid talking about last night? Bit risky though, wasn't it? What if we'd actually been gagging for a foursome?"

"That's where he came in. Shutting it down. Maybe."

"Huh. So . . . a bit suss, then, innit?"

Phil was silent a moment. "Maybe. Or it could be a game they like to play. Shocking the straightlaced. I've met couples like them before."

From the direction of his gaze, there was some worrying stuff going down in the middle distance. Not that I could see any, mind. Had that been a reference to something that'd happened when he was with his first husband, the late and unlamented (by me, at any rate) Mysterious Mark? Or was it just me seeing the ghost of honeymoons past everywhere I looked?

I took a deep breath. "Right. We'll put them down in the column for keeping half an eye on and move on to the next lot, yeah?"

Phil nodded and shook himself minutely. "Yeah."

We went back to work, going over to say hi to people and then subtly steering the conversation in the direction of violent death.

It wasn't easy. Our interviewees were surprisingly resistant to that last bit. Maybe they reckoned that, having paid a fortune for a few weeks of blissful relaxation, nasty real-world events shouldn't be allowed to taint the experience? I lost count of the number of times I heard a variation of, *Oh, but that was an accident, wasn't it? Tragic, of course, but nothing to do with us. Now, have you been to the museum in Naples?*

We'd made it barely quarter of the way around our fellow guests when Will the waiter approached us, mid table-flit, with a bearer-of-bad-tidings expression on his face. "Excuse me, sirs, but the manager would like a quick word."

Me and Phil exchanged glances. "Do you know what it's about?" I asked.

"Uh, the manager will explain?" Will clearly did know and, equally clearly, didn't want to be the one to tell us. "If you wouldn't mind coming this way?"

Phil made a resigned face, and I shrugged. "Guess we can find time in our busy schedule."

Chapter Sixteen

Will ushered us into a small office to one side of reception, then shook the dust off his feet and left us to it. There was a short, balding bloke sitting behind the desk, his chair pushed back to accommodate his paunch. I was almost certain he was the guy who'd welcomed us on arrival, but I couldn't swear to it, having been a bit punch-drunk from travel at the time. Or, as Phil would no doubt put it, having had eyes only for my antipasto.

He stood up as we entered, a surprising amount of spring in his step, and gave us a tight little smile. The mine-host bonhomie was conspicuously absent tonight. "Good evening. Mr. Morrison and Mr. Paretski, yes? I am Enrique Udinese, deputy manager here. Thank you for coming to see me." He shoved out a hand.

Phil gave it a thorough examination before he shook it. "*Signor* Udinese. Good evening."

"How are you enjoying your stay? It is your honeymoon, I believe? Of course we are delighted you have chosen to spend it with us."

I'd have been more delighted if he'd get to the flippin' point.

"It's a lovely hotel," Phil said noncommittally. "Is there something we can do for you?"

"Ah, yes." Enrique's face twisted into a parody of polite embarrassment. "I regret to inform you that I have received complaints you are upsetting the other guests."

Phil folded his arms. "How's that, then?"

"Not being too gay, are we?" I threw in cheerfully, hoping it'd jumpstart some plain speaking.

Enrique's eyes widened in alarm. "No, no! Of course, we have no prejudice here. But I am told you have been asking questions about the unfortunate incident last night."

Huh. Plain speaking apparently only went so far with this bloke. "You mean Wayne's death?"

"Indeed," Enrique admitted with a visible wince. "Of course, it was most tragic, but the guests do not wish to be constantly reminded of the incident."

"Of course," I echoed. "We wouldn't want to let justice get in the way of fun in the sun, now would we?"

"Justice? I don't understand. What happened to Mr. Hills was a deeply regrettable accident, but such things will happen when guests relax, perhaps a little too freely."

Phil's expression hardened. "You're implying he was drunk?"

The manager spread his hands. "People here are on holiday. They come here to rest, to enjoy, to eat, to drink. Sometimes they drink too much. It is the English national sport, I understand." He gave a small laugh.

We didn't.

"Of course we extend our deepest condolences to Mr. Hills and his family. And his friends, also," the manager said quickly. "But we have a responsibility to all of our guests. And so I must ask you to stop what you are doing. Let the dead rest in peace."

"What do you suggest we tell Siri?" Phil's tone was hard. "She's the one who asked us to look into Wayne's death."

"His companion? The poor woman, I'm sure she is distraught. It is natural to wish for a . . . what is the word?"

"A scapegoat?" I put in, surprising myself.

"Yes. That is it. Exactly. She wishes for a scapegoat to bear the blame for her lover's death, but sometimes there is only bad luck. A few drinks, nine times out of ten, will cause no harm at all, but there is always the tenth time. You must persuade her to take comfort in his memory and in the knowledge that his death was merely unlucky chance."

Sounded like arse-covering to me, but I let Phil take the lead seeing as this was his job, not mine.

He fixed Enrique with a steely glare. "And if we don't want to do what you say?"

"Then with the greatest regret I must ask you to find alternative accommodation. But I trust it will not come to that?"

Phil nodded. "Noted. Thank you, Signor Udinese. I think we'll be off to bed now."

We would?

"Have a good night, gentlemen," the manager oozed as Phil took my arm and led me away.

I wondered who'd run to teacher to tell tales. As we made our chastened way through the bar, my eye was caught by the Snipes, now sitting at the table in the corner. Mrs. S. had a distinctly smug look on her well-made-up face as she intercepted my gaze.

A sudden chill rippled down my spine. Who had more to gain from shutting off any investigation into Wayne's death than the murderer him- or *her*self? Was all that marital bickering and honeymoon-couple propositioning simply a cover for the Snipes' murderous intentions? Was offing some poor random bastard just another kinky game to them?

Maybe I was reading too much into a smirk, and the real villain of the piece was old Enrique himself? Unless they were all in on it together—the Snipes, the local mafia, the hotel management and, for all I knew, Martin too. I was sure I'd seen a mystery movie where it'd turned out they'd *all* done it.

"I think my brain's blown a gasket," I said out loud—although not *too* loud—to Phil. "I've got conspiracy theories coming out of my ear-holes. Next thing you know, I'll be accusing you of giving old Wayne the heave-ho."

I was expecting a laugh, or at least a huff of one, but Phil's lips tightened and he didn't let out a sound.

"Oi. You all right? I know *you* didn't do it—I was with you, remember?"

He nodded. "Yeah. Come on. Time we called it a night."

"Going to put a proper spanner in the works, this is, innit?" I muttered as we headed back to our room. "How are we supposed to investigate Wayne's death if we can't even talk about it?"

Phil glowered at the far end of the hallway like it'd said something rude about his mum. "There's other avenues to explore."

"Yeah? Like what?"

"For a start, we can dig a little deeper into Wayne himself. Use contacts back home."

"What, like talk to his old mates from school? Oh, wait."

"Funny. I was hoping to talk to someone who's associated with him in recent years. Don't know much about what he was up to lately, do we? At any rate—" Phil paused. Had he changed his mind about what he was going to say? If so, why? "I'm pretty sure Siri's got more to tell us," he went on. "Whether she knows it or not."

"At least she's not likely to go moaning to the manager about us asking questions."

Phil unlocked our door and held it open for me. "No. And there's the two old ladies."

"You mean Cassie and Jane?" I grinned, walking into the room and throwing myself down on the bed with an *oof.* "Don't let 'em hear you calling them that. What about them, though?"

"Not sure." Phil scrunched up his face in a strangely attractive frown. Or maybe I was biased. "Got a feeling they're not telling us all they know."

"Investigatorly intuition?"

"Maybe. May be nothing. But it can't hurt to get them to open up." Then he yawned and stretched. "Bed?"

I was answering his yawn even as I nodded. "Yeah. All that tramping around in the heat takes it out of you. Not sure I'll be up for another day like today if I don't catch up on sleep first."

"We'll see if we can find something to do tomorrow where you can put your feet up." Phil's tone was all consideration but his faint smirk gave him away.

"Are you implying I'm a delicate flower?" I demanded.

"Would I?"

"Yes. Yes, you would. I'm going to hold you to that, you know. Tomorrow, we're taking it easy."

Yeah, right. Because it wasn't like we had a murder investigation to be getting on with. I hauled my arse off the bed and headed to the bathroom.

When I came back, I wished I'd been a bit nippier with the old tooth-flossing and other nighttime rituals. Phil was standing by the window with his arms folded, doing his thing of keeping a watchful eye on the darkness outside again.

I hoped he wasn't expecting any further bodies to hurtle past, but I couldn't discount the possibility. His mood seemed to have turned more sombre as the light fled.

Then again, his ex–best friend had died, hadn't he?

I padded over to sling my arms around his waist from behind. "Hey, just 'cos Wayne wasn't my favourite person doesn't mean you can't be cut up about him dying like that." To tell the truth, I was feeling a little cut up about it myself, which I was having trouble getting my head around.

Like I said, I hadn't even liked the bloke.

I felt bad for thinking that, though. Hadn't Wayne done his best to let bygones be bygones? To be, against all expectation, friendly? To make up for what he'd done in school when, let's face it, we were all a tad rough around the edges?

Phil leaned back against me, his hands resting on top of mine. "I'm not cut up about it. I just . . ." He sighed, and I hugged him tighter. "It's complicated."

Maybe it'd help him feel better right now if he thought of Wayne's death as a case to be solved? To look at it logically, rather than emotionally. Of course, we were a smidge hampered by knowing bugger all about what had happened on the terrace. I frowned. "If it *wasn't* an accident . . . do you think the local mafia had anything to do with it? The lads from the café with all the bling who turned up in the hotel that night? Maybe they never left." I couldn't recall spotting them on the terrace when we'd gone up there after Wayne fell, but there had been a *lot* of people milling around.

"It's possible," Phil said it matter-of-factly, like he'd been way ahead of me with that idea. I tried to think if Wayne's supposed business associates had looked particularly grim and/or murderous either time we'd seen them. They'd been . . . well, businesslike at the café, hadn't they? Apart from the flirting with the waitress, but maybe that was just default macho-lad behaviour in Italy. All I could remember from passing them in the corridor was being miffed that

Phil had been paying them so much attention. Which was probably a sign that I really needed to get over myself.

"Wonder what he was doing with them. Some kind of property stuff, I s'pose? That was his field, wasn't it?"

"He had fingers in a lot of pies."

Why was Phil being so cagey? I let go of him with one hand and moved so I could see his face. "Think we ought to mention it to the boys in blue?"

"Not sure going to the police with vague suspicions is going to do us any favours." His jaw tightened. "And by us, I mean me."

"Meaning *you*? Meaning what, exactly?"

He folded his arms and gazed out to sea. "Meaning, if I—or you, for that matter—go around shouting that Wayne was murdered and it was a couple of local lads who did it, it's going to look like we're trying to deflect suspicion."

"You mean, from *us*? Why the hell would there be any suspicion to deflect?"

Phil turned to fix me in the eye, and his expression was grim. "Because a few hours before he died, me and Wayne had a fight."

Chapter Seventeen

I stared at Phil. "You had a fight with Wayne? When?" We'd been together all day. Nearly all day, at any rate.

"I ran into them in town while you were sunning yourself on the beach. They got a later train back than we did."

"So what the hell was it about? And how come you never told me?" Because he hadn't said a dicky bird—not even about bumping into the dearly departed.

"I'm telling you now." Phil sighed and gave the darkness another stern glare. "He was using you."

"What?"

"Trying to, anyhow. Had a go at persuading me to work on you to play ball."

"What?" I squawked again. *Bloody hell, Parrotski. Get a grip.* "Exactly what kind of ball game are we talking about?"

"Remember all that interest in the unexcavated bits of Herculaneum when we were on the tour together? Wayne had this mad idea he could get you to find stuff for him. There and Pompeii. Art treasures and God knows what. So he could sell them."

"What? Where would he even get an idea like that?"

"Reads the news, doesn't he?" Phil's shoulders hunched a little. "And I might have mentioned a couple of things about your gift at that reunion, okay? People asked."

"But . . . they'd never let us go fossicking around in their ancient ruins. The authorities, I mean. Don't you have to be a proper archaeologist to dig there?"

Phil closed his eyes briefly. "Don't think he was planning to ask for permission."

He said it gently, and I felt like an idiot. I still had an arm around his waist, so I gave him a squeeze.

"I couldn't believe it. I could've killed him." Phil grimaced. "You think a bloke's changed, and then you find out he's the same self-serving bastard he always was."

"Hey, he had me taken in and all," I said softly. "Huh. I guess that apology he gave me for being a shit when we were kids wasn't worth a thing after all." I sighed. "I honestly thought he was being sincere too."

Phil snorted. "Sincere about wanting you to forgive him so you'd go along with his scheme, maybe. You're always so willing to see the best in people."

"Yeah, well don't beat yourself up because you gave it a try for once. And what about Martin?"

"What about him?"

"If I'm seeing the best in him, I'd hate to think what his worst is like."

Phil frowned, then shook his head. "Back to Wayne. He'd have needed local partners. Guess who they must be."

"The blokes with the bling?" It all made sense.

Phil nodded. "He'd need them to deal with security at the site, do the actual digging, fence the goods."

"The goods I was supposed to find for him. For fuck's sake, my so-called gift doesn't even *work* like that." Had Wayne seen me as some kind of psychic metal-detector? He'd have been well disappointed when he found out the best I could do was track down things that had been hidden. Oh, and water, which didn't tend to bring in the big bucks. "Those poor sods in Pompeii were in the middle of a natural disaster. They weren't going to be *hiding* stuff."

"I told him that. Not sure he believed me." Phil paused. "Although Samuel Pepys buried his cheese."

I stared. Had the stress finally got to him? "Uh, really?"

"Yes. Really. It was during the Fire of London. He buried his cheese in the garden so it'd be safe until he could go back for it. People do that sort of stuff—bury their valuables to keep them from being looted, and plan to go back for them later."

"Since when is *cheese* a valuable?"

"Since 1666?" Phil smirked.

I glared.

"There's an Italian bank that still accepts Parmesan as collateral for loans," Phil added.

"All well and good until mice move into the vaults, I guess." I frowned. "So okay, maybe the idea wasn't totally daft. But how did Wayne reckon he was going to talk me into ransacking the Roman ruins? Call me old-fashioned, but even setting aside the moral issues, it'd take a hell of a lot to persuade me to risk getting sent to jail on my flippin' honeymoon."

"Money." Phil's face hardened. "I told him your principles weren't for sale."

"Good," I said, a sneaky voice inside me wondering just how *much* money might have been involved.

Not that I'd have taken it, mind. But I'd have kind of liked to know what value dear old departed Wayne had set on my morals. Obviously, it'd say far more about him than about me, but . . . come to think of it, I decided I didn't want to know how cheap Wayne had thought my principles were.

"So you and him had an argument about it?" I was hoping that by *fight* he'd meant a verbal disagreement and not your actual fisticuffs. "On the street?"

He winced. "In the art gallery."

"Bet that went down well."

"Too right. We were asked to leave."

"No raised voices allowed to disturb the ambiance of the artwork?"

Phil reddened. "There might have been a bit of a scuffle."

And they say you can never go back to your schooldays. I bit my tongue, seeing as he was clearly doing a bang-up job of kicking himself for it already. "Where was Siri during all this?"

"Hanging off his arm looking awkward." Phil paused. "Pretty sure he was using her too. Trying to get her to soften you up."

"But I'm gay." And there was something I never thought I'd need to point out to my husband on our honeymoon.

"Not like that. Making friends with you. So you'd feel bad about saying no."

Would I have? Maybe I would have, at that. "I'd still have said it."

"I know that. Wayne doesn't—" he gave me a crooked smile "—didn't know you like I do."

"Should hope not," I said weakly. "So do you reckon it's going to come back and bite you in the bum? Having this public row with him?"

"Depends. We don't know what people saw up there, do we?"

"But the police know we weren't up there when he fell."

"They know that's what we told them."

"But people must have seen us leave."

Phil shrugged. "Maybe we went back up *before* he fell, not after. Everyone would have been too busy watching the fireworks to notice."

"Yeah, but we didn't."

"It's only our word on it. Not like they've got cameras in the hallways here." He stepped away from me. "We should get some sleep. We'll find out more about it tomorrow."

I thought about it, as I lay in bed, spooned by my husband, neither of us sleeping. Well, you would, wouldn't you?

Could I really find hidden Roman treasures? Not to, you know, steal them like Wayne and his mafia mates wanted to, but simply to . . . find them. I could maybe head up to the edge of the excavations and have a listen. See if the vibes were talking to me.

Trouble was, these weren't going to be *good* vibes, were they? People stashing stuff in fear for their lives would have been pouring a whole lot of sick terror into whatever they hid. I'd feel that—if I felt anything at all, that was. After two thousand years, there was a good chance the traces wouldn't be strong enough for me to pick up anymore. Did weird psychic stuff have a half-life? I'd never tried to pick up on something so old before. The thought of traipsing around farmers' fields with my mental equivalent of a metal detector had never much appealed, mostly because I'd have felt a right tit doing it. Maybe I could borrow an actual metal detector so as to look slightly less like a weirdo.

Of course, if it turned out the vibes *didn't* weaken with time, maybe I could go hunting for dinosaur fossils to see if they really had been stashed there four thousand years ago by a god with a sense of humour. Knock the whole creationism thing on the head once and for all. Or not, as the case might be. Huh. If I found clear evidence of an honest-to-Him bloke upstairs looking down on us mortals and having a few yuks in the process, I was going to have some serious issues with the guy.

But going back to the Roman stuff: even if I found something, then what? It wasn't like I'd be able to dig it up myself without going down Wayne's road of illegality. I pictured myself trying to persuade some Italian archaeologist his next excavation ought to be *here* instead of *there*, and rolled my eyes. Yeah, right. I'd be given my marching orders before you could say *Loco Inglese.*

And even if they believed me, your actual experts on Roman remains weren't going to give a monkey's about hoards of gold, were they? They were after the knowledge.

I thought about it a while longer and frowned. Okay, so archaeologists were human too. Although the ones on *Time Team* tended to look somewhat less evolved than your average person in the street. They probably *would* give a monkey's about hoards of gold. But they weren't going to disrupt all that careful sifting of the evidence on the dodgy half chance of a bit of bling.

But . . . more than anything else, it just seemed *wrong*. Going poking around into all those disaster-hit Pompeiians' back gardens, trying to find the cool stuff they'd left behind when they fled in terror or died trying. And yeah, maybe that was precisely what the archaeologists were doing, but at least they had reasonably pure motives for it all. Knowledge and stuff. Not some kind of get-rich-quick scheme.

Weirdly, I felt let down. Like I'd expected better of Wayne. But it was mixed with a guilty sense of relief too. Because I'd been feeling bad about all the times I'd tried to avoid him, the way I hadn't liked him, despite all his friendly overtures, his attempts to make amends. And now I knew he'd deserved it.

But falling a hundred feet onto tarmac and then being run over by a truck? He hadn't deserved that. Nobody did.

I had strange dreams again that night. In one of them, Wayne survived his fall, but broke his pelvis like I had back when we'd been in our teens. He was quite chuffed about it—said we had to be friends now since we had matching limps.

Then he handed me a shovel and told me to dig up the bodies so he could steal the rings off their fingers.

All in all, I was glad to wake up in the morning.

Chapter Eighteen

Phil gave me a funny look as I slid out of bed the next day. "Did I do that?"

I yawned. "Do what?"

"You've got bruises on your arms."

I squinted at the small but distinct finger marks on my upper arms. "Huh. No, that must have been Siri last night. Girl's got a grip on her." I sent him a leer. "Why, wanna mark me up a bit? Stake your claim?"

Phil huffed, amused. "Been there, done that." Then he rolled his eyes, probably at my blank expression. "Looked at your ring finger lately? In case you've already forgotten that whole getting-married bit?"

"Oh, that," I said, and was hit by an unwelcome flashback to the ring cycle portion of last night's dream. As passion killers go, it worked a treat. "Right. Good point. Breakfast?"

I hopped out of bed maybe a little more hastily than might have been flattering to my newly wedded husband.

Phil, bless him, didn't seem to take it to heart. "You and your stomach," he said fondly, shoving off the duvet and starting to search for clothes.

The day having dawned bright and glorious—is there any other kind of summer's day in Italy?—we decided to take our coffees outside after breakfast. There was a better chance of finding a quiet spot to discuss the plans for the day out there. That was the theory, anyhow.

So we grabbed our cups, hardened our hearts to the pain on the waiter's face when he saw us carrying our own drinks, and set off towards the terrace. But as we passed through the bar en route, we bumped into Jane and Cassie, presumably on their way to get their Weetabix.

"You're not going outside, are you?" Jane asked sharply.

"Uh, yeah?" And good morning to you too. "Shouldn't we?"

"*I* certainly couldn't stomach eating or drinking out there. Not after What Happened." You could hear the capitals in her voice. Not to mention the disapproval. How very dare Wayne have the bad manners to join the choir invisible in full view of decent people trying to enjoy their holiday.

Cassie snorted. "It's not like anything we do or don't do *now* is likely to bring the young man back to life."

I could imagine Wayne preening at being called a young man, him with his receding hairline and all. Then again, he'd probably have preferred to live to be an old one. "Yeah, it's put a dampener on the fun in the sun, and no mistake," I commiserated.

"We soldier on," Jane said firmly, which sounded a bit rich coming from someone who'd only moments ago declared the terrace out of bounds for emotional reasons.

"Had you got to know him?" Phil asked.

Cassie laughed, which struck me as a little heartless in the circs. "Oh, he *tried*. But Jane here sent him away with a flea in his ear, didn't you, dear?"

Jane pursed her lips. "I would *not* have put it quite that way."

"No? What happened?" Phil's tone was mild.

"I dare say most people wouldn't appreciate being given a sales pitch while trying to relax on holiday. But I was *not* rude to him. I simply made it very clear I wasn't interested."

"Bet you wish you'd been friendlier now, though, don't you?" Cassie said, unhelpfully.

I ignored her and gave Jane a sympathetic smile. "Yeah, he did the same to us. Some people find it hard to switch off, I guess. Although you wouldn't catch me going around offering to fix anyone's drains while I'm on my hols. So, uh, have you got plans for today?"

Jane's face softened. "We're taking a boat trip. Out to Capri. Do you suppose we could persuade that poor girl to join us? As it seems she's staying here for the time being. I hate to think of her brooding in her hotel room all day. Do you think she'd come?"

"Maybe if you invite Martin first," I muttered, nonetheless touched by her obvious concern for Siri.

Cassie's eyes widened. "Oho, so *that's* what that's all about, eh? Out with the old and in with the new? No time wasted there." She was smiling as she said it, but did her tone hold a hint of . . . what? Bitterness? It was gone before I could be sure.

Jane tutted. "I'd never have dreamed of taking up with another man after my poor Ralph passed away."

"Have a lot of offers, did you?" Cassie said, and laughed in a rather unsisterly fashion.

From the death glare she sent her, Jane agreed.

"No one's suggesting there's anything untoward going on between Siri and Martin," I said hastily.

"Yes, they are." Cassie gave me a roguish grin and—ye gods—a wink.

I might have blushed. "I, uh, I just meant he's been taking care of her, that's all."

Jane sniffed, then sent me a sharp glance as if daring me to try the hanky trick again. "Does she even know him?"

"She does now. So, boat trip to Capri?" I reminded her desperately. I didn't glance at Phil, but I swear I could *hear* him smirking by my side. "What time are you heading out on that?"

"Ten o'clock," Cassie said cheerfully. "Are you thinking of joining us too?"

I hadn't been, although the trip had been on our to-do list for the honeymoon. This time I did look at Phil. Okay, so he might be chafing at the bit to get on with the investigating, but wouldn't a boat trip be an ideal opportunity to ask a few questions without putting any hoteliers' backs up? Jane, for one, would be more likely to talk the further we got her away from the Terrace of Terror. "What do you think?"

"Don't see why not. I'll find out if Siri and Martin want to come, and we can all go together." Phil downed his coffee and headed off, leaving me in the company of the sisters.

Who then promptly bogged off to get their breakfast. While I could hardly blame them for that, it left me feeling like a total Billy-No-Mates, sitting in the bar with only my lukewarm coffee for company. I felt around in my pocket for my phone. Still bugger all signal, so my social media remained unchecked. I was probably missing loads of important memes.

I sighed and shoved my phone back into my pocket. Noticing Will the waiter smirking at me, I glared at him, then thought, *What the hell.* "Hey, were you on the terrace the other night?"

The smirk disappeared, and Will's gaze shifted like he was scanning for an escape route. He'd missed a patch when he'd shaved this morning, and his Adam's apple stood out sharply as he swallowed. "Er, which night would that be?"

"The night you lost one of your guests, maybe?"

Will took a step back. "I'm, er, sorry, but we're not supposed to talk about that." Then he legged it behind the bar and disappeared through a side door.

Great. So now we weren't allowed to upset the staff either? Didn't he—or the hotel management, who were presumably pulling the strings—*want* Wayne's killer brought to justice? It all smacked of a cover-up to me, but then getting known as a murder hotel probably wouldn't be good for business, apart from with a very select and possibly undesirable clientele. Or was there more to it than that? Will was a big, strong lad, if a bit on the gawky side. It wouldn't be hard for him to tip your average sedentary bloke over a balcony. Wayne hadn't been what you'd call politeness itself to the staff here, and I'd bet he hadn't been openhanded with the gratuities.

Heh. Tip or be tipped. I half laughed, then realised I was joking about (a) a tragic death that had devastated Siri and (b) the possibility I was being served my drinks by a murderer. That wiped the smile off my face pretty quickly.

I took my coffee and my inappropriate self outside, which was where Phil found me a few minutes later, sitting on my lonesome and trying not to stare at either the bit of the balcony where Wayne had gone over, or Mr. and Mrs. Snipe being all passive-aggressive with each other at the next table along while they blithely ignored the bloke whose husband they'd tried to chat up last night.

"Boat trip's a go." Phil slid into the seat next to me.

"Yeah? Siri wasn't upset about you taking time off from the investigation?"

He huffed. "Told her I might need her to distract one of the sisters so I could get the other one on their own."

I laughed. "Which one do you reckon did it? They've both got dead husbands. And Cassie doesn't seem to have liked hers much." I winced. "Uh, not that I think having a dead husband means you're a murderer."

"Glad to hear it," Phil said dryly.

Had his late first husband, The Mysterious Mark, been as prone to foot-in-mouth disease as I so evidently was? I scrabbled for a change of subject. "So are we walking down to the harbour? Could take a while at old-lady speed."

"You've got a short memory. Remember Jane and her luggage when we first got here?"

Huh. He was right—she'd been pretty nippy. "So we're jogging down?"

"No. I ordered a taxi."

"For all six of us?"

"I ordered a large taxi."

"That's the man I love. Nothing if not thorough." I leered at him. "In all matters. Reckon we've got time for a quick—"

"No."

I glanced at my watch. He was probably right. "Spoilsport," I said anyway.

"Realist." Phil sent me a fond smile. "Although it's good to know my charm hasn't totally faded."

"Never," I said sincerely, and heaved myself out of the chair to go and tell the ladies about the taxi.

Chapter Nineteen

What with Phil's shoulders and Cassie's hips, even a large taxi was pretty tight for elbow room.

Martin, being an opportunistic so-and-so, bagged the front seat by the driver while the rest of us were wasting time being all polite and British. All that space was wasted on him though as he sat there rigidly, disapproval coming off him in waves. I was guessing it'd been Siri who'd had the casting vote on whether to come, not him. Had he even been there when Phil had spoken to her?

"Capri will be absolutely rammed with tourists," Martin was saying. "We'd be better off going to Ischia."

He pronounced it *Ishia*.

"*Iskia*," Jane said firmly, "is not where we want to go today."

"How about you, Siri?" My voice came out sounding so fake-hearty I cringed inside. "You always wanted to go to Capri?"

"Oh, yeah," she said distractedly. "I never heard of the other one. Isky-whatsit. Is it, like, supposed to be famous for anything?"

"Ischia is famed for its thermal spas," Jane conceded grudgingly.

"Oh." Siri frowned. "But you can go to a spa anywhere. Didn't all the famous people used to go to Capri?"

"And the queer ones," I added to prove I'd read a guidebook too.

"Oh, that's cool," Siri said with her first sign of animation this morning, as Martin scowled and turned back to glare out of the cab's front window. Seeing as we were nearly at the harbour, he got a close-up view of a hairpin bend and a brick wall, which served him right.

"Do you, like, go to places for the queer history?" Siri frowned. "Is it all right if I say 'queer' if I'm not queer? I mean LGBT."

Bless her. "Probably best to steer clear if I'm honest. Some of the older gay guys had it chucked at them as an insult, back before it got . . . What's the word I'm looking for? Rehabilitated?"

"Reclaimed," Phil said, sounding amused.

"Right. And, uh, to answer your first question, a bit, maybe? I guess it adds something, knowing a place was important to people like me."

She actually smiled. "That's lovely. Isn't that lovely, Martin?"

"Delightful," he said tersely, not even bothering to face her.

Jane sniffed. It seemed we still had some work to do to break her of that.

Thankfully, it didn't take long to reach the harbour. The taxi disgorged us, only moderately sweaty and dishevelled, and I cast a longing look at the iced-lemon-drink seller before trotting dutifully over to the ticket office with the others.

The breeze on the open water was blissful, and despite a fairly crowded boat, I enjoyed the trip across the bay. But when we got off the ferry in Capri, I had to concede Martin had had a point. The place was *seething* with tourists. Jane, who seemed to know what she was doing, marched us off to the queue for the funicular on the other side of the road.

"Where are we even going?" I whispered to Phil. "Does anyone know, or are we just queuing for this funicular because it's there?"

He huffed. "Thought you'd read the guidebook? We're going up to the main square."

"Hope there's more room to breathe up there," I muttered.

There wasn't. When we fought our way out of the funicular and onto the Piazzetta—which, disappointingly, turned out to be the main square rather than a place to savour pizza—it was all elbows to the fore. I was dripping with sweat already and Phil, too, had a tinge of pink in his cheeks. Martin had acquired damp patches under his armpits, and Cassie mopped her brow with a cheerful floral scarf. Jane looked as chilly as ever, though.

Siri . . . Siri looked overwhelmed and bewildered.

"Hey, can we get out of the crush?" I suggested.

Jane nodded. "This way." She strode off, leaving the rest of us no choice but to follow.

It did get better and in a surprisingly short time. Once we'd left the narrow, cobbled streets behind us, with their many restaurants and shops selling expensive tat—and, all right, quality stuff too—we soon emerged at a pretty little garden perched high on the cliffs, the other side of the island from where we'd landed. It was full of flowers, and pink seemed to be this year's colour. Dotted around were gleaming white statues in styles both ancient (beardy blokes in togas) and modern (a nymph feeling up her own tit in a pond).

"Be a great place for wedding pics, this," I mused. Although the sun was as hot as ever, there was a gentle breeze that made the place blessedly cool compared to the heaving town square.

Cassie's ears pricked up. "Excellent idea. We must get some honeymoon shots of you two. Go and stand over by the bougainvillea."

"Uh . . ." I scouted around helplessly, and then gave Phil a *help me* look. He shrugged, clearly as florally illiterate as I was. "You're no help," I muttered, although to be honest I was relieved to not be the only idiot in the village this time.

"The pink stuff," Cassie said with a roll of her eyes and a shooing motion. "No, not that pink stuff. The other pink stuff. There. Don't they make a lovely picture?"

She beamed around at our companions. Siri gave us a watery smile, Martin tapped his feet, and Jane, predictably, sniffed. Cassie, oblivious, pulled out a compact camera and chivvied me and Phil into various poses including, embarrassingly, a kiss.

We probably came off as more wooden than Pinocchio, but she seemed satisfied after that. "I'll email you the pictures once I've downloaded them," she announced, sounding tech-savvier than I'd somehow expected.

"Could we perhaps do some sightseeing now?" Jane demanded.

Annoyed at her impatience to be off—because it *was* our honeymoon, we didn't have all that many pics of us together, and it hadn't taken *that* long—I stepped forward with a grin. "We ought to get some pics of you and Cassie together first. Go on, you two go and stand by the bargain-whatsit."

Jane reddened. Cassie beamed and grabbed her by the elbow. "Another excellent idea. Come on, Jane, I know you can smile if you put your mind to it."

I used my phone to take several pics of the two of them, Cassie round and cheerful like a happy dumpling, and Jane tight-lipped and unbending. A stern stalk of celery, maybe? I wondered what her problem was. Why go on holiday at all if you're determined not to have any fun while you're there?

After I'd finished with the sisters, I quirked an eyebrow at Siri. She hugged herself as she shook her head. "Don't take any pictures of me. I look horrible."

"Of course you don't," Martin said gallantly, throwing an arm around her shoulders.

"What he said," I agreed. To be honest, she didn't look so bad today. Her puffy eyes were hidden by a large pair of sunglasses, and she was wearing another sleeveless dress, this one a brighter colour that lifted her complexion a bit. With her hair back in a simple ponytail, she gave off faintly fifties vibes that fit in well with the location. "But if you don't want pics, why don't we take a gander at the view instead?"

I led the way up to one of the viewpoints and leaned over the railings.

The views . . . Well, my gob was properly smacked. I felt like I'd travelled sixty or seventy years back in time, and Audrey Hepburn was going to trip around a corner anytime now. As long as she brought Cary Grant with her, I had zero problem with that. We were high up on the cliffs here, and the bright blue sea sparkled in the sunlight unbelievably far below us, dotted with blinding-white yachts. To the left, vast rocks jutted up into the sea like a giant's teeth, their true scale only revealed by the boats that sprinkled the water around them and could have been grains of leftover rice scattered on the same giant's vast blue dinner plate.

Up on the cliff tops with us, more of those umbrella pines spread their welcome shade, and spiky cacti grew wild among the rocks. It was hard to understand why everyone else crammed themselves into the tiny town. This was the real Capri, right here. The one that had first enticed people here from all over and seduced them into staying.

Granted, the handsome young local fishermen might have had a hand in it too, from all accounts. Sadly, if there were any of those around today, they were too far away to make out.

Directly below us, there was a snaking road that looked flat from so high above, but had to be pretty steep from all the hairpin bends. I wondered what it must be like to drive along, and if it would be worth hiring a car to find out.

Then a hand gripped my arm tight enough to hurt. All I could think of was how stupidly vulnerable I'd made myself. And how utterly, bloody terrifying—not to mention, fatal—a fall from this height would be.

Chapter Twenty

"T-Tom?" Siri's voice was faint. "Don't lean over so far. Please."

My heart racing like a bloody Ferrari, I stepped back hastily from the railing, almost treading on Martin's lurking toes. I couldn't help shooting him a suspicious glance. "Uh, yeah. Course. Sorry. Okay, I've seen enough. Everyone ready to move on?"

"Quite ready," Jane said firmly, and glared at Cassie until she stopped taking photos of the view.

Siri was still hovering, so I put my arm through hers as we made our way back down through the garden. She hadn't *meant* to give me a coronary. "Sorry about that. Bit thoughtless of me."

"Oh, no—it's me being silly." I couldn't read her face with those sunglasses covering half of it.

"Don't be daft. Uh, I mean, you're not being silly. I'm touched you were worried about me." Out of the corner of my eye, I noticed Phil had engaged Martin in conversation.

This could be my chance to talk to Siri without his evil influence. Martin's, that is, not Phil's. I drew in a breath, trying to think on my feet—only to have Martin prove he was way ahead of me there. He stepped smartly away from Phil, saying something in a brusque tone, and then put his arm around Siri's shoulders. "Now, now. We mustn't keep the honeymoon couple apart."

Siri disengaged herself from me with a shy smile. "Sorry, Tom. You go and have your couple time with your lovely husband, yeah?"

Me and my lovely husband exchanged frustrated glances as we paired back up. "Get anything out of Martin?" I murmured.

"About as much as you got out of Siri by the looks of things. That bloke could teach a Tory politician a few tricks for evading the question."

"Great. Any idea where we're heading now?"

Jane had struck out in the lead, apparently with a goal in mind.

"Carthusian Monastery." Phil said it with certainty.

"Yeah? How d'you know that?"

He huffed. "There was a notice up about it at the entrance to the gardens. By that stall selling perfumes they make there."

Oh. Right. I'd seen that, then forgotten about it immediately, not being of the perfume-buying persuasion. Or the monastic one, for that matter. "Wait, monks make perfume? I thought they were all into brewing their own alcohol. You know, 'cos there's bugger all else fun to do in a monastery."

Phil shrugged. "Don't ask me."

I grinned. "Makes you wonder if they've always been as celibate as they're cracked up to be. What do monks want perfume for, if not to keep their lady loves sweet?"

He raised an eyebrow. "Could have been to keep each other smelling sweet. No one took daily showers in those days."

"Must have got pretty ripe in this climate," I mused, trying and failing not to get turned on by the thought of a lot of sweaty blokes living in close proximity. I sent Phil a sidelong glance, but if he was thinking the same thoughts I was, he was doing a much better job of hiding it.

We didn't have to go far—just a hop, skip, and a jump down what would have been an alleyway under grey British skies. Here, it was a sun-bleached passageway, the unrelieved brightness of all that white stone making me squint.

The monastery, when we got there, was even quieter than the gardens had been, although probably for better reason. I'm sure it was one of the sights, but I'd rather have been outside looking at the views. The painted murals were pretty enough—or rather, the fragments of them that remained—but after the ancient art at Pompeii, I couldn't get excited about saints and angels only a few centuries old.

Tom Paretski: antiquities snob.

Cassie loved it all, exclaiming at each new bit of artwork and snapping away with her camera, but Jane, oddly, seemed ill at ease. Despite being the one who'd dragged us all here.

One thing the monastery did have going for it was the relative cool inside its high stone walls. The echoey chambers we wandered through were mostly bare, but one of them held a grand piano that stood out stark black against the white stone. When we got closer, I saw a pattern of dusty paw prints running across its lid and felt an unexpected pang of homesickness. "Hey, do you think the cats are missing us?"

Phil smirked. "They're getting fed, aren't they? So I'd say that's a no."

"Bet Merlin misses your lap." I leered. "I'd miss it if it bogged off and left me for two weeks."

"Not the rest of me, then?"

"Oh, I dunno. You've got other good points." I let my gaze roam over them deliberately, then jumped a mile as Jane sniffed right in my shell-like.

"This is a *place* of *worship*," she hissed.

About to hit back with an *Oi, we're married, it's allowed*, I stopped when I realised she seemed genuinely upset. "Uh, sorry?" I muttered instead.

"Catholic countries take these things seriously," she said sternly.

"Got it. Best behaviour from now on. No being gay in the house of God."

Jane's cheeks went a little pink. "It's nothing to do with you being . . ." She made a vague hand-wavy gesture that I guessed meant *queer as a three-Euro note*. "I'm aware one has to move with the times. It's a matter of . . . of decency. Respect. I'd say the same thing to any young couple."

"Course you would," I reassured her. I didn't look at Phil, but I swear I could hear the faint rumble of an eye roll from his direction.

Then I wondered if my imagination was picturing it directed at her or at me.

I was overthinking this. I grabbed my phone to take a quick snap of the paw prints. It'd be something to show the cats when we got home. I turned back in time to confirm that Phil really did roll his eyes at me for that, and I was about to call him on it when my gaze caught on a bloke the other side of the room.

Given that he was still by the door, rather than ambling around ogling the artwork like everyone else, I'd have assumed he'd just walked in, but there was an odd stillness about him that made me think he'd been there for longer than that.

He was wearing sunglasses almost as big as Siri's, and unlike her, he hadn't taken them off in the dimmer light indoors. Maybe the light glinting off his heavy gold necklace had been giving him eye strain. I couldn't work out whether I'd seen him before, or if he simply reminded me of someone. Like our maybe-stalker in Pompeii, perhaps, although this bloke was almost certainly taller and more heavily built. With a touch of déjà vu, I reflected he could be a well-dressed tourist or simply a local on his lunch break.

Nope—tourist, I decided, as the guy started taking pics with his phone. He was quite methodical about it, working his way around the room quickly but smoothly, no bit of artwork left unsnapped. On the one hand, it was a relief to see we weren't being followed, but on the other, it was worrying that my subconscious apparently now felt threatened by any man who wasn't a total slob.

Odd, though: I got the impression he wasn't really into any of the murals he was photographing. Not like Cassie, who *ooh*ed and *aah*ed over every new splash of colour, or Jane, with her quietly appreciative gaze as she shadowed her sister. It was like he was taking a visual record, instead of merely looking at stuff.

Until he faced me and Phil. Then he suddenly seemed more intent. I think it was a body language thing, maybe? That stillness about him again.

Of course, he could have been waiting for the daft British bloke to stop staring at him and get out of the way of his shot. Feeling uncomfortable, I jerked my head at Phil, and we moved over to one side. When I glanced back to see what the bloke had been so interested in, all I could see was that modern piano. Okay, the paw prints were cute, but there were no medieval murals or even any interesting stonework.

I turned back again to see Sunglasses walking smartly out of the room.

"Did that bloke take a picture of us? Deliberately?" I whispered to Phil, nodding at his retreating figure. "Or am I being paranoid?"

Phil was frowning. "Was that the man you saw in Pompeii?"

"No. At least, I'm pretty sure it wasn't. Think he could have been one of Wayne's mafia mates?"

"You didn't recognise him?"

I blinked. "What, so you did?"

He nodded. "He was one of the men who were at the hotel the night Wayne died."

"Well, bugger."

"Yeah."

I seriously needed to start paying more attention to people I passed during the day. Hah, maybe I should start photographing them all like Sunglasses apparently did. "So I wasn't just being paranoid in Pompeii? But why the hell would they be following us around?" I thought about it. "Shit, you think they killed him, and they're after us because we're looking into his death? Because swimming with concrete boots on is definitely not on my list of fun things to do on our honeymoon."

Phil drew in a breath, but whatever he was about to say was lost as Jane stomped up to us. "Have you finished in here? The rest of us are ready to move on."

I glanced around and realised that while me and Phil had been muttering in a corner, the rest of our ill-assorted little group had indeed bogged off and left us.

"Before we go," Phil said, stepping forward, "can we have a word?"

"About what?"

"About the night Wayne died," Phil went on, ignoring her frosty tone. "I don't know if you're aware, but Siri's asked us to investigate the matter."

"She's upset, poor girl," I put in. "Can't believe it was an accident."

"Then what was it?" Jane snapped.

I shrugged. "She thinks maybe someone did him in."

Jane's lips thinned to the point of nonexistence. "We will *not* talk about such matters *here*. This is God's house."

"Yeah, but the bloke upstairs is supposed to be all about justice, isn't he?" I coaxed. "Tell you what, how about we take it outside? You want to help Siri, don't you?"

Put like that, she had to cave and she knew it. "Very well." Jane stalked out of the room and into the . . . technically, I guess it was a corridor, but it was a bit too grand and stony for that. Then again, it seemed too plain, functional, and lacking in Hogwarts-type flourishes to be a cloister, not that I'm an expert.

"What do you want to know?" she said impatiently.

Phil fixed her in the eye. "Do you remember seeing anyone unusual out on the terrace that night? Anyone who didn't seem to belong?"

"Locals, maybe, rather than guests?" I put in, then buttoned my lip at Phil's sharp look.

Jane's brow furrowed, so at least she was giving it some thought. "It's possible? I remember thinking there seemed to be far more people there than I'd seen before. Was there someone in particular you had in mind? These locals—were they men?"

"I'd rather we concentrate on what you can recall," Phil said quickly. "Can you think back to the scene? Picture where you were standing and who was near you."

"I think . . ."

"Close your eyes if it helps."

She did. The harsh lines eased from her face, and she looked younger and, dare I say it, oddly vulnerable. "There might have been some men there who weren't tourists." Her eyes flashed open, and the old Jane was back. "But I couldn't describe them to you."

"General impression?" Phil tried. "Young, old?"

"No. No, there's nothing. Now if you don't mind, we should be getting back to the others."

Jane turned on her heel and walked off smartly. Me and Phil sent each other significant glances, although exactly what his was supposed to signify I wasn't sure. *Mine* was all about the necessity of checking our bed very carefully from now on for dismembered horses' heads. Then we trotted dutifully after her, missing the next open room entirely—not that I was bothered—and emerging into a whiteout. When my eyes adjusted, I could see it was a sunlit courtyard. Martin and Siri were hovering around Cassie, who was sitting on some steps fanning herself.

Jane tutted. "She *will* keep overdoing things."

"Everything all right?" Phil asked as we approached them.

"Fine, fine." Cassie heaved herself to her feet.

"Do we need to get you back in the shade?" I asked.

"God, no. Anything but. The air in these places is terrible. No, I'll be fine. Just get me to some open space."

Me and Phil exchanged glances, and he stepped up to take her arm, earning himself a roguish laugh. "I'll be sure to come over all unnecessary more often if this is what it gets me," Cassie cooed with an exaggerated simper.

"Oi, no funny business with my husband." I grinned to show I was joking, although I really wasn't. "I want him back in the same condition you got him."

"Is it like a fruit stall—if I squeeze him, he's mine?" Cassie cackled.

Blimey, she'd perked up no end. "Sorry, this one's not for sale," I told her.

"You couldn't afford me anyway," Phil added, getting into the spirit.

Cassie laughed again. Jane sniffed.

Siri burst into tears.

Chapter Twenty-One

Martin took Siri aside for a few minutes, during which the rest of us stood around shuffling our feet with various degrees of awkwardness and/or guilt. Or maybe that was just me. With hindsight, Phil's and my display of cheery coupledom hadn't exactly been the height of tact.

"I'm taking Siri back to the hotel," Martin announced when he returned with the lady in question, his arm firmly around her shaking shoulders. "She needs some time to herself."

"What do you bet she doesn't get it?" I muttered to Phil.

He returned my cynical glance.

Jane spoke up. "Cassie, I think we should go back too."

Cassie turned mulish. "Go back? Already? We haven't seen half the island."

"We don't want to overexert ourselves," Jane said primly, leaving no one in any doubt that when she said *we* she meant *you*.

Eyes flashing, Cassie squared up to her sister. "*You* may be ready to consign yourself to an old folks' home, but *I'm* certainly not."

"Tell you what," I put in hastily, "how about we all go and have a nice cold drink somewhere and then decide what we're going to do?"

On the plus side, that seemed to defuse the tension nicely. On the more negative side, though, going for a nice cold drink involved returning to the crowded, sweaty town. Out of sheer self-preservation, we ducked into the first café we saw. It was a cool place in both senses of the word, the walls covered with large black-and-white photos of all the Hollywood legends who'd, presumably, graced the island with their presence. More importantly, it had the blessed relief of air-con.

What it didn't have was Siri and Martin, who'd buggered off without so much as an *arrivederci*, presumably to catch the next boat back to Sorrento. So much for our hopes of getting anything out of Martin this trip. Left with Cassie and Jane, me and Phil must've looked like a couple of lads who'd brought their old mums out for a treat—at least, I fervently hoped we looked like that, and not like a cougar-toyboy double date.

I was pleased to see they had café freddo on the menu, and chivvied Phil into having one too. Cassie went for a Spritz. Jane, being Jane, insisted on a pot of hot tea.

It was an odd situation, us being strangers thrown together by circumstance, with Wayne's death being one of the few things we had in common. Obviously me and Phil wanted to talk about it, and I was pretty sure Cassie wasn't averse, but Jane stomped any mention of *unpleasantness* down flat.

Thoughts of our local mafia mates kept popping up to distract me. Every time someone new stuck their head around the open café door, I glanced up on autopilot to see if it was our unwelcome shadow. But the bloke with the bling seemed to have buggered off.

Which made me wonder in itself. Did that mean it wasn't me and Phil he was shadowing, but Siri? For the first time I was glad Martin had velcroed himself to her side. At least he ought to be some protection if she needed it.

But it didn't make sense, them following Siri, did it? Not with what we knew about their association with Wayne. Unless they thought maybe she'd been the one to bump him off so she could go into the antiquities-robbing business with me herself?

It was all making my head ache, so it'll be no surprise that the conversation over our drinks was a bit on the stilted side. Although give Cassie her due, she did her best to liven it up with a few ribaldly inappropriate quips that had her sister fairly puffing steam out through her nostrils.

Luckily, all those cups of tea coupled with the cool temperature had the predictable effect on Jane's elderly bladder. Even luckier, Cassie didn't insist on going with her.

As Jane disappeared behind the door marked *WC*, Phil leaned forward. "Cassie, would you mind if I ask you a few questions about the night Wayne died?"

"Why—sorry you missed it, are you?"

Me-owch. Apparently Cassie *did* have inhibitions, and they were all stripped away by a couple of Spritzes.

"Why do you say that?" Phil asked evenly.

She rolled her eyes so hard the rest of her head went along for the ride. "Oh, *please*. It was obvious he was sniffing around your young man here. Wanted to have his cake and eat it, I suppose. I've known men like that before, to my sorrow." She snorted like a horse. "Pillar of the bloody community in public, and going at it hammer and tongs with some poor boy in secret. It's Siri I feel sorry for."

I blinked and wished I'd gone for something alcoholic too. "No, you got it all wrong. He—" I broke off as Phil laid a hand on my arm.

"Do you think Siri was upset about that?" Phil asked as if I hadn't spoken.

Cassie snorted. "She'd have to be, wouldn't she?"

"Did you see any evidence of this?"

Why the hell was Phil going down this line? We knew what Wayne had been after me for, and it was nothing like what she was implying.

"Oh, she's the sort that hides it all behind her lipstick and eyeliner," Cassie said dismissively, and chugged the last half of her drink. "Where's the waiter gone? I need another of these."

I sent Phil a glance, and then managed to signal the waiter by holding up her empty glass and pointing. He nodded.

Meanwhile Phil was saying, "Can we go over what happened on the terrace?"

Cassie barked a laugh. "Hah. *Go over*." Then she blinked at her glass. "Hmph. Maybe I should stick to plain water from now on."

Great. I caught the waiter's eye again and tried to convey *cancel that last order* via improvised sign language. He appeared equal parts confused and alarmed by my throat-cutting gestures.

"On the terrace?" Phil was prompting.

"Oh. That. Yes, well, if you ask me, he'd had a few too many."

"Why do you say that?"

Cassie's generous lip curled. "I could tell by the look of him. Typical man. Drinks too much to prove his masculinity. As if *that's* anything to be proud of."

I wasn't sure if she meant holding your alcohol or being male. Probably the latter, knowing her.

Phil didn't seem troubled by the issue. "Were you near Wayne when he fell?"

"Was I near him . . .? Jane would know." She glanced up and brightened. "Jane, were we near to that young man when he offed himself?"

"When he *what*?" I blurted out, glancing up to see Jane returning from the loo.

Cassie rolled her eyes a little less exuberantly this time. "When he jumped. Well, I say jumped. More like he didn't stop himself falling. Couldn't live with the double life anymore, I expect. Ashamed of his desires."

"Cassandra, you've had quite enough to drink," Jane snapped, reaching our table at the same time as the waiter, who'd brought us a Spritz *and* another café freddo.

"It's okay, this one's mine," I said quickly, snatching up the Spritz and shoving the café freddo in Phil's direction.

Cassie didn't seem to notice. She heaved herself to her feet with a "My turn now," and headed off only slightly unsteadily in the direction Jane had come from.

"She shouldn't be drinking at all on her medication," Jane muttered as she sat down.

"Will she be all right?" I had visions of Cassie coming over unnecessary again, but this time without anyone there to catch her when she fell.

"She'd be perfectly fine if she only did what she was supposed to," Jane said, which wasn't exactly an answer. Still, if she didn't feel the need to go haring off to look after her sister, it probably wasn't my place to do it.

"Uh, if you don't mind my asking, what's the matter with her?"

"Failing to take care of herself, that's what the matter is. She was always like this, you know. Rushing headlong into things without thinking of the consequences. That's how she ended up married to that dreadful man."

"At least she had her big sister to take care of her, eh?" I tried to jolly her along. "And she's taking her medication, yeah?"

"For the most part. Although her doctor keeps warning her she needs to make lifestyle changes too, or she's at real risk of a stroke or a heart attack. She will *insist* on drinking, and she really shouldn't."

"Is she a lot younger than you?"

"Ten years. To the day." Jane's face softened. "I remember it so well. My tenth birthday. My father handed me a tiny warm bundle, so light I could barely feel the weight, and only her chubby little face showing. He said, 'Here's your birthday present, Jane.' And from then on, she was mine."

I blinked and tried to imagine a modern ten-year-old being so chuffed. Maybe if the baby had come clutching the latest iPhone in its podgy fists? "It's great you've stayed so close over the years. Me and my sister, Cherry, we've got a similar age difference, but we were never what you'd call close until recently. She's expecting, now—got married back in February." I wasn't sure why I was telling her this. "In a cathedral and all."

"Oh, how lovely." Jane's eyes were worryingly misty. "Is he a godly man, your brother-in-law? So few men are, these days."

"Uh, yeah." I was about to tell her about Greg being so godly he went to work in a purple frock, but perhaps fortunately, I was interrupted by Cassie making it back miraculously unscathed, and we all decided to call it a day. While we'd only scratched the surface as far as the sights of Capri were concerned, it looked like Phil and me had got as far as we were going to with the investigation, in present company at any rate.

I couldn't help feeling, as we made our way back to the funicular, that we'd learned precisely bugger all. Unless you counted that Cassie was probably the least reliable witness I'd ever encountered. She'd not only got the wrong end of the stick where Wayne and me were concerned, she was determined to waggle it under everybody's noses. And as for Wayne succumbing to a fit of self-loathing and killing himself... If there was anyone less likely to do that than Wayne "Aren't I Wonderful?" Hills, I didn't want to meet them.

We didn't press her further, though, as she clearly still wasn't herself—not to mention, Jane was clinging to her like an overprotective limpet.

"Are you two all right there?" I asked Jane at one point, worried she might not be up to the weight her not-so-little sis was putting on her arm.

"We're fine, thank you."

"Sure? If you want me and Phil to take turns helping Cassie—"

The lady herself turned on me with tetchiness in her tones. "Oh, for heaven's sake, stop fussing! You're worse than Jane."

"Just wondered if your big sis might need a break, that's all," I said, giving her a cheery smile.

"I'm perfectly fine, thank you," Jane said primly. "I may be old, but I'm not *frail*. Caring for an ailing husband is hard, physical work, you know. I'm quite up to taking Cassandra's arm for a short walk."

I gave up then. At least it was all downhill this way.

I managed to get Phil to myself on the boat as we chugged back over the bay to Sorrento. We leaned on the railings, gazing across the sea to where Vesuvius loomed peacefully, looking like butter wouldn't melt in its crater. Out on the water, the heat of the day was once again tempered by the breeze of our passage, and it was pretty bloody near perfect. "Do you believe all that bollocks Cassie came out with?" I murmured. "Think it was just the Spritzes talking?"

Phil huffed. "Who knows?" He paused. "I wondered about Wayne, at first. Whether he was like me."

I literally took a step back in amazement. "You did? Uh . . . did something happen between you two that I ought to know about?" On second thoughts, maybe blissful ignorance would be a better policy.

I got an eye roll for that. "I said *at first*. Wayne was straight as they come. And I've told you before, we were only ever friends. Carry on like this and I'll start thinking *you* had some kind of fascination with him."

"That's a definite *no* from me." I managed not to shudder, but it was a close-run thing. "All right, what about our friendly neighbourhood stalker? What do you reckon that's about? You don't reckon they did him in, do you? And now they've heard we're looking into it? Bloody hell, think they're going to put the frighteners on us?"

Phil was gazing straight at Vesuvius, the force of his glare enough to stop any eruptions in their tracks. "It's possible. There's a good chance they're just keeping tabs on us." He huffed. "It's strange, though. If they killed Wayne, why not follow up straight away with a direct approach?"

"What, more direct than murder? Why would they want to knock Wayne off, anyway? Him being their golden goose and all. Assuming they believed his mad plan would work."

"A direct approach to you. And it's the goose that laid the golden eggs. The goose wasn't golden, and Wayne wasn't the goose anyhow. *You're* supposed to be the goose."

"Honk bloody honk." I closed my eyes briefly at a particularly piercing glint of sunlight off the blue waters of the bay. "So what did that make him? The Pied Piper?"

"That was rats, not geese. And *unnecessary*, that's what." Phil huffed a cynical laugh.

"You mean, cut out the middle man and all that?" I did shudder this time. "Seems a bit . . . I dunno. Aren't the mafia supposed to be big on honour? So Wayne comes to them with a money-making scheme, and they tell him, 'Cheers, mate, we're having that, have a nice death'? Nothing very honourable about that."

"Firstly, I'd be amazed if this is the actual Cosa Nostra or the Camorra we're dealing with. I shouldn't think Wayne had that kind of contacts. This'll be some small-time local crew. And secondly, maybe he fell out with them over the details. Maybe he was asking for too big a cut or finder's fee, however he put it." Phil looked away. "It's the sort of thing he'd do. Push it too hard."

Was that what he'd done with Phil that'd led to them falling out—or at any rate, drifting apart? Pushed something too hard?

We had more important things to worry about right now than the ancient past, though. "So you reckon they're following us around to make sure we're not up to anything without cutting them in on it? Are they going to be making me an offer I can't refuse?"

"I think it wouldn't hurt to be on our guard." The darkness in his tone made me shiver.

"But . . . you think these blokes actually believe I could find stuff for them?"

"Might do. Googled yourself lately? There's plenty about you online, ever since you made the papers after the fire at the Dyke.

People can read that stuff just as easily from this country as they can back home."

I squinted out at the coast of mainland Italy, now looming large on the horizon. I wasn't sure I liked the idea of people anywhere in the world knowing stuff about me and my so-called gift. Especially since, people and the internet being what they were, most of what they knew was probably wrong, or at best wildly exaggerated. "International celebrity, that's me," I said with a touch of bitterness. All right, maybe more than a touch. "I ought to start charging for autographs. Hey, if we ever split up, you can write a tell-all about me and make a fortune."

Phil slung his arm around my waist, there on the boat where anyone could see us. "Not going to happen," he said firmly.

I leaned into him, warmed inside and out.

Chapter Twenty-Two

We took it easy when we got back to the hotel, lazing in the folding chairs on our small balcony and writing postcards. If our stalker was still on our tail—not that either of us had spotted him since the monastery on Capri—he'd have to kick his heels in a bar somewhere. I, for one, was going to stop worrying about him for now.

Well, that was the plan. I realised my mind wasn't totally in the game when I found I'd scrawled bland lines about the weather to Mum and Dad on the back of the card I'd earmarked for Gary and Darren.

"Don't reckon I ought to send this one to my parents, do you?" I asked Phil, holding it up.

He laughed. "Put it this way, if you're planning to send your mum a dick pic, don't sign it from me as well."

"It's not a dick pic. It's a photo of an antique statue of an actual Roman god."

"Who's carting his enormous dong around in a wheelbarrow. It's a dick pic."

I sighed, chucked the dick pic on the tiny table between us, and picked up a nice, boring card showing the Bay of Naples to rewrite my murder-free message to Mum and Dad. There was no point in them worrying. My mind drifted again during the task, and I remembered what I'd been thinking about earlier. "How come you and Wayne didn't stay friends?" Because they'd been solid as a proverbial back when I'd known them in school. "Was it the gay thing?"

Phil sent me a piercing gaze, then looked away. "No. It wasn't *the gay thing*. Not directly, anyhow."

"What, then? Did he badmouth your mum? Screw over your sister?" I asked it idly, and wasn't prepared for the force of Phil's reply.

"What the hell do you *think* happened?"

"I dunno, do I?" Narked at his tone, I'd raised my voice to match his. "I wasn't there. I was in the sodding hospital with a knackered pelvis, wasn't I?"

He closed his eyes, and when he spoke again, it was almost too soft to hear. "Yeah. Yeah, you were."

I didn't get what he was trying to say—and then suddenly I did.

He'd kept the newspaper clipping for over a decade—the one about the accident. I'd come across it by chance way back when we'd first reconnected, around half a lifetime ago.

All right, a couple of years ago. Mind you, a lot had happened since then.

"You broke up with Wayne because I broke my hip?" I managed.

Phil huffed. "I didn't *break up* with him. For the ninety-ninth time, we weren't a couple. But yeah, I stopped wanting to be friends with him after that. It was the first time we'd done anything that had . . . consequences. That we knew about," he added, turning a bit red, as well he might. I'd told him a while back how badly the teenaged bullying had affected my state of mind.

"But he wasn't even sorry about it when we found out how bad you were hurt. Christ, he laughed, the git. Said that'd keep you out of our way for a good long while." He turned to give me a weak smile. "I promised myself it'd be different—*I'd* be different—when you came back to school. But you never did."

It rocked me, knowing how soon he'd had a change of heart. Then again—"You told me you only came out to people we were at school with at that reunion last year."

He shrugged. "Wasn't any point, back in sixth form. You weren't there."

That was . . . I couldn't quite get my head round it. I had this weird image of me and him becoming friends at seventeen instead of a dozen years later. That *childhood sweethearts* remark I'd made to Jane . . . that could maybe even have been true.

How different would our lives have been, in that case?

Then I shook my head. Nah, never would've happened. If Phil Morrison had so much as said a friendly *hello* to me, I'd have assumed he was just being a git as usual and run a mile.

Limped a mile, whatever.

Phil reached across the table and gave my hand a squeeze. "And yeah, I know you'd have shot me straight down if I'd asked you out back then." He took a deep breath. "I spent most of my A-level year pissed off with you. For not coming back to school. Not giving me a chance to show you I could be a better man."

I squeezed back. "Yeah, well, I was pissed off with you for a long time and all. Funny how things turn out, innit?"

We had a stroke of luck after dinner. Leaning over the terrace railings (I know, I know) and gazing idly at the view, I happened to notice a pair of distinctive braces walking smartly down the road towards the town. Martin, his shirt sleeves rolled up and his jacket slung over one arm, was headed off somewhere. I gave Phil a nudge. "Oi, looks like Siri's getting that alone time at last. Want to go and check she's okay?"

Phil nodded, a satisfied smile barely visible on his lips. "Best go now, before she decides to take a shower or get an early night."

We legged it down to her room. Siri answered on the first knock and broke into a sad smile when she saw it was us, so she couldn't have been as desperate as all that to get away from everyone.

"Tom, Phil. Come on in. Sorry it's such a mess."

"Don't worry about it, love," I told her as we trooped into the room and I tried not to step on her knickers. The place was a bit of a tip, but you could hardly blame the poor girl. Picking up your stuff off the floor probably didn't seem all that important when you'd just lost the love of your life.

Some of the clothes lying around looked too masculine for Siri's taste. Had I seen Wayne wearing them?

Or, as might be, Martin?

Siri cleared a load of stuff off the end of the bed and perched there, so I joined her. Phil parked his arse on the (thankfully sturdy-looking) counter that housed the telly.

I gave Siri a hug. "How are you doing? Feeling any better?"

She nodded. "Yeah. It was really kind of you all to take me out today. Can you thank Jane and Cassie for me? And tell them I'm sorry I had to go and ruin it. You must've all thought I was a right miserable cow."

"Oi, none of that. Me and Phil and the ladies had a drink in a caff after you left, and no one had a bad word to say about you. Not sure I'd have managed to be so brave if it'd been . . ." I gestured vaguely in Phil's direction.

Siri sniffled and nodded. "You found out anything yet? About who did it?"

"We're still working on it." Phil leaned forward. "Which is why I need to ask you some more questions about that night."

She looked up at him, her eyes moist. "But I don't know anything."

I gave her a squeeze. "You might know stuff you don't know you know. I mean, you might have seen something that could give us a clue even if it seems unimportant in itself."

"The smallest details could be significant," Phil chimed in. "We know this is hard for you, but we need you to take us through the scene again."

Siri took in a deep, shaky breath, then gave a brave little nod. "You mean from . . . from when he fell?"

"How about you start a bit earlier than that. Say from when Wayne joined you and Martin on the terrace."

She took another couple of deep breaths, then launched in. "Okay, so, I was dead pleased to see him, yeah? 'Cos he'd been poorly."

Or he'd been having a secret meeting with the Bling Boys.

"How did he seem when you saw him?" Phil asked gently.

"Well . . ." Her brow furrowed. "It was difficult, 'cos of the fireworks, you know? And they'd turned the lights right down. But he must've felt better, 'cos he'd been drinking."

I blinked. "He was drunk?"

"No! No, I just meant . . . I smelled it. On his breath. When he kissed me." Her lip quivered. "I wish I'd never told the police that. Maybe they'd have done a proper inquiry, then? Not written poor Wayne off as another drunk tourist who'd had an accident."

I gave her a sympathetic look. "Don't blame yourself. They'd have found out anyway. From the bar staff or blood tests or something."

To be brutally honest, which obviously I wasn't going to be in Siri's hearing, knowing Wayne had had a few before he fell did make the accident theory a lot more credible. And to be fair to the local plod, they were probably sick to death of scraping binge-drinking foreigners out of the messes they'd got themselves into.

Phil's tone was even as he carried on. "So Wayne came up to where you and Martin were sitting, and he kissed you?"

If I knew Wayne, he'd done it to make a point. As in, *Hands off, she's mine*. Which, to be fair, I suppose a lot of blokes would do if they'd been expecting to rescue their significant other from solitude, only to find them cosied up with an overly attentive stranger.

"Yeah," Siri confirmed. "And I said something like, he'd got there just in time—you know, for the fireworks—and Martin said we should watch them from the balcony so we could see the boats all lit up in the bay."

Huh. So the boat-watching had been Martin's idea, not Siri's?

"But Wayne didn't want to do that. 'Cos of his inner-ear thing. So Martin said I should go with him."

I bet that had gone down well with Wayne.

"Was Wayne happy with that idea?" Phil asked, reading my mind.

Siri's mouth twisted. "He . . . Look, he hadn't seemed happy from the moment he got there," she burst out in the end. "And—and I was cross with him, all right? 'Cos I'd been so happy, and he was ruining it by being grumpy." Her whole face crumpled. "I didn't know what was going to happen!"

I patted her knee as she sniffled. "Course you didn't. Nobody could have known."

Except one person, obviously. Or maybe more than one?

"And then . . . And then he fell, and it was awful, and I was all on my own."

I blinked. Beside me, Phil had gone still. "Martin wasn't with you when Wayne fell?"

"He was, but . . . he'd gone to get us some drinks. He only stepped away for a moment, yeah?" She hugged herself. "And then I was looking down at the road, and it was horrible, and all I could think was that I wanted Wayne to give me a cuddle and make me feel better. But it . . . It was . . ." She ducked her head.

I slung an arm around her and gave her that cuddle. She felt bonier than she ought to, and I wondered how much she'd eaten today.

"Did Martin have the drinks with him when he joined you again?" Phil asked.

She stared at him with watery eyes. "Drinks? Why would I care about drinks when Wayne was dead? What does it even matter?"

"I'm trying to build up a picture of the scene," Phil said patiently.

"Oh." She bit her lip. "Um, no? I don't think he did. But he probably put them down somewhere. Or left them behind. Or maybe he hadn't got them yet."

Phil persisted. "How long would you say he left you alone?"

"Only a moment." Her brow creased, and she shook off my arm. "Why? You can't think he done it!"

Our witness was rapidly turning hostile, which was unfortunate. Especially as she was also our employer.

Uh, *Phil's* employer. Strictly speaking.

"Course we don't think he did it," I lied. "But he might have seen something while he was away from you. You know, that you couldn't see, 'cos you were looking out at the fireworks."

"Oh. Yeah, I guess? But he didn't. I mean, he would've said if he did, wouldn't he?"

Would he? Even if he *hadn't* taken the opportunity to shove Wayne off this mortal coil for reasons as yet unknown, we still didn't know how on-the-level dear old Martin was. And I personally wouldn't have trusted him to hold my drink while I nipped to the gents.

"Sometimes people assume what they've seen isn't relevant. But it all helps to complete the picture." Phil leaned forward. "Can we go back to when Wayne appeared on the terrace? What made you think he wasn't happy?"

Siri frowned. "Um, I dunno? He held my shoulder a bit tight when he bent down to kiss me hello. And he wasn't very friendly to Martin."

Yeah, I wonder why? I managed not to roll my eyes.

"Look, I know what you're thinking." Siri jumped off the bed and glared up at Phil, like a plucky Chihuahua squaring up to a Rottweiler.

"You think he was jealous, right? Wayne had *nothing* to be jealous about. I'd never've done that to him, and Martin's a gentleman. And, anyway, he's gay."

Chapter Twenty-Three

"Martin's gay?" I blurted out. My bloody gaydar: permanently on the blink.

"He told you that?" Phil asked. I sent him a sharp glance. Was he implying something? Like, say, that anything Martin told her should be taken with a pinch of scepticism?

Siri narrowed her eyes. "Well, yeah. Or I wouldn't've known, would I? I'm not a lesbian."

I guessed she meant she hadn't been initiated into the ritual of the Secret Queer Handshake™. That made two of us, apparently. "Okay, moving on—"

"You're acting like that policeman," Siri cut me off with a hurt look. "He was like that and all—inseminating stuff about me and Martin."

Did she mean insinuating? I'd have to ask Phil when I got him on his own. "Nobody's suggesting you were walking out on Wayne," I said, trying to pour a splash of extra virgin on the Bay of Biscay. "We don't know Martin very well." Not to mention, neither did she. "We can't help being, uh, cautious about the bloke and his motives."

"Martin hasn't got any motives," she snapped back. "So don't you go saying he has."

"Everyone has their own motivation for what they do," Phil said, which didn't seem particularly helpful right then.

"We just don't want to see you getting hurt, any more than you already have been," I put in quick.

Siri slumped back down on the bed next to me like her strings had been cut. "That's so sweet of you, Tom. But Martin's one of the good guys, yeah? You're not going to find out who k-killed my Wayne by being all suspicious of him."

"But it would help if you could persuade him to talk to us." Phil's tone was more conciliatory this time. "Like we said, he may have seen something important."

"Where's he off to tonight?" I asked as casually as I could.

Siri shrugged. "He went back to his room. He's got some calls to make. Why?"

I tried to be subtle with the significant glance I sent in Phil's direction. Should we tell her he'd lied about that? Phil gave a minute shake of his head.

I gave myself a pat on the back for effective nonverbal communication, which was preferable to making a note to have a word with him about this mind-reading lark.

"Business?" Phil asked as if he didn't give a toss either way.

She nodded.

"What line's he in?"

"Oh, he's in the same line of business as Wayne." Siri gave a wobbly smile. "Don't say nothing to him about it, 'cos he's never *said*, but I think he's having some problems. He's been asking all kinds of stuff about how Wayne does—how Wayne did things like get new customers and that. I had to tell him I don't know much about all that."

"You were never involved in Wayne's business ventures?" Phil asked.

"No. Never. Well, I used to go on trips with him, and sometimes there was these sales presentations they do, but I never got involved in all that."

Was that really Martin's deal? He simply wanted to pick Siri's brains about business? It didn't sit right with me. Why would he assume she'd had anything to do with it? Presumably he'd been in the foreign property trade long before they'd got together, and she had her own career.

Then again, maybe he'd been intending to use Siri to get friendly with Wayne? He'd made a bloody catastrophic job of it, if so. All he'd achieved, in the brief interval between him getting chummy with Siri and Wayne getting dead, was putting the bloke's back up something chronic.

"What about his business associates here in Sorrento?" I asked.

She bit her lip. "I know he had some. But I never met them."

Phil decided to take over. "How much do you know about what he had planned here? Involving Tom?"

Siri brightened. "Oh, I know about *that.* But it wasn't business. He just wanted you to help out these archaeologists he knew."

"Did you ever meet these . . . archaeologists?" Even Phil couldn't keep the incredulity out of his voice.

Thankfully, from her lack of reaction, it sailed straight over Siri's head. "No. Wayne said I shouldn't bother 'cos I'd only be bored. Like when he was doing his business stuff."

Exactly like, I reckoned.

Phil cleared his throat. "Can you think of a reason for Wayne to go over to the balcony, if it wasn't to be with you?"

That was a good point. I was a bit miffed I hadn't thought of it.

Siri's face crumpled. "I don't know! I wasn't with him, was I? Why are you asking me all this stuff?"

"We just want to—"

She jumped up again, nearly knocking me off the end of the bed. "I can't talk about it anymore. I don't feel well."

To be fair, she didn't look well. Her face had gone all blotchy, and she was trembling like a bargain-whatsit in a breeze. I stood. "Are you going to be okay on your own?"

I crossed my fingers she wouldn't ask us to get Martin.

Then I uncrossed them, because it was no skin off my nose if he got caught out in his lies, was it? She didn't ask for him, though. She simply gave a tearful nod and turned to stare out of the window.

Phil didn't seem too happy, but he apologised for upsetting her and followed my lead out of there.

"What the hell was all that about?" I muttered as we made our way back to our own room. "Think it's the strain getting to her?"

"Guilt," Phil said shortly.

I tripped over my feet and would've face-planted on the hallway carpet if Phil hadn't caught my arm and steadied me. "What? You think *Siri* ki—"

"Keep your voice down." Letting go of my arm, Phil sent the surrounding doorways suspicious glares, as if there might be a mafioso—or a copper—taking notes behind any one of them. "And no, of course I don't. But she's blaming herself."

"Why do you reckon that?"

"You saw how defensive she got about any suggestion there might be something going on between her and Martin."

I barely got my gob open before he was cutting me off.

"And before you leap to her defence, no, I don't think she was playing around with him. But I do think Wayne reckoned they were getting too friendly, and maybe Siri wasn't above using that to keep him keen."

I opened my mouth again—then paused and gave him a hard stare. "Going to let me get a word in edgewise this time?"

Phil huffed a laugh. "Maybe. Go on, then."

"Okay, how's that work, then? She uses Martin to get Wayne jealous—yeah, remind him he ought to appreciate her while he's got her, I can see that—but what's it got to do with her feeling guilty about Wayne's death? You're not telling me you think he topped himself, are you?"

"No. My guess is, she thinks Wayne was trying to get over his fear of heights—"

"You mean, his inner-ear thing," I put in drily.

"—so he wouldn't look bad next to Martin, and that's why he went over to the balcony. On his own, so if he couldn't hack it, she and Martin wouldn't see."

"Huh. You know, if this inner-ear thing was for real, maybe it all went down like that and it really was an accident? He got all dizzy and toppled over?"

"That's presumably what the police here think. Although it sounds like they're putting the dizziness down to alcohol."

"But you don't?"

Phil was silent a mo, as we let an excited French family pass us in the corridor. "It could have been. But he was using that inner-ear excuse back in school, and I can remember his dad telling me it was bollocks and he was just a wuss about heights."

Bit mean of daddy dearest to go grassing Wayne up to his mates. Still . . . "What's even the difference, though? If he was that scared of heights, it could make him dizzy anyway, couldn't it?"

We'd reached our door, and Phil gave a nod as he opened it. "It's possible."

"And poor old Siri's desperate to find someone else to blame." I shut the door behind us and flopped down flat on the bed. "Maybe it'd be best if we focussed on convincing her it wasn't her fault, rather than going around searching for some imaginary murderer?"

"I said it *might* be that." Phil was gazing out of the window again. Whatever he'd paid for our room with a view, he was apparently determined to get his money's worth.

I pushed myself up on my elbows. "So now you're saying it *was* murder? I'm confused."

"I'm saying we don't know, and Siri asked us to look into it. So that's what I'm going to do." His shoulders tensed. "There's something not right here, I know that."

"Private eye's instinct?"

He huffed and came to join me on the bed, lying down next to me and rubbing a hand over his face. "Maybe. Christ, this is frustrating. I feel like I'm hamstrung, here. No in with the police, so no way to check out the background of Wayne's local contacts."

"Is that why we've been concentrating on the Brits?"

"Yeah. But all we know about them is what they tell us. Wayne too. I could do with more information on them—financial situations, whether they've had any bother with the law in the past." Phil turned his head to gaze at me. "Was wondering if you could give Dave Southgate a bell."

"Course—but I thought you had your own mate on the force you could touch for info? Back home, I mean."

"He's on holiday right now." Phil reddened slightly, and no, the irony wasn't lost on me either.

"I'll call Dave," I said.

Because I had to use the hotel phone—my mobile still being blissfully signal-free—Dave answered with a businesslike, "Southgate."

"Dave? It's me. Tom. Uh, Paretski."

"Think I wouldn't recognise your dulcet tones? What are you doing ringing me on your honeymoon? Morrison run off with a waiter, has he?"

"Ha ha. No. We, um, need a bit of help, that's all."

"Bloody hell, Paretski. If you've been caught shagging in public in a Catholic country—"

"It's nothing like that! We need some information, though. There's, uh, there's been a death."

"Thought you could turn that sniffer-dog thing on and off? Rule number one of a successful honeymoon, mate: don't go looking for bloody bodies."

"I didn't go looking for him. It wasn't even me who found him. He fell past our window. He was a mate, actually. Well, Phil's mate. A long time ago."

"So what was he doing on your honeymoon with you? Or do I not want to know?"

"Oi, not what you're thinking. But, uh, it's a long story. Point is, his girlfriend reckons he was pushed, and we were hoping you could dig into his background for us. Recent stuff, that is. See if anything jumps out—'scuse pun—as to why someone would want to bump him off."

"Don't rate the Italian police, then? I should be offended. Spirit of international cooperation and all that."

"They're not investigating. They've put it down as an accident."

"And you don't trust their judgement because?"

"It's not me. It's Siri."

"Great. You're taking advice from your bleeding iPhone now?"

"Not that Siri. The real one. Wayne's girlfriend. Can we get to the point?" This phone call was going to cost us a fortune.

"Eager to get back to frolicking in the sun with your lawfully wedded husband, are you?"

"Too right. Look, will you do it? His name's Wayne Hills, and he had some kind of a business flogging property in Europe. Possibly some dodgy dealing there, if he was running true to form. Might have a few red flags in that computer system of yours. I can probably message you his address and stuff," I added with a hopeful glance at Phil, who nodded.

"Fine, I'll see what I can do. Anything else I can do for you? All-expenses paid tour of Interpol headquarters? Strippagram by the local fire department?"

I winced. "Uh, yeah. There's this bloke who's been sniffing around the girlfriend. Martin Kingsman. If that's his real name. Out here on his own, and he seems . . . I don't know. Dodgy." Phil waved his phone under my nose, and I saw he'd managed to snap a sneaky pic of Martin while we were in that garden on Capri. "I'll send you a photo of him. British, sounds like a southerner, maybe midthirties, on the posh side."

"Got it. Two dodgy geezers, one living, one snuffed it." Dave gave a heavy sigh down the phone that nearly blew my eardrums out. "Look, not that I want any details, but is everything going okay with you and Morrison?"

"Yeah, why wouldn't it?"

"Because you're playing hunt-the-murderer on your honeymoon instead of hunt-the-sausage?"

"Dave, I know where the sausage is. I don't need to hunt it. And everything's fine. But . . . we got to know the girlfriend, okay? And she's really cut up about it all."

"You and your bleedin' damsels in distress. I wouldn't mind so much if you actually had the first idea what to do with a bloody damsel."

"Oi, I know how . . . damsels work!" I caught Phil's frankly amused eye and looked away hurriedly. "I'm just not interested, that's all. Anyway, how's it going with you and the missus? Nipper started walking yet?"

"So bloody close I can taste it." He'd been saying that ever since young Lucas had learned to sit up on his own. "He's a champ, that one. Must take after his dad."

I laughed. "You wish. Listen, I'd better go before this call bankrupts me. You'll give us a bell if you find out anything, yeah? Oh, and call the hotel. I think my mobile service provider's taking a holiday and all." I gave him the number, and we said our fond farewells.

Okay, so he told me to at least *try* to stay out of trouble, and I pretended I wouldn't know trouble if it jumped up and bit me on the bum. But it came to the same thing.

"Right, that's all in motion," I said brightly as I put my phone down.

Phil didn't seem as cheered-up as I'd hoped at the prospect of Dave doing his job for him. "Sounded like he was worried about you," he said flatly.

"What . . .?" I reran the conversation in my head. "Oh, well, yeah. No one likes to think their mate's had a murder on his honeymoon."

"That was all, was it?"

"Why wouldn't it be?" I frowned. "You don't still reckon he hates you, do you? That's water under the bridge. Trust me."

Phil ran a hand through his hair and turned away. "Ignore me. Just feeling like I'm doing a crap job on all fronts at the moment."

"Bollocks. You're doing great." I sent him a comforting leer, but it was wasted on the broad expanse of his back. "Better than, on certain fronts in particular. Speaking of which, bed?"

He let out a gentle sigh and turned to face me, his shoulders relaxing a little. "Yeah. Bed."

Chapter Twenty-Four

Next morning, after we'd enjoyed a few of the traditional honeymoon activities, Phil levered himself up on one elbow and raised an eyebrow at me. "Fancy getting up to something a bit more energetic today?"

I gave his naked form an appreciative leer. "More energetic than what we just did? The other guests are going to be complaining about us again."

"Get your mind out of the gutter. I was thinking of something uplifting—literally. The hotel's running a tour to Vesuvius this morning, and if we get a move on, we could join it."

"A coach tour? Like for old-age pensioners? Doesn't sound all that energetic to me."

"It's not that kind of coach tour. They drop you off at a car park halfway up, and you have to climb up to the crater from there."

I made a face. "We're not talking ropes and crampons, are we? Because that sounds a bit *too* energetic for my liking."

"First it's too easy, now it's too hard . . . Who are you, Goldilocks? It's a steep path, that's all. My mum could do it in her slippers. And still have the breath to nag us for not visiting often enough."

"All right, you've sold me." Fresh air and exercise would do us both good. And hopefully take Phil's mind off his perceived failings while we were waiting for Dave to come up with the goods.

Of course, he wasn't the only person around who could benefit from some distraction. "We ought to ask Siri if she wants to come too."

Phil nodded, like he'd been planning to do that all along. "Keeping an eye on her and Martin wouldn't be a bad idea."

"Yeah. We could ask him if he enjoyed his evening on the town," I said pointedly.

"Maybe. We don't know he was being dishonest with Siri. He might have changed his mind about going out after he spoke to her. Or not wanted to hurt her feelings."

"S'pose," I muttered, unwilling to let go of my mental image of Martin as a bad 'un.

Phil huffed a laugh. "Come on. We'll knock on Siri's door on the way to breakfast and ask them. Course, they might have other plans."

If they did, they were happy enough to abandon them. And by *they* I mean Siri—Martin was there all right, but he had a sour expression on his admittedly not-unhandsome mug from the moment he saw who it was.

After breakfast, we all gathered in the downstairs lobby to await the bus. Siri was giving off brave yet fragile vibes in a T-shirt and capris combo accessorised with flip-flops, while Martin, in his braces and smart shoes, appeared well overdressed next to her. Me and Phil were working the rugged-and-handsome look, obviously.

There were around seven or eight of our fellow guests who I only knew by sight, most of them in proper walking boots. I eyed my trainers with misgivings. Then again, the Snipes—yeah, they were here too, like the proverbial bad pennies—were in the sort of gear that seemed more suited to the streets of Milan, although at least his jacket was linen and her jewelled sandals didn't have much of a heel.

Mrs. S. gave me an unfriendly smirk when she caught my eye, and I glanced away hurriedly.

Siri piped up, "This is going to be really interesting." I wasn't sure if she was trying to convince herself or her sullen squire. "I've never seen a proper volcano before. Not up close, like."

"Seen a lot of improper ones, have you?" I quipped. "Showing their lava, letting off gas in front of all and sundry?"

Okay, it was a poor joke, but it made her giggle, which had been the point.

"Wouldn't it be awful, though, if it went off and we were on it?" Siri carried on, her dark eyes big.

"Don't worry," Martin said a touch brusquely. "It's perfectly safe."

"Yeah, we're fine." I resisted the urge to cross my fingers behind my back. "They've got, uh, scientists with machines that watch them—"

"Seismographs," Phil put in.

"Yeah, those things. So they'll get plenty of warning before an eruption happens." I hoped.

Siri beamed up at us both. "You're dead clever, knowing so much. W-Wayne was always having to tell me stuff too." Her smile faltered, and a sniffle threatened.

Martin slung an avuncular arm around her shoulders. "The world would be a boring place if we were all experts in every field. I dare say not a man here would be able to produce a perfect set of nails like you can."

She brightened, and I actually found myself warming towards Martin—a little bit.

I didn't like it. Luckily, the coach turned up at that point to take my mind off my distress.

I used the journey to flip through the guidebook. "Hey, we could have done this by train and bus. Probably cheaper."

"The coach has air-con."

"And it's worth every penny." I peered through the tiny gap between the seats to spy on Martin and Siri, a few (empty) rows in front of us, but couldn't make out anything untoward going on. They seemed to be talking about something serious, from the way they had their heads together, Siri's nodding as if she was taking every dodgy word Martin uttered as gospel.

Then again, maybe I really was being too paranoid about the bloke. I turned back to my guidebook. "Says here, Vesuvius is the only active volcano on the European mainland. Last erupted in 1944 and is overdue to go off again."

Phil raised an eyebrow. "Worried?"

"Nope. Like I told Siri, I've got total faith in the seismo-whatsits. Course, it'd be sort of romantic. Like a Shakespearian tragedy."

"What, getting killed on our honeymoon? I prefer my romance alive and well, thanks."

"Hey, we could end up like those poor bastards in Pompeii, buried under ash locked in a final embrace. Our love preserved for all eternity."

Phil looked a bit green at that point.

"Or not," I went on quickly. "If we're on the volcano itself when the big bang happens, maybe we'll just get vaporised by the pyroclastics."

He snorted. "You're so reassuring."

When we all piled out of our air-conditioned coach at journey's end, the heat of the day felt pretty pyroclastic already. There was literally nothing there apart from the car park, and we were all keen to stretch our legs, so we didn't waste any time hanging around.

The path up to the crater was wide, all the better to accommodate the tourists, and made up of dark grey gravelly stuff. Scree, is that what you call it on mountains? I'm pretty sure it's got another name when you see it in front gardens owned by people who can't be arsed to mow a lawn. Whatever it was, combined with the slope, it soon made for slippery footing, and I didn't envy Siri in her flip-flops.

I could see Martin, who'd courteously offered her his arm, was getting frustrated with her slow progress, although he was doing his gritted-teeth best not to show it. Phil, too, was chafing at the bit, striding ahead with those long legs of his and then having to wait until we caught up. Then again, *I'd* felt stiff climbing out of those coach seats after so long. The close confines must have been even more annoying for him.

This was daft. "Tell you what, why don't you two go on up, and I'll follow with Siri?" I suggested, taking her other arm.

Martin seized his chance with both hands—which he was able to do, having dropped Siri like a ton of hot potatoes. "If you don't mind, my dear . . ."

"I don't want to hold you up, neither, Tom," Siri said bravely. "I can manage."

"Nah, I wouldn't mind slowing down myself." I slapped my hip, which had, in fact, set up a protest at what I was asking of it, although admittedly a minor one. "Old war wound."

As Martin drew level with him, Phil turned to give me an unreadable look over his shoulder. "You sure you're up for this?"

"Course." I waved him off. "I'm not in any hurry, that's all. You go on ahead. Race Martin to the top."

Martin raised a speculative eyebrow in Phil's direction. "I'm in if you are."

It got him a glower. "What are we, twelve?"

"Suit yourself." Martin shrugged and powered on up the hill.

It might have been my imagination, but I was pretty sure Phil lengthened his stride.

Siri giggled. "Men. Not you, obviously."

"Think of me as one of the girls." Hey, I'm secure in my masculinity, me. Mostly. "So how are you holding up, anyway? Martin taking good care of you?"

"He's been, like, a rock. And you and Phil. Bugger. 'Scuse French." We halted while Siri recaptured an escaped flip-flop. "You've all been so good to me. And you on your honeymoon too. You've got to make sure you enjoy it. You get loads of holidays, but you only get one honeymoon."

"Unless you're Phil," I said without thinking.

We stopped again, as Siri's grip tightened on my arm. "How come?"

I shrugged, not sure why she was so shocked—people got remarried all the time, didn't they? "I'm his second husband."

"You're never!" She dug her nails into my arm, then mercifully relaxed her grip. "Innit weird, though? All the wedding stuff and that, he's done it before, hasn't he? You must keep wondering if it's really as special to him as it is to you."

I'd been doing a reasonable job of *not* wondering that lately, but now it was front and centre in my mind again. Cheers, love.

"So, what, is he divorced, then?" she went on.

"Uh, his first husband died."

"Oh my God, that's awful. Oh, Tom, I'm so sorry."

"Um, I never actually knew the bloke."

"No, I mean, it's like—how can you compare with someone who's dead?" Siri gazed at me with wide, earnest eyes. "I know even if, like, years from now, I get together with another bloke, he'll never mean as much to me as my poor Wayne." The eyes grew moist, and she gave a gentle sniffle.

Right. "Guess I'll have to settle for . . ." What, second best? I was buggered if I was going to be runner-up to a bloke who hadn't appreciated Phil while he had him.

Siri patted my arm. "I'm sure he loves you as much as he can."

What could I say, but—"Cheers, love."

We walked on a few paces, my arm hot and clammy where she was holding on. The sun was merciless, and I wasn't the only one feeling it—people to the right and left of us were slowing their pace and mopping their fevered brows. I wondered how Phil and Martin were doing on their macho march to the top. I couldn't even see them anymore.

Siri spoke again—or, rather, she whispered. "Who are we following?"

"Uh, what?" I panted—I mean, said.

"That's why we came here, isn't it? So you and Phil could follow a suspect?"

She looked so hopeful I didn't have the heart to tell her we were mostly just enjoying our hols while we waited for info. Inspiration struck when I glanced around and my gaze caught on the Snipes, who weren't moving any faster than we were. "See that couple? Her with the halter dress and sunglasses, and him in the linen jacket?" Which any sane person would have taken off by now. "They're the ones who complained about us asking people about the night Wayne died."

I could almost hear the little cogs whirring as she worked the rest of it out herself. "Ohhh . . . So maybe they had a reason, yeah?"

I nodded and did my best to tamp down the guilt that threatened to rise. After all, I technically hadn't *lied* to her, had I? Not like Martin.

Probably.

"I never liked them two," Siri whispered after a mo. "She's dead snooty. I've had people like her in the salon, and they always complain and never tip. And he gives me the creeps."

"Oh?"

"Yeah, he came up to me the first night they were here and was being all friendly, but I didn't like the way he was looking at me. Like he was trying to see through my clothes. And then *she* came along and was really nasty."

I was starting to think maybe I should be suspecting them in earnest. "Was Wayne with you?"

"Yeah, he came over while I was talking to the bloke."

"Mr. Snipe," I said without thinking.

"Oh, is that his name? Anyway, Wayne came over, and then she joined us and sort of sneered at him. Called him a typical Brit on holiday, and you could tell she didn't mean it in a good way." Siri coloured. "Then they went away, but I heard him saying something about how I'd never make it onto *University Challenge*, and then they laughed. I know I'm not that bright, 'cos I was always rubbish at school, but it wasn't nice of them to, like, laugh about it, was it?"

Was there a Roman god of justice? If so, hopefully my brief but fervent prayer would ensure painfully turned ankles for the Snipes. "They were talking out of their arses. 'Scuse Italian. And sod *University* bloody *Challenge*. I'd rather have a conversation with you than with those two any day."

"That's so sweet of you." Siri squeezed my arm, then concentrated on her footing for a few steps further. "Wayne used to have a laugh, sometimes, about me being thick, but he was nice about it, you know?"

"Uh, yeah," I lied.

"I always knew he was smarter than me. And it's good, innit, having someone who can teach you stuff? Like you and Phil."

I blinked. "Uh . . ."

"I'm not saying you're thick," she said quickly, possibly sensing my mood. "But he knows a lot, doesn't he?"

"Yeah. He's got an app." I might have said it a bit shortly.

Apparently Siri didn't notice, because she giggled. "You're so funny. Ooh, do you think they're at the top yet? It's a long way, innit?"

It *was* a long way, especially at the speed we were going. Supposedly a thirty-minute walk, I reckoned it'd take us at least forty-five. Hopefully we'd get there before Phil and Martin passed us on their way back down.

When we finally reached the top of the path, though, we found them waiting for us. They weren't speaking to each other, and I didn't think it was because they'd run out of things to say. Neither bloke had a smile on his mug. Martin was flushed and sweaty, while Phil was doing a sterling impersonation of one of the stones on the path.

"Who won?" Siri asked brightly.

"We'll call it a draw." Martin glanced over at Phil and smirked.

Phil glowered. "We weren't actually racing."

Martin full-on beamed. "How's your hip bearing up, Tom? Phil was telling me about your accident."

From Phil's glare, it was going to be a toss-up whether it was him or Vesuvius that erupted first. I doubted it'd been his choice of conversation topic. It certainly wouldn't have been mine, but maybe I'd asked for it with that *war wound* comment.

I sent them both a sunny smile, hoping to stave off any mass fatalities. "Never better. Taking it slow with Siri turned out to be just the thing."

"Are we going to look at this volcano now we've come all this way?" Siri didn't quite tap her foot, but she was definitely a little fidgety around the flip-flops.

Martin roused himself and offered her his arm. "Of course. Shall we?"

Me and Phil watched them set off on the path around the crater—nice and level, this one. We gave them a couple of minutes to get out of earshot before we set off after them.

"Get anything out of Martin on the way up?" I asked. "Or was he the one asking all the questions?"

Phil scowled, which was as good an answer as any. "You learn anything new from Siri?"

"Uh. No. Unless you count our old friends the Snipes trying it on with her until they worked out Wayne would be part of the deal? We talked about dead ex partners. That was all." Yeah, I could maybe have done without mentioning that to Phil.

We walked on in silence for a few yards while I tried to think of a nontouchy subject. Luckily for me, there was a bloody great volcanic crater right in front of our noses. We stopped to peer at it over the fence at the edge of the path.

"It's a bit . . ." I grimaced.

"Un-volcano-like?" Phil suggested with a twist to his mouth.

"Yeah. That. I mean, I wasn't expecting a lake of boiling lava, but this? If you didn't know, you'd think it was a nice spot for a picnic." Okay, that was an exaggeration. The inside of the crater was barren and rocky, with only a few scrubby plants cropping up here and there. But it did appear thoroughly innocuous.

"Probably looked a lot like that when they were building Pompeii."

"Huh. Guess so. Still, any hobbits looking to get rid of the One Ring would be right out of luck."

Phil huffed. "Geek."

"Oi. It's a universal story of, uh, overcoming adversity. And Orcs. Gary made me watch it." I shuddered in memory. "All three movies back-to-back. The extended editions. Have you got any idea how much popcorn a grown man can put away in eleven hours?"

"Doesn't seem to have ruined your girlish figure."

Thank God, his sense of humour was returning. "Not me. Him. I couldn't touch the stuff after the first bucket. 'Specially when I noticed he was letting Julian drool all over it." Julian was Gary's St. Bernard, which he treated like a big hairy baby.

Or at any rate, he always had done. Maybe that was about to change with the arrival of the real thing? "Hey, has Darren mentioned anything to you about him and Gary having kids?"

"No." Phil gave me a sharp look, and the half smile he'd been sporting morphed into a frown. "Has Gary been talking about it?"

"Sort of. Maybe? He sent me this weird text a couple of days ago, which sounded like they might be? Something about the patter of tiny footsteps, and how he was all excited about it."

"Knowing Gary, he could have been talking about the postman bringing his latest mail-order sex toy. Have you asked him about it?"

"Never get a bloody signal, do I?" I pulled out my phone on the off chance—we were on the top of a flippin' mountain; I could probably semaphore him from here. Then I groaned. "Sod it. Must've forgotten to charge it last night. Well, that's that. Unless you want to ask Darren?"

"What, and cause a domestic if your mate's been talking out of turn?"

Huh. I'd thought Gary was *our* mate by now. "Not talking. Hinting. Being enig-wotsit at best. But yeah, I guess you're right. We'll find out soon enough."

We were silent for a few minutes, ambling along the path. Ahead of us, visible past a handful of other meandering tourists, Martin was making animated gestures as he talked to Siri. Or more likely *at* Siri.

"Gonna be weird, though, innit?" I said as we skirted the ice cream kiosk set handily halfway around the crater. I wouldn't have minded one, but Phil didn't seem to be in the mood to wait in line and I wasn't *that* bothered.

"What?"

"Gary and Darren being parents. Like Cherry and Greg"—my sister had announced they were expecting at our wedding—"and Dave and his sprog. We'll be the only ones left not juggling nappies soon."

"It bothers you." Phil stopped to look me in the eye, his expression unreadable. "Is it because you actually want a kid, or it just that you're feeling left out?"

I took a deep breath. It was a valid question in the circs. "I dunno . . ." We walked on a few paces. "I mean, we've always said we'd have 'em one day. And it's the natural order of things, innit? First comes love, then comes marriage, then comes . . . well, you know the rest."

"Sod the natural order of things." Phil's tone was unexpectedly harsh.

I blinked. "I thought you wanted kids?"

"I do. But not because everyone else is having one or because that's what we're supposed to do." He strode away from me down the path, those long legs eating up the ground and spitting it out again.

I stopped dead and stared after him, until my own legs unlocked themselves and I could follow.

Chapter Twenty-Five

I felt like a kid myself, scurrying after him. "Oi, that's not what I meant!"

"Isn't it? Every time I've mentioned kids, you've been all 'Yeah, course, some day.' Now you think Gary's getting one, it's suddenly a priority."

What was he getting in such a paddy for? "Oh, for fuck's sake! It's a kid, not the latest bloody iPhone!"

Phil whirled—then seemed to check himself. "Yes. That's the point."

I blinked at him. "So if we're on the same page about it, why are we arguing?"

He sighed, those massive shoulders slumping as he shoved his hands into his pockets. "I don't want to have a kid with someone who doesn't want one."

"And why the hell would you think that about me? I've *always* said I wanted kids eventually."

Phil let out another long breath. "Things change. People change once you make a commitment. They start taking you for granted. Or maybe they just stop hiding how they really feel. I've been here before, okay?"

For a moment I couldn't work out what he meant. Then I saw red. "What, because your last husband let you down, you think *I'm* going to? Why did you even marry me if you reckoned that was going to happen? If you think I'm *hiding* stuff?"

"This is nothing to do with—"

He broke off as an elderly couple dodged round us, looking embarrassed, and I realised we were (a) causing a scene and

(b) blocking the path. I shuffled over to the railing, and after a mo, Phil joined me.

"I'm not bloody *Mark*," I muttered.

"I know." Phil's voice was toneless.

"I know you know. What I *don't* know is whether you wish I was, sometimes. Oh, not the actual Mark, 'cos from what I've heard he was a total shit. The one you *thought* you were marrying." It came out of my mouth before I had a chance to think it through. Did I genuinely feel like that? I hadn't known I had. But it had to have come from somewhere.

Phil drew in a sharp breath—and then Mrs. Snipe's mocking tones drowned out whatever he'd been going to say. "Oh dear, I hope there isn't trouble in paradise."

"We're fine, ta," I said breezily at the same moment Phil grunted a terse "No."

I couldn't see her eyes behind those overlarge sunglasses, but her mouth twisted sardonically. "If either of you needs consoling, you know where to find me."

Then she swept off to rejoin her husband, who was tapping his foot a few yards off.

I gave Phil's granite features a sidelong look and decided I'd had enough. Life was too short, and the day was too flippin' hot. He could talk himself out of the bad mood Martin had evidently put him in. "Going to catch up with Siri. Make sure she's okay."

Then I set off at a jog.

I felt like a right berk when, just as Siri and Martin turned their heads at the pitter-patter of my not-so-tiny footsteps, I trod on a loose stone and turned my ankle, jarring my bad hip with a jolt of fire. The resulting epic stumble had their eyes (and presumably Phil's too, with my luck) going wide in concern. At least I managed not to face-plant on the gravel.

"Tom, you shouldn't be running!" Siri said loudly enough to make sure any English speakers on the volcano knew I was too infirm to be allowed out on my own.

"Perhaps this has all been too much for you," Martin said solicitously, as he disengaged from Siri and offered me his arm instead.

"I'm fine," I said through gritted teeth.

I had half an ear out for Phil running over, probably to offer to assist the rest of them with swaddling me in bloody bubble wrap, but no heavy footfalls came.

Which was good, all right? Meant he hadn't seen me almost fall.

Probably.

I mean, even though we'd had a bit of a barney, he'd have come straight over if he'd seen me stumble. Wouldn't he?

In my moment of marital doubt, I actually found myself taking Martin's arm. It was harder and more muscular than you'd think. He'd only have to go on a low-fat diet for about a week to get as ripped as Phil was; it was all there under the self-indulgent softness.

"There, that's better," he breathed in my ear, and I remembered Siri had said he was gay.

Which was neither here nor there, obviously. Me being married and all. And it wasn't like I found him attractive. I just, you know. Could see why someone *might*.

"Let's get him to a bench," Siri said.

I found my tongue. "No, it's good. Better if I walk it off."

"As you wish," Martin purred. "We'll wander around the top, here, for a while. No hurry to go back down."

"Cheers." The pain was definitely easing, but I'd be lying if I said I wasn't glad of his support, unasked-for though it was. Should have known I was going to end up paying for it.

"It must be hard, having such a physical reminder of a traumatic time in your youth," Martin oozed as he navigated us around a couple taking pictures of the crater. "I'm not at all sure that husband of yours is taking good enough care of you. Someone who'd bring you on a working honeymoon—"

"Oi, he wasn't working until—well, you know." Bit insensitive of him to bring it up in front of Siri.

"No? Oh—I understood there was something of a business nature going on with the sadly departed Mr. Hills." With his unoccupied hand, he patted Siri's shoulder, getting a brave smile in return.

"No. There wasn't." This time, the shortness of my tone was down to annoyance, not pain. I freed my arm. "Think I'm okay now. Cheers for the help."

"You sure you're going to be all right?" Siri's voice followed me as I walked back the way I'd come, and I gave her a wave without turning my head. I was doing a quick scan for Phil, not sure if it was so I could avoid him or so I could go and try to make things up with him. I spotted him across the other side of the crater. He was eating an ice cream.

Bastard.

That was *that* decision made. I ambled (okay; hobbled) back along the path slowly, giving him plenty of time to bugger off. Which he did. *Fine.* I busied myself taking panoramic photos of the views with my thankfully still-charged camera. They wouldn't come out because of the haze and several people managed to walk in and out of my shots, ending up as weirdly elongated human centipedes, but right now I could do with all the laughs I could get.

Eventually, Siri and Martin caught up with me and suggested it was time to go back down to the coach. I had a strong suspicion they reckoned I couldn't make it on my own, but thankfully Martin didn't try to grab me this time.

The views on the way down were spectacular, which was all to the good, seeing as the company wasn't all that congenial. Presumably they'd been spectacular on the way up too, but I'd been focussing on Siri then, and at the end, the crater itself.

And my grumpy husband, of course.

The sides of the volcano were lush with flowering bushes in bright yellow and dark green, with here and there a flash of pink or white from smaller plants tucked away. Looking down from above, the effect was of a carpet of colour. It was probably sending up a waft of floral perfume, but unfortunately that was drowned out where I was by the mingled aromas of dust, sweat, and suntan lotion.

Further down there was a stretch of unbroken green that ended where human habitation began in a blur of hotels, houses, and the like clustered around the shores of the Bay of Naples. The shoreline itself curved in a big, arching bow to where the city of Naples must lie, and further on from that were faint mountain shapes almost lost in the mist that could have been either islands or headlands—my command of the geography wasn't strong enough to tell.

That was the good news. The bad news was that my hip was still miffed with me for not watching where I planted my size nines, and had decided to be a git about it. Usually it's okay in warm weather, but since my almost-pratfall, the joint jarred painfully every time I took a step on that side. What with the downhill gradient and that treacherous stony path, the way down was harder than the hot, sweaty uphill climb had been.

I let Siri and Martin drift ahead, not fancying any more of Martin's insinuations under the guise of concern.

"You all right?" Phil rumbled in my ear, having snuck up on me somehow. I'd been sure he was ahead of us.

"I'm fine." Unfortunately coinciding with a painful jolt from my hip, it came out a bit sharper than I meant it to.

Sod it. He could deal.

"Your hip's troubling you."

Cheers for pointing that out. I'd never have noticed. "I'm *fine*." I darted a sidelong glance over at him in time to catch the tensing of his jaw, which gave me a nasty little stab of satisfaction.

"You should go on ahead," I told him. "Don't want to hold you up."

He narrowed his eyes. "*Fine*," he muttered, and strode off.

Bastard.

I sat next to him on the coach, when I finally limped aboard, because finding a different seat would have been childish. I did, however, contrive to spend the journey with my nose stuck firmly in the guidebook.

Apparently this was just fine (God, I was starting to hate that word) with Phil. He stared out of the window for the duration and didn't say a dicky bird.

Chapter Twenty-Six

My hip, which had been treated to a nice rest on the coach trip back, showed an utter lack of gratitude by stiffening up like a bastard. Climbing down the steep coach steps after Phil's broad form, I felt about a hundred years old. It didn't help that I was way overdue for my lunch, or that some spritely old bird who could have been Jane's sister from another mister was tutting away behind me, "Come on, young man, look lively."

"In a rush, are we?" I said with my best attempt at a cheery smile.

"Need a hand, do we?" she countered, with a steely glint in her eye. "Dear me, I'm sure young men were *much* fitter when I was a girl."

"Must have been all the exercise they got back before cars had been invented," I shot back.

Okay, I didn't actually *say* it. My mum didn't bring me up to be rude to little old ladies, not even ones who were asking for it. But I thought it really loudly in her direction.

All in all, I was in no mood for what happened when I limped as unobtrusively as I could into the hotel's downstairs lobby, having stood aside to let the lady go round me before she could come out with any further comments. I'd barely set foot indoors when some local lad who seemed familiar hopped up from one of the seats around the water feature.

"Signor Paretski? I would like to have a word with you."

Phil stepped out of the dark shadow where he'd been lurking in wait for me. The local lad sent him a glare suggesting he could kindly piss off for the duration.

In my current temper, I was tempted to agree—but only tempted; I'm not that daft. "No, thanks," I said shortly, and carried on walking towards the lift. All I wanted was to cool off with a shower, and maybe self-medicate with a Spritz.

"*Signore*, if you will give me a moment of your time—" He put a hand on my shoulder to halt me, and my blood tipped the final couple of degrees to boiling point.

I whirled, about to give him a piece of my mind—but Phil got there first. "Get your hands off him," he growled, his fists clenched.

I wasn't sure who I wanted to wallop first. "I don't need you fighting my battles," I ground out at Phil.

"Jesus, will you listen to yourself?" Phil grabbed the local lad, who'd been glancing uneasily from one to the other of us, and physically propelled him out of the hotel before coming back in, doing a cartoon-style hand-dust.

"Finished being all macho, now, have we?" I asked sardonically. "Or were you planning to carry me up to the room slung over your shoulder?"

A nervous giggle from Siri alerted me to the fact that we weren't, after all, alone in the lobby. "Um, Tom, Phil? We're going to get some lunch in the restaurant. I was going to ask if you wanted to join us?"

"No, ta, love. You go ahead," I told her before Phil could open his gob and accept on our behalf. I didn't much fancy making small talk with bloody Martin at this precise moment. Or large talk, even.

Course, now I came to think about it, Phil didn't look much in the mood for company either. We let Siri and Martin take the lift without us, although we could all have squeezed in, and shuffled our feet waiting for it to come back down again while avoiding each other's gaze.

Well, this was all a bit crap, wasn't it? Even in my most pessimistic moments, I hadn't thought the honeymoon period would be over before we'd got through the first sodding week.

I wanted to call Gary and get a second opinion on whether I was worrying about nothing, but my flippin' mobile was still out for the count. Not that there was much chance of getting a signal on it anyway. And yeah, there was the phone in the hotel room—but it wouldn't be that easy to get to it without Phil being in the room with me, would it? Plus, an international call from the hotel phone would most likely cost me an arm, a leg, and my first-born kidney, especially the way

Gary could go on. Probably ought to save it for official investigation stuff.

I was making a proverbial out of a whatsit. It wasn't worth the aggro just to have Gary cooing *there, there* noises down the phone at me.

Not to mention . . . Gary had never been exactly enthusiastic about me and Phil, right from the start, had he? It would've felt disloyal, ringing him up to say that yes, actually, Mrs. S. had been right and there *was* trouble in paradise.

Oh, bloody hell, I thought as we opened the door to our room. It was a last resort, but there was nothing else for it.

I was going to have to talk it out with Phil.

I didn't rush him on it. I gave him time to kick off his shoes and flop down on the bed, and I took a mo to plug my mobile in to charge before I hit him with, "What the hell have you been in such a mood about all morning?"

His expression turned even more mulish than it had been already. "Nothing."

I hesitated, then lay down on the bed next to him, propped up on one elbow. "Come on. It's me you're talking to. Or, you know, not."

Phil sighed and scrubbed both hands over his face. "Why *are* you with me?"

My elbow almost gave way. This again? "What do you mean?"

"You hated Wayne."

Yeah, but . . . "What's that got to do with the price of *pesce*?"

"*Why* did you hate him?" He sounded like my old chemistry teacher quizzing me on the finer points of Bunsen-burner safety, specifically the reason it's *not* a good idea to turn the flame on your school jumper to see if you can get the navy blue to turn a cool bright orange, particularly while wearing said jumper.

"'Cos he was a git," I said cautiously, not wanting to trap myself into any (more) embarrassing admissions of my own idiocy.

"Yeah. He was a git. To you, back in school." Phil stared at the ceiling. "Thing is, so was I, wasn't I?"

"Well, yeah. But that's water under the bridge." Was *that* all he was worried about? "Forgiven and forgotten, all right?"

"Forgiven, maybe. Never going to forget it though, are you?" His gaze strayed, unmistakeably, to my bad hip, which was, by the way, still aching from its downhill trek, ta for asking.

"Look, we've had this out before. You never meant for anything bad to happen. Not *that* bad, anyway."

With a restless motion, Phil pushed himself up to sitting and perched on the side of the bed. "Neither did Wayne. But you never forgave him."

Did he have to rub my guilt in my face? "I was *trying*, okay?"

"Maybe you shouldn't forgive either of us."

I stared at him. "Maybe you should stop talking bollocks. What the hell's brought all this up again now?"

Phil turned away and muttered something I didn't catch, but which definitely had the word *Martin* in it.

"I bloody knew it." Okay, so I hadn't, but it was all starting to make sense now, so it felt like I *should* have known it. "It was on the way up that volcano, wasn't it? Him picking away at you. Telling you all kinds of crap." Bloody hell, I wished I'd been a fly on the nonexistent wall for that conversation. Some species of stinging fly, preferably of the sort Martin was violently allergic to.

"It was nothing that's not true. You, me . . . how can it be healthy with that for a start?" Standing up, Phil folded his arms and locked his gaze on mine. "And he had another valid point. If I'd looked like Wayne, would we be together now?"

I blinked. "I can't believe you're asking me that."

It was a lie. I could believe it all right. Because not only was it a question I'd avoided asking myself ever since we'd got here and met Wayne again, it was a question I didn't have an answer for.

Don't get me wrong. I was in love with Phil—every single bit of him, inside and out. Even when he was being a pigheaded git, like now. All right, the physical aspects were a bloody good bonus, but they weren't what I was in love with. If he came over all Deadpool tomorrow, I liked to think it'd make zero difference to how I felt about him.

But if you'd taken Phil's personality and put it in Wayne's unappealing body back when we'd first reconnected a couple of years ago, given him the grating voice and the irritating smirk . . . would

I have bothered to give him a second chance? Nobody likes to be thought shallow, do they? Especially if they're worried it might be true.

Phil's shoulders slumped. He sat back down on the bed and took my face carefully in both hands. I barely managed not to fall off the other side in surprise. "Christ, I'm sorry," he breathed.

He was sorry? "'S okay," I mumbled.

"No, it's not. It's just . . . Sometimes I look at you, and I wonder how the hell we ended up here, together."

"Uh . . . You mean that in a good way, right?"

Phil huffed a laugh, his breath warm against my forehead. "Yeah. I mean that in a good way. I don't deserve you."

"And again, possible ambiguity there," I teased gently. I was starting to think things might be okay, and a speck of inspiration was washed into my brain on a surge of heady relief. "Listen, you know I like how you look. Always have done. But you've got to remember, back when we first met up again on that case in Brock's Hollow? Couldn't stand you. You got on nerves I hadn't even known I had."

"Is this supposed to make me feel better?" He was smiling, though.

"Yeah. 'Cos we ended up spending time together in spite of ourselves, and I got to know the real you. And *that* was when I fell for you proper." I grinned and patted his cheek. "You're pretty, but you're not *that* pretty. Get over yourself. Oh, and by the way, you got to know the real me too. Not hiding anything here. If you were expecting any surprises, you're out of luck. What you see is what you get."

That told him. There was a certain meltiness in his eyes as he gazed at me. Then he snorted. "Martin's good, I'll give him that. Had me doubting myself, doubting you . . . doubting us."

"Big stripy git. What's even in it for him? Apart from schaden-wotsit?"

"He's not an idiot. He's got to have noticed we're suspicious of him hanging around Siri. Maybe he wanted to give us something else to worry about." Phil's arms slid around my waist, pulling me close. "Which he did."

"Screw him. Or rather don't. In fact, nobody should screw him. Ever." I searched Phil's face, frowning a little when I detected a smidge of concern still lingering. "But we're okay now, right?"

"Yeah. We're okay." He paused. "Tom . . . don't take this the wrong way, but how do you really feel about having kids? Sooner, rather than later? I just want to know. So I can stop worrying about it."

I took a deep breath. "Honestly? I don't know. Do I want 'em? Yeah. Am I ready for it now? I dunno. Sometimes it feels like maybe we should get on with it, 'cos it's going to take a bit longer what with neither of us having a handy uterus. But I don't know. What do you feel about it? Sooner or later?"

"Sooner," he admitted, and it *sounded* like an admission, like he thought I wouldn't be happy with his answer. "But it doesn't have to be right now. Seeing you with that little girl at Herculaneum . . . It hit me: that's what I want for us. A family. But it's not something to rush into. I want to do it when we're both ready for it."

I was smiling when I spoke again. "Okay, then. No harm in looking into things when we get back home. Find out about the hurdles we have to jump." In the best-case scenario, it was likely to take a couple of years before we managed to find a surrogate and get sprogged up. Longer, probably, if we took the adoption route. It wouldn't be sensible to wait too long—but we had time to get used to the idea.

Phil pulled me tight against him and kissed me like he was drowning and I was air.

Chapter Twenty-Seven

It was a blissful moment of reconnection, so of course my stomach decided to ruin the mood by rumbling loudly. I told it to shut up and got on with the task at hand, but then it rumbled again, this time even louder.

Phil stopped kissing me and laughed. "You and your stomach. I suppose we'd better go and get some lunch."

"Uh-uh," I murmured into his neck. "Not sharing you yet. We can get room service."

"You'll have to wait longer. Sure you're not going to starve to death?"

I grinned. "Could be a close-run thing. You'll have to think of some way to distract me from the hunger pangs while we wait."

Phil nodded solemnly. "Think I can do that. Hang on a mo." He reached over to the bedside table and grabbed the copy of the *Daily Fail* they'd given us on the flight over. "Here you go. Cryptic crossword still needs doing."

"I'll give you bloody cryptic," I said, and tackled him.

He went down easy, and I straddled him on the bed. "Here's a clue for you. Three down. *Something that needs attention.* Two words: first word *My*; second word four letters, starting in *C*."

Phil smirked. "Trying to tell me you want cake for lunch?"

"Git." Then I blinked and rolled off him. "Lunch. We should order that first."

I ignored his laughter and chucked over the room-service menu as he muttered, "Priorities," in a long-suffering tone.

The choice was limited, of course, so we both opted for pasta arrabbiata with a side salad. I gave Phil a look as I put the phone down.

"Veggie pasta? You're going to want double rations of meat at dinner to make up for this."

He raised an eyebrow. "Or you could make up for the lack right now."

"Uh-huh. Maybe I should ring them back and tell 'em not to bother with the parmesan, as it's already pretty cheesy round here?"

"You know you love it."

"I know I love you." It just slipped out. Honest. Everyone knows it's not me who's the mushy one in this relationship.

Usually.

Phil stroked my face again, his touch gentle. "Christ, where would I be without you?"

See? *He's* the mushy one. The prickling at the corner of my eyes was down to allergies or something, and I kissed him deeply because I wanted to, not because I couldn't trust my voice to answer.

All right?

We might be newlyweds but we'd been sleeping together a while now, and I'd thought I'd wanted the usual: fun times. A load of joking around. A bit of slap and tickle. Affectionate, yeah, but just the right side of rough. Instead, Phil gave me tender, and it was fucking perfect. Like in those old-timey wedding vows: *with my body I thee worship*. He took it slow, easing my clothes off and kissing his way down my body, setting the nerves aflame with sensation—and anticipation. When his lips finally closed around my cock, I *felt* worshipped and honoured and, Jesus, really fucking cherished. He'd lost his own shirt at some point, and I drank in the sight of those broad shoulders, that well-muscled chest.

Getting my hands on him was even better. Mine. All mine. For always.

What the hell had I done to deserve all this? I ran my hands through his hair. Was it softer than usual? Hard to think when he did that thing with his tongue. I moaned—and then he stopped and lifted his head. "Want to come this way?"

"You want decisions at a time like this?" I joked weakly.

He smiled. "Up to you, but I'd like to be inside you."

Oh God yes. It hit me right in the chest, a burst of longing. "Yes. That."

Again, he didn't rush, getting me ready with practised hands and then sliding into me from behind, slow and even. It was almost too much, and I was glad he couldn't see my face. He'd get worried and stop, and oh God I needed him not to stop. His front moulded to my back, a perfect fit, and he took me with steady, powerful thrusts.

When his hand wrapped around my dick, electric sensation shot up my spine, and I let out a sound we'll pretend wasn't a whimper.

"Good?" he asked and, thank God, didn't seem to expect an answer. "Never going to let you go," he added, as if I wasn't already overwhelmed.

"Never going to let you," I choked out, and then he twisted his hand and I was coming all over the sheets.

Phil milked me through it, then sped up. A few brisk thrusts and he was gasping, filling up the condom inside me.

God, I loved him.

Clearly Priapus and his Olympian mates were smiling upon us that afternoon, as room service didn't arrive until after we'd finished. I was still floating on a blissful sea, my hip hardly hurting at all, when the knock came at the door. Suddenly I remembered I was ravenous, and I pulled on my hotel bathrobe and legged it to open up.

We briefly considered eating on our tiny balcony, but as the midafternoon sun was beaming straight at us like a fifties sci-fi death ray, we sensibly decided to protect our pale English hides and picnic in the room instead.

It had the added advantage that we didn't need to get dressed.

Halfway through my pasta, I paused. "We were a bit shirty with that local Mafia type, weren't we? Hope that's not coming back to bite us in the bum."

Phil nodded. "Should have used the opportunity to ask a few questions."

"Yeah. On the other hand, he'd probably want to go somewhere quiet for a chat, wouldn't he? Not sure I'd fancy that, after what happened to Wayne. Even if I am their totally not-golden goose."

"Two of us, one of him. He couldn't have forced us to go anywhere." Phil stared into space, visions of lost opportunities for interrogation presumably dancing in his head.

I patted his thigh. "Hey, you'll get your chance. It's a fair bet they'll try again."

On second thoughts, that wasn't as reassuring as I'd made it sound.

After we'd eaten, it was too late to think about sightseeing, so we grabbed our cossies and headed up to the rooftop pool. And yeah, I know it's a bad idea to go swimming on a full stomach, but we could work on our tans while we let the food go down—not to mention, work on interrogating any fellow guests we might find there.

We were in luck—not only was Siri there, unencumbered by Martin for once, but so were Cassie and Jane.

Jane, dressed in the sort of calf-length cotton frock with puffed sleeves I'd last seen in pictures of Lady Di from the eighties, was managing the rare feat of making a sun lounger look uncomfortable. She lay there stiffly with her arms by her sides as though she was on a visit to the dentist.

Cassie, by contrast, was decked out in a crimson one-piece swimsuit with white polka-dots and could have jumped straight off a saucy seaside postcard. All that was missing was a weedy, downtrodden husband and/or a crab pinching her ample bum. She was sipping a tall drink and leafing through an airport bonkbuster, although the droplets of water scattered about her person suggested she hadn't long come out of the pool. I gave her a cheery wave.

"There you are!" she bellowed, as if we were late for a date. "Come and join us."

"In a mo." By way of excuse, I gestured to where Siri was sitting on her lonesome the other side of the pool, her bikini visible through one of those floaty smock things women wear to keep the sun off their shoulders. She was sporting her goggly sunglasses again, so half her expression was hidden, but the line of her mouth seemed a little disgruntled.

"How are you doing, love? What's got your goat?" I asked, sliding into the chair next to her.

"Tom! Oh, it's nothing. Hello, Phil, you all right?"

Phil gave her a smile and a nod, then moved off a pace, gazing at the view with a hand shielding his eyes from the sun. Either he didn't want to queer my pitch or he'd developed a sudden interest in the finer details of the bay.

I leaned in closer to Siri. "Course it's not nothing. Go on, you tell your Uncle Tom."

Her brow furrowed. "Isn't that racist?"

"Uh, I don't think so." Great, now I wasn't sure. "Maybe if you're American? Anyway, what's got your frown on?"

She lowered her voice. "It's those old ladies over there. You know, the ones who went to Capri with us—well, one of them. The funny rude one."

I stifled a laugh. "Cassie? What's she been up to?" I snuck a glance in her direction, but currently she wasn't doing anything more nefarious than, by the looks of Jane's scandalised expression, regaling her with a salacious excerpt from her book.

"I was sitting here, and she got out of the pool and sat next to me"—she gestured to the lounger on the other side of her, which I'd avoided because of a sizeable wet patch—"and started telling me I can't trust Martin."

I hesitated. Was this the time to tell her Martin had lied about where he was last night? "Well . . . he's an older bloke, and you're—"

"Yeah, but he's *gay*. And I told her that, and she said it was beside the point. She thinks he's, like, some kind of con man?" Siri's eyes were wide and bewildered.

Phil abandoned the bay to its own devices and leaned over my shoulder. "Did she say why?"

"Why what?" Martin's jovial tones, coming from behind our little huddle, made me jump.

Chapter Twenty-Eight

I wasn't the only one, either. Phil's hand tightened on my shoulder, and Siri gave a guilty little start too. She covered it with a beaming smile. "Oh, nothing. We was just talking. You were a long time," she added, clearly deciding the best defence was a good offence.

Martin shrugged, his unbuttoned shirt rising and falling around a not-untoned chest. "I ran into that English couple from this morning and we had a chat."

"Oh, you mean the Snipes?" Siri sent me a significant glance.

Crap. I'd forgotten I'd told her they were suspects. Not to mention, misled her about their names.

Martin was frowning. "No, the Harrisons. I don't think I know the Snipes. Seems an odd name. Northern, perhaps?"

I stood up. "Right, we'll leave you to it. Promised we'd go and join the ladies over there." I gestured at Cassie, who obliged with a cheery wave.

Phil joined me in circumnavigating the pool to where the ladies were. We could have dived in and swum over, but it seemed a bit posy and, anyway, we were carrying towels and sun cream. I didn't think Jane would appreciate us lobbing them over and shouting, *Catch!*

We went where the welcome would be warmer, and plonked ourselves down in a couple of chairs next to Cassie's lounger.

"Finally the scenery improves," Cassie said with a roguish grin, giving Phil a good once-over.

I'd have felt slighted, but it wasn't like she was wrong.

"How's your book?" I asked, nodding to the lurid cover.

"Oh, you know. The usual. Everyone shagging everyone else's wives and husbands. Good clean fun." She laughed.

Jane sniffed.

"Not so much fun in real life," Phil said mildly.

"Dearie, some of us have had quite enough of real life. I prefer fantasy, where nobody ever gets too badly hurt."

It was the perfect opening. "I hear you're worried about Siri getting hurt?" I said lightly.

Cassie heaved a sigh. "If she *will* hang around with a crook and a swindler . . ."

I grinned. "Which one's me and which one's Phil, in this scenario?"

"They're both Martin, dearie, as I'm sure you're aware. Wouldn't trust the man as far as I could throw him."

It occurred to me she could probably throw him pretty far, so long as it was vertically downwards with gravity on her side. I winced.

Cassie's eyes turned hawklike. "Dodgy tum? You have to watch for that on holiday. Too much unfamiliar food."

"No, I'm fine, ta. Just . . ." I grimaced. "Nothing you want to hear about."

Her eyes widened, and she grinned like a shark. "Oh! *That*. Plenty of lubrication, that's what you need."

"Cassandra!" Jane snapped.

My face had to be the colour of Cassie's cossie. "We're, um, we're fine, ta," I managed.

Phil leaned forward. "Going back to Martin, is there a reason you don't trust him?"

"Martin? Oh, yes." She blinked, visibly changing mental gears and not without a certain reluctance at that. "For one thing, he's exactly the type, isn't he? And did you know what he—"

Jane stood up. "Cassandra, it's time we got out of the sun. I told you to reapply your sunscreen when you got out of the pool, and now you're turning red. You can't keep taking chances with your health."

Cassie made a hilarious mock-guilty face at me, but to be fair to Jane, she *was* going a bit pink.

"Come along," Jane insisted. "You can talk to Tom and Phil later. And *not* about their private affairs," she added, the beetroot tones of her face probably giving mine a run for its money.

They left.

"So much for grilling our fellow guests," I muttered to Phil. "Move on to plan B?"

"Which is?"

I grinned. "Grilling ourselves. I'm not going back without a tan. Everyone would think we spent the entire honeymoon in bed."

"Worried about your reputation?"

"Worried about Gary's jokes, more like. Right, time to slap on the sun lotion." I fitted my actions to my words, then settled down in my chair, where I could keep a surreptitious eye on Siri and Martin on the other side of the pool. Just in case.

The sun was truly baking, but it was a dry heat and not too sweat-inducing if you didn't move a muscle. Knowing the pool was always an option if it got too hot helped too.

Phil lay facedown on Jane's vacated lounger, which meant I got to admire his broad, well-sculpted shoulders, back, and perfectly formed arse. Yum.

"Do you reckon there's anything in Cassie dissing Martin?" I kept my voice low. "Wish we'd heard what she was going to tell us about him. Think she might have seen him up to something he shouldn't have been?"

Phil's shoulders shifted minutely. "Not sure. Maybe it's just a personality clash. You've got to admit, Martin gives off a certain con man vibe."

I grinned. "I know *you* don't like him."

"And you do?"

There was something about Phil's tone that made me pay attention. "Not a lot, no."

"So I was imagining those admiring glances, earlier?"

Suddenly the heat wasn't a problem anymore. "Oi, you know I'd never look at another bloke! Uh, figuratively. I mean, my eyes have got to go somewhere, and all right, maybe he's not the ugliest bloke in the hotel. But I'd never—"

I broke off as I realised he was laughing, silently.

"You absolute bastard," I told him in relief. "You're lucky I don't tip you in the pool."

He turned over to grin at me. "You love me."

Git. Even as I cursed him mentally, my heart swelled.

"Yeah. Yeah, I do."

An unspecified amount of time later, I woke up to a prod in the ribs. "Oi!"

"No falling asleep in the sun," Phil rumbled in my ear. "That can have consequences."

I stretched. "Don't I know it. One time I burnt bright red, all except where Gary drew a dick on my chest in sun lotion. It took weeks for that to disappear."

I glanced over the other side of the pool. Siri and Martin had disappeared—so much for keeping an eye on them. *Oh well.* "Time for a quick swim?"

We took a few lazy turns round the pool, then sat out until we'd dried off again before heading back to our room.

Five minutes after we got there, nicely browned all over, the phone rang.

It was Dave, of course, which I found out after I'd picked up with a cheery *buongiorno.*

"Bloody hell, the boy's gone native. Gonna ditch that van of yours for a Vespa?"

"Yep, and start baking pizzas just like Mama used to make. How's it going back in the old homeland?"

"Not as good as it is over there, by the sound of it. I'd ask what's got you in such a good mood, but I'm guessing I don't want to know. Anyway, I've got some of that information you asked for. Seeing as I obviously have nothing better to do than be yours and Morrison's dogsbody."

"Slaved away for hours on a hot computer, did you?"

Dave snorted. "Gave it to a minion to ferret out. What's the bleedin' point of being a DCI if you've got to slog through data your own bloody self?"

"So what's the word on Wayne. *Is* there any word on him, or did he come up smelling of roses? Oh, and mind if I put you on speaker? It's only Phil here with me."

"As long as he understands this *didn't* come from me."

Phil grunted his assent, and Dave went on, louder and tinnier this time. "Yes, there's word all right. And definitely no smell of roses. More like the crap you put on 'em to make 'em grow. Your Mr. Hills came up as a person of interest in a fraud case a year or two back. Suspected of selling holiday homes in Spain that didn't belong to him, didn't have planning permission, and didn't bleedin' exist, either. Wily bastard, though. Corporate structure like . . ." Dave paused. "Like Penrose and Escher did LSD and designed a Russian doll together."

"Like what now?"

"Don't ask me. That's what the minion said. Something to do with mathematical artists, whatever the bleedin' bollocks those are."

"Sounds like this minion's wasted on the police force."

"Or the force is wasted on her. Anyway, upshot is, the briefs advised we wouldn't be able to prosecute. Despite Hills clearly being guilty as sin and criminally smug to boot."

I shot Phil a glance, but this revelation about his erstwhile best mate didn't seem to be devastating him unduly. If anything, he looked resigned. I turned my attention back to Dave. "Anyone obviously pissed off about it? Apart from your lot, that is?"

"No one I'd expect to hop on a plane for the purpose of murdering him on his summer hols. Although it's got a sort of poetic justice about it. Victims were ordinary people. Could have been your mum and dad, wanting somewhere in the sun to pop over to when the cold weather hit back home."

"Can't imagine my dad doing anyone in. And my mum would be more likely to complain at the poor sod until he threw himself over the railings to get away from her." I started wondering about Phil's mum, and came to the disturbing conclusion I couldn't rule murder out where she was concerned. Good thing I wasn't planning on breaking her son's heart. "Okay, cheers for that," I told Dave. "What about Martin Kingsman?"

"Ah, well, here's where it gets interesting. Your Mr. Kingsman turns out to be one of Morrison's lot."

"Uh . . . in what way?" I frowned at Phil, but he'd closed his eyes, a complicated expression on his face.

"Bloody private investigator, isn't he?"

Chapter Twenty-Nine

"Martin's a PI? Investigating what?" I stared at Phil. His eyes were open this time, but they weren't looking at me.

"How the bleedin' hell would I know? Strangely, he *didn't* drop in for a cup of tea and a chat about his plans before he left the country."

"He'd have files about the cases he was working on though, right? Phone records from talking to clients, etcetera . . ."

"Oh, I'm sorry. There I was thinking you knew I was a copper, when you're clearly under the misapprehension I'm a hack working for the *News of the* bloody *World*. We—that is, officers of the law—can't swan around tapping the phones of private individuals at the drop of a bleedin' hat. There's laws about it. See *Law: Officer* thereof."

"All right, all right. I forgot. Not that you're a copper, obviously. Just that you need warrants or whatever. It's hot here. Fries the brain cells." This was a barefaced lie, seeing as I was speaking to him from the hotel room with the air-con on full blast. What with my mostly unclad state, it was actually a little on the nippy side. I gave brief consideration to asking Dave to see if he could make an exception in Martin's case, but Phil would probably see that as setting a dangerous precedent regarding the rights of private investigators to, well, privacy. "So we've got no way of finding out what he's here for?"

"You could always—and I realise this may come over as something of a novel idea—try *asking* him. Seeing as you're there with him and all."

"What if he lies? Says he's just here on holiday?"

"Maybe he *is* there for the sun, sea, and sangria, you ever thought of that?"

"That's Spain, sangria. Over here it's Spritzes."

"Sounds bloody German to me, but what do I know?"

"And there's a question. But it'd have to be a bit of a coincidence, wouldn't it? Him—a private investigator—coming over here to get a tan and the alcoholic beverage of his choosing, and Wayne popping his clogs in the middle of it all."

Dave swore under his breath. "That heat really has fried your brain, hasn't it? Less than a week married, and already you've forgotten what your new husband does for a living."

Oops. Yeah, I supposed if it was true for Martin, it'd have to be true for Phil. And while it wasn't a coincidence Wayne was here at the same time as us, I was pretty certain it hadn't been my beloved who'd sent him on his way to the afterlife. "Okay, point taken. Is there anything else you *can* tell us? Has he ever been suspected of any dodgy practices?"

"If he has, it's never made it onto our systems. Closest thing he's got to a criminal record is when his wife got done for doing fifty in a thirty-mile-an-hour zone."

My eyebrows hit the ceiling "Hang about—he's got a wife?"

"It's not that bleedin' unusual."

"It is if you're gay. Uh, and a bloke, obviously. These days, anyhow. Are they definitely still together?"

"She's listed at the same address. Him, her, and the four kiddies."

"Four kids?" My voice might have jumped an octave or two. If the marriage had been an attempt to prove himself straight, old Martin had certainly been putting the effort in.

"Ages eight to fourteen. Sounds like you need to get your gaydar seen to."

"Not my gaydar." Not this time, anyway. "He's been telling Wayne's girlfriend he's gay."

"Yeah? I hear some women go for that. You ever tried it?"

"What, pulling a woman by pretending to be gay? Think very carefully about what you've just suggested, Dave."

"I'll take it that's a no, then. Right, anything else I can do for you? Seeing as how I live to serve."

"No, that's— Oh, wait a mo." Phil was making hand signals. I sent him an *it's all yours* gesture, and he stepped up to the mic, figuratively speaking.

"Could you check out a couple of our fellow guests? They're sisters. Probably in their sixties or seventies. Jane Higginbottom and Cassandra Austin—Austin's their maiden name. Spelled with an *i*. Both widowed. Jane was married to Ralph Higginbottom. We don't know Cassandra's husband's name."

"Going after little old ladies now, are we? What is this, *Arsenic and Old* bloody *Lace*?"

"Just a hunch."

Phil clammed up after that, so I added a, "Cheers, mate. We owe you."

"Too bloody right you do. Now, some of us have jobs to be getting on with, so how about you and that husband of yours get back to your own dubious practices? You're supposed to be on your honeymoon, you know."

"Nah, don't worry, we did all that earlier."

"And that's another one for the list of things I did *not* need to know."

I laughed. "Thanks again for the info. We'll buy you a pint or six when we get back. Don't be too hard on the minions, yeah?"

He snorted again, muttered something about *mathematical bloody artists*, and hung up.

"Well, that was *very* interesting," I said. "Nice to know we weren't being paranoid about old Martin. I get why he might want to lie about the wife and kiddies—all the better to take advantage of attractive young ladies—but why do you reckon he's lying about his job? That's got to mean he's up to no good, right?"

"Maybe. Or maybe he wanted a holiday without everyone walking on eggshells in case he was investigating them."

I frowned. "That ever happen to you?"

He nodded. "That, or you get people who want to know all the ins and outs, how it's done, if it's like it is on the telly. Sometimes it's easier to say I work in security. Don't you get people wanting to talk about their plumbing when they hear what you do?"

I shrugged. "Yeah, but I might end up getting work out of it, so it's swings and roundabouts. I s'pose at least I don't get people worrying I've been nosing around their pipes." There was an innuendo begging to be made there, and I was socked in the gut by a pang of homesickness for my mates in general and Gary in particular.

Phil slung an arm around me and pulled me close, which was a pretty effective remedy. Especially with us both still being mostly naked. "No nosing around anyone else's pipes, got that?"

"Long as you keep your investigations to the strictly professional."

My tone was fond, but Phil still sighed and moved away a fraction. "Professional. As if. I'm off my game, here."

"Oi, your game's fine. You're not even supposed to be on it, right now, remember?"

"I should've twigged that Martin's a PI. The way he got me talking about you . . . I should have known."

"You're not used to being on the other side of it, that's all. Did you reckon he was gay?"

"Was keeping an open mind. Dave wasn't wrong. You get men playing the part, so women won't think they're a threat. Then when they make a move, the girl thinks she's special."

I sat up straight in alarm. "Shit—we've got to tell her."

"She won't thank us. Or believe us, necessarily."

"Yeah, but what if he . . . you know, makes that move?"

"Didn't say we shouldn't do it. Just be prepared for the fallout."

I nodded slowly. "Could this have been what Cassie was on about? Maybe she caught Martin in a lie—saw a pic of his kids in his wallet, maybe, or he spoke without thinking?"

Phil huffed unhappily. "If that's the case, I'm beginning to think I'm in the wrong job. *I* should have seen the signs—certainly sooner than an untrained old lady."

"Oi, you've been distracted, all right?"

He frowned. "You mean by Wayne's death? I still should have—"

"No, by *me*. Your gorgeously distracting and newly wedded husband—ringing any bells? And yeah, Wayne dying, obviously," I added, realising I was possibly making too light of his ex-best mate's decease. Then I frowned. "Or . . . maybe Cassie found out something that suggested Martin killed Wayne? I mean, if you were coming on a murder holiday, you'd want to tell a few porkies, wouldn't you?"

"We definitely need to talk to her."

"Yeah. Sooner the better. Siri, first, though. She needs to know Martin's been lying—and she could be in trouble if she tells him what Cassie said."

Phil shook his head. "Doubt she will. She didn't want to tell him what we were talking about when he came up here, did she? I'm guessing she either doesn't want to hurt his feelings, or she doesn't want to get Cassie in trouble."

"Probably both," I admitted. "There's a girl with her heart in the right place. Shame you can't say the same for the men she goes around with."

After changing into something more respectable, i.e. actual clothes rather than swimming cossies, we headed down the corridor to knock on Siri's door.

I got a nasty dose of déjà vu when Martin opened it, his face unwelcoming. "Keep it down. Siri's having a nap."

"And what are you up to?" I demanded in the fiercest whisper I could manage.

"I fail to see what that has to do with you," was the rejoinder.

Phil stuck a metaphorical foot in the door. "We'd like a word with you."

We would? I guess if life gives you lemons, make limoncello.

Martin's eyes narrowed. "The feeling isn't mutual."

"Unless you'd like us to wake Siri up to tell her what we know about you?" Phil carried on with a deceptively mild tone.

Martin went completely still for a mo. Then he shook himself minutely. "Not here. Give me a moment and we'll go to the bar." He stepped back and shut the door in our faces.

I spent the next few minutes thinking we'd been suckered and that Phil should have added an *actual* foot in the door, but then the door opened again and Martin slunk through it. "Come on, then. I haven't got all day."

I rolled my eyes at Phil, and we followed him to the lift.

As soon as we were sitting at a secluded table in the bar nursing a couple of Spritzes (me and Phil) and a Scotch on the rocks (Martin), Phil went straight on the attack. "How's the investigation going? And while we're on the subject, how did you manage to sell this trip to your client—or your wife and kids, for that matter?"

Martin froze . . . then deliberately relaxed. "Ah. I suppose, as a fellow practitioner of the investigative arts, I might have expected you to eventually, well, *practise*." He gave me a sidelong glance of his own before turning back to Phil. "How did *you* manage to sell this trip to your husband? Oh—but he *isn't* your husband, is he? I might have known that backstory was too melodramatic to be real."

I bristled. "Oi, that's my life you're talking about!"

"You mean this really is your honeymoon?" Martin gave Phil a considering once-over. "I suppose you're hardly the first man to have fallen for his assistant."

"Tom's not my assistant," Phil barked, while I was still busy spluttering in indignation. "And we're not here to talk about us. Who are you investigating, and why did you lie to Siri?"

Martin leaned back with an annoying smirk. "*Obviously*, I'm investigating her business dealings. In the absence of the inconveniently deceased Mr. Hills. Don't try to tell me you're not doing the same."

I did the gape of the gob-smacked mackerel. "Uh, what?"

"Siri's our client," Phil said with quiet emphasis.

"Well, yes, if you will go around revealing your profession to everyone you're looking into, it's probably inevitable one of them will end up hiring you. It must make keeping timesheets terribly complicated—do you keep it simple and bill each of them for the same hours?"

"Siri's our only client," I snapped.

"Of course she is," Martin purred.

"What were you doing last night, when you told Siri you'd be in your room?" Phil asked, and I remembered the flow of information was supposed to be going our way, not Martin's.

Hey, give me a break. I never went to police school.

"Drinking a very nice bottle of Chianti and chatting with some rather *belle signorine*. You may enjoy being gay 24-7, but I find it gets wearing after a while."

Phil's face got stonier. "What were you investigating Wayne for?"

Martin raised an eyebrow. "Oh, I'm sure you can guess. Being old friends, as you were."

The implication was clear. Not to mention insulting. "Whatever dodgy deals Wayne was up to were nothing to do with us," I said firmly.

Phil leaned forward, all the better to loom over our Mr. Kingsman. "What do you know about his dealings with a local gang here?"

There was a sharp intake of breath, quickly covered up. "Absolutely nothing, I can assure you." Martin sounded plausible enough. But then again, he made a profession of sounding plausible.

"So what were you looking into him for?" Phil said mildly.

Martin spread his hands. "I couldn't possibly say."

"Try harder," I suggested.

Martin stood. "I'm afraid not. Some of us do believe in client confidentiality, you know. *Ci si vede, belli.*" He knocked back his drink and walked out on us. No, it was worse: he bloody *sauntered* out on us.

I stared after him, gob well and truly smacked. "We've got to tell Siri the truth about that bastard," I ground out, then took a gulp of my Spritz, wishing it was stronger.

"Agreed." Phil glared at his drink. "Not now, though. He'll have gone straight back to her room. Come on, let's finish these out on the terrace."

Chapter Thirty

It was a good plan. Stepping out into the late-afternoon sunshine was a balm to my irritated soul, and I could feel the tension drain away under that cloudless blue sky. Gazing out over the Bay of Naples evened up my sense of perspective nicely. So what if Martin was an annoying git? This was our honeymoon, and it was just us two for now—me and the bloke I loved. "Have I mentioned this was a good choice of destination?" I murmured.

"What, even with . . ." Phil waved his hand in a vaguely encompassing gesture.

"Not blaming you for that, am I?"

"You could, you know. If I hadn't let Wayne know where we were going . . ."

"Right, 'cos clearly you should have foreseen he'd invite himself along with us. Anyway, I'm not gonna complain about meeting Siri. She's like the little sister I never had."

Phil huffed. "Believe me, they're not all they're cracked up to be."

"You asking me to comment on your family? Because right now? Not going there. I want a relaxing evening for the two of us. Nobody else, not in body or in spirit."

Phil smiled. "I'll drink to that." He did and all, knocking back the last of his Spritz. "Fancy getting another drink, then heading into town? We can have a wander, then get dinner in a local restaurant. It'll make a change."

And more importantly, get us away from the circus our honeymoon had turned into. "See? I always knew you were good at this making-plans lark. Same again, then."

Proof that my beloved was back on form: he glanced up, caught the eye of the waiter, and ordered our drinks in two shakes of a thingy's whatsit.

We took our time over the second Spritzes. After our late lunch, neither of us was ravenous, and it was a treat to watch the sun sink lower over the bay as the early diners bustled around us. It actually felt like a proper holiday.

Soon enough, though, Phil put down his empty glass and stood up. "Ready to go?"

I finished my drink, stood, and held out my arm. "And then some."

It was worth making the effort to go out for the pleasure of the walk down there alone. A cooling breeze wafted up to us from the water, bringing the scents of the sea. Despite the number of people out and about in cars, on motorbikes, and on foot, it seemed curiously peaceful, as if the town was breathing a sigh of relief after the heat and bustle of the day. Settling down for an evening of good food, good wine, and good company. It was the sort of atmosphere that made Brits do something daft like selling up and emigrating to sunnier climes, forgetting how much they'd miss the tea, the telly and, yeah, the terrible weather back home.

I mean, come on. Sunshine every day? It's not natural. What do Italians even find to complain about?

We didn't do the arm-in-arm thing on the way down, obviously. For a start, we'd have got in people's way something chronic. And for another . . . Well. You know. Better safe than sorry.

Proof Phil hadn't entirely managed to forget about the case for the duration came when he turned and stared back at a church we'd passed, and paused a mo, frowning.

"What's up?" I asked, as you do.

"Not sure. Had a feeling . . . It's probably nothing."

"PI's instinct?"

"Something like that."

"Think that mafia bloke's after us again?"

"Maybe. Thought I might have seen someone duck into that portico." We took a couple of steps in that direction—then some totally random and definitely unfamiliar bloke emerged, shoving his phone into his trouser pocket. He gave us an uncurious glance and strolled on by.

Phil grunted. "Just me being jumpy. Come on, let's get you fed."

Of course, this being Sorrento, we were spoilt for choice when it came to restaurants. We had a gander at the menu posted up outside a lively-looking place we came across in the old town. I liked the sound of their seafood, but Phil judged the place too touristy. We'd barely started the debate on it when a sharp-dressed woman in her twenties barged in with a strongly accented, "Excuse me? You want good food? You go there. Not touristy." She pointed over the other side of the alleyway, where a set of stone steps led up to a restaurant we hadn't even noticed was there. Then she strode off back to her equally well-clad companion, her heels unerring on the cobbles.

Me and Phil looked at each other, shrugged, and headed up the stairs.

There weren't many tables free in Casa Incognito (I managed to forget its proper name, which I'm blaming firmly on events that happened later), most of them being occupied by families speaking Italian, so I reckoned we'd come to the right place for some good, authentic local cuisine.

I wasn't wrong. I had a moment's panic when I realised the menu was all in Italian, but a combination of Phil's app and the waitress's English got us there in the end. Not for the first time, I wondered if I should have another go at learning a foreign language. They couldn't *all* be as hard as the French my despairing teachers tried to drum into me at school, could they? And at least Italian had plenty of vowels, which was more than you could say for Polish.

We both had starters of succulent local prawns served with creamy mozzarella burrata, which I followed with a main of chicken, potatoes, and artichokes, redolent with oregano and apple cider vinegar. Phil went for a cod dish with chickpeas and broccoli, which I can confirm tasted a lot better than it sounded. Hey, if you're not going to do the cutesy sharing-meals thing on honeymoon, when are you?

Pleasantly full after all that, and floating on a crisp, aromatic sea of Campanian white (Greco di Tufo, if you're interested) we regretfully declined the panna cotta and paid the bill.

Ambling back down the stone steps to street level, I was disappointed there was no one checking out the menu at Ristorante Turistico so we could pay it forward. Then again, even tourist hangouts have bills to pay. As we left both establishments behind, the dimly lit, cobbled street gave the area a timeless quality despite the muted roar of traffic that penetrated from the main road.

It put me in a retrospective mood. "We could be a couple of old Romans, strolling home from the . . . what did they call 'em? Thermopylae?"

Phil huffed a laugh. "Thermopolium?"

"That's the one. Or was that a fast-food place? They must've had 'em, though. Restaurants. Everyone likes a meal out."

"And the odd bottle of wine or two," Phil rumbled, sounding amused.

"Oi, I wasn't the only one drinking it," I pointed out. Then something caught my eye in the near-darkness, and I frowned. "Bloody hell, I thought I saw Martin. How many bottles did we drink?"

"Where did you see him?"

"Going round the corner over there. Not sure it was him, though. Could have been anyone in a stripy shirt, to be honest. Still. What do you think he's up to? Chianti and *señoritas* again? Wait, no, it's *signorinas* here, innit?"

Phil was staring over at the corner I'd gestured to. "He'd better not be following us," he muttered grimly.

"Huh. You don't reckon it's us he's privately investigating, do you, and all that about Siri was bollocks?" I thought about it. "But why? We're on honeymoon, not here on business."

Phil shook his head slowly. "It doesn't—"

He broke off as a shrill cry sounded in the alley to our left—a woman's voice, high-pitched and desperate. I whirled round. In a pool of yellow light shed by a lantern on a wall bracket, some bastard in a glinting gold necklace had his hand at a young girl's throat.

At times like that, you don't think. You just act. I bolted down that alley towards them, Phil at my side shouting "Stop right now" in that loud, authoritative voice they teach them at police school.

We'd almost reached them when three other guys stepped out of the shadows. Two of them grabbed me by an arm each, wrenching my shoulders, and I gasped as an honest-to-God gun was jabbed into my gut, narrowly missing my ribs and half-winding me, causing more shock than pain.

The guy with the woman let her go and stepped aside while the fourth bastard bashed Phil on the side of the head with something. Hard.

Chapter Thirty-One

Phil didn't fall, but he staggered. The sight of him stumbling, eyes unfocussed, almost made me think, *Sod them all*, and rush the bastard who'd hit him.

Almost.

I'd have done it if it hadn't been that the bastard and the bloke with the bling now each had a gun trained on my husband from a couple of feet away—no prizes for guessing what they'd belted him with. That, and knowing it wasn't Phil they wanted. It was me.

This wasn't some random robbery-with-excessive-violence. I recognised them now—these were Wayne's local mafia mates. One of them was almost certainly the guy who'd been shadowing us on Capri.

And Phil, my husband of less than a week, was expendable in their eyes. My strong, passionate Phil, who read poetry on the Underground, had an app for Italian on his phone, and was a not-so-secret romantic. He could die here at the drop of a hat, because these fucking gits didn't need him.

"Don't hurt him," I blurted out, much too late.

"Then you do what we say," the Blingmeister growled, and kicked Phil's knee out from behind, forcing him to fall heavily to the ground. Phil's arms didn't seem to be totally under his control, and he only just managed to save himself from hitting the cobblestones face-first.

"Phil!" I rasped, my throat dry. I was going to fucking *kill* these bastards.

The gun in my side jabbed harder. Apparently the thug wielding it hadn't heard of elementary gun safety—or if he had, he didn't hold with it. "Quiet. You want him to live, you come with us."

It'd been a hell of a lot more reassuring when the bloke in *The Terminator* said it.

"Signor Hills is dead now." His face half-shadowed in the dimly lit alleyway, Mr. Bling had a glint in his eye I couldn't interpret. "We deal direct. Man to man. Perhaps that is better, no?"

I felt like I'd swallowed a bucketload of those iced lemon drinks we'd got down by the harbour. Or downed a whole pot of café freddo. So Wayne had died to cut out the middle man?

These guys weren't messing around.

"O-okay." I took a steadying breath. "But if anyone touches Phil again, all deals are off. I mean it. If he gets hurt again, you can all sod off."

"Then it is simple. We don't want to hurt your—" He smirked, as if the idea was amusing. "—husband. You do what we say, everyone is happy."

Yeah, I was sure me and Phil would be jumping for sodding joy. I didn't say so, though. I just nodded.

At some point during all this, a dark transit van had drawn up at the end of the alleyway, closing it off from anyone who might be tempted into taking an unwise short cut. Me and Phil were ushered towards it. As we neared the main street, the gun jabbing into my ribs removed any temptation to shout for help. Particularly as I was one hundred percent certain they'd shoot Phil first. After all, I was their golden goose, wasn't I?

Christ. Was I ever going to hear Phil correcting my metaphors again?

A still-stumbling Phil was bundled into the back of the van, two of the heavies with him, and my stomach felt hollow as we were separated. They made me sit up front, squished in between the driver and Mr. Bling. And Mr. Bling's gun. "They'd better not hurt him," I said again.

I might as well have saved my breath. Mr. Bling ignored me and rattled something off in Italian to the driver, who nodded and pulled away.

"What—" It came out a bit hoarse. I cleared my throat. "What, exactly, are you expecting me to do?"

"What you agreed with Signor Hills."

Funny, because I didn't remember agreeing sweet bloody F.A. with the late, unlamented Wayne. I opened my gob to tell Mr. Bling so, then closed it, on the basis that arguing with my kidnappers wouldn't do me any good and might do Phil actual harm.

Mr. Bling was speaking again by then anyhow. "You find the . . ." He waved his non-gun-toting hand with a hint of frustration, presumably at not finding the word he wanted. Maybe he didn't have an app on his phone. "You do good, maybe I pay you." He laughed, as if it was a joke.

I didn't bother asking what would happen if I did bad.

The van swept out of Sorrento and onto the main road. I felt sick with my own helplessness, furious at myself—not to mention Wayne—for getting us into this mess.

Every car we passed was a kick in the gut. A lost opportunity to attract attention, somehow get help . . . Except it wouldn't work like that, would it? Even if anyone saw me waving as they zoomed past going the other way—unlikely, in the darkened interior of the van—what were the chances they'd (a) realise I wasn't just messing about and (b) remember enough details to be worth telling the *polizia*?

If I'd been on my own, maybe I would've taken the chance. But not with Phil there to carry the can.

The journey seemed to take forever, but it was still over far too soon. In the darkness, I couldn't tell where we were as the driver pulled to a halt. It didn't look like Pompeii—we'd driven through a modern town, with its streetlights and neon signs—but what had I really seen of the place, apart from the train station and the ruins? There wasn't much traffic, but it was getting late. There weren't many people walking around, either, not that I could risk trying to get help from anyone anyway.

Part of me still couldn't believe this was happening. Me and my newly wedded husband—on our bloody honeymoon, no less—about to reenact *Raiders of the Lost Ark* at gunpoint. I try not to think ill of the dead, but right now I was hoping wherever Wayne was, it was warm and toasty with a side order of pitchfork-prodding.

I couldn't decide if it was a plus point that our kidnappers seemed so comfortable waving firearms around. Yeah, less chance of us getting winged by a wild shot due to nerves—but a lot more chance of us getting killed by a carefully aimed bullet to the head. Which was looking likelier all the time, because they'd have to be idiots to leave us alive to tell tales whether or not I managed to come up with the goods.

And—spoilers—I wasn't going to be able to come up with the goods. My so-called gift doesn't work on stuff that's only been lost, and what were the chances of me picking up any hidden-things vibes that were close enough for these bastards to be able to dig through to?

I guessed we now knew what Martin was up to here. Somehow, he must be in league with these bastards—had followed us, and tipped them off to where we were. The only surprise was that he wasn't here with them to get the rewards. Maybe they'd paid him off already.

Maybe he'd read my mind and knew what I'd do to him if I saw him again.

When Mr. Bling prodded me out of the van, I managed to get my bearings. Ahead of us was a tree-lined walkway, with a big drop on one side. Not Pompeii. Herculaneum. Were they starting small, or was there better security at the big-name site?

Better, or less corruptible, perhaps. It took only a minimum of conversation with the guy at the gate before we were inside the historic site, so clearly he'd been planted there or paid off in advance.

At least Phil was looking slightly more human, thank Christ. His eyes were brighter, although he still seemed unsteady on his feet as he trooped along with the rest of us. I hoped like hell he was faking some of it. They'd tied his hands behind him, I realised after a mo. They'd better bloody well catch him if he tripped and fell.

Maybe I should be grateful they hadn't tied mine.

"What do you even want me to do?" I asked Mr. Bling as we descended the long ramps into the site.

"To find the treasures." Mr. Bling beamed, maybe because he'd found the word at last.

"Look, I don't know what Wayne told you, but it's not that simple—"

"Is simple. You find the treasures. Or your man . . ." No longer smiling, Mr. Bling spread his hands. "You don't want him to be hurt? You find the treasures."

I swallowed and tried very, very hard to believe in Phil's buried-cheese theory. "Okay, but where am I supposed to start? And how are you planning to get the stuff, anyhow? Can't see anyone with a shovel." *Great, Paretski, antagonise the gunman.*

I failed in that, anyway. He laughed. "Don't worry. We have what we need."

The ruins were spotlit, although sparingly, throwing dramatic shadows from ancient archways. Wouldn't someone from the modern town notice there were people moving around in here when there shouldn't be?

Or were private nighttime tours a regular thing, just business as usual?

I wondered how far sound would carry up into the modern streets, and how loud it would have to be to be heard. Say, for instance, a gunshot? Nausea swept over me. As we reached the Roman streets, I stumbled on the cobblestones, and Mr. Bling grabbed my arm. "*Sta' attento*! You have bad leg, yes?"

Christ. Was there anything these bastards *didn't* know about me? I hoped the fires in Wayne's particular corner of hell were extra flamy.

Then I felt bad, because he might have betrayed me to the mafia, but he'd died from it too. Course, chances were we'd end the night even on that score. My gut roiled, and I swallowed. "Are we going somewhere in particular? Because if you want me to do my thing, walking around at gunpoint—"

"You will see. Soon."

We carried on down the main street and took a left, and I realised where we were heading. I should have guessed. We were making a beeline for the blocked-off tunnel entrances I'd seen on the tour—except they weren't blocked off anymore. The wooden doors, when they came into sight, were open, and there were lights on inside.

"Do a lot of this, do you?" I asked. I'd read somewhere you were supposed to engage with your kidnappers, and everyone likes talking about themselves, don't they?

"Here? No. But Pompeii, yes. A few years ago. Frescoes. A difficult job. A man is careless, and *poof*!" Mr. Bling clicked his fingers. "You have only dust, and the client is not happy."

"You've got a client?"

He gave me a strange frown, as if I ought to know this. "Of course not. We wait to see what you will find. Then I will find a buyer.

You should look for gold, silver, even bronze. Jewellery, vases, coins, small statues. Things that are easy to take away."

Right. As if that was how it worked.

We are so fucked.

Chapter Thirty-Two

"Doesn't it bother you, what you're planning to do here?" I asked desperately as we walked on towards the tunnel. "If we go straight for the good stuff, a lot of historical evidence is going to get destroyed. This is your own heritage you're raiding."

"So? In Italy, we have plenty of heritage. The historians do not need it all. And most of the treasures that go to museums end up in back rooms and are never on display. If I sell to a private collector, they will be seen and admired." Mr. Bling laughed and clapped me on the shoulder. "And we have you to show us where to dig, so we destroy less. It is all good."

I didn't answer. For one thing, I had a feeling we were never going to agree on the subject, and for another, we'd reached the tunnel entrance.

The mouth opened up to a sort of antechamber, off which a narrower tunnel led. There was another guy inside there already, standing next to a shedload of heavy-duty kit. Picks, shovels, various lighting paraphernalia, and a box covered in warning labels that looked nastily like it might hold explosives. These bastards must have robbed their local mining-equipment wholesaler and set up shop here before they'd even set off to nab me and Phil.

They'd been that confident they'd get us. To give 'em their due, they hadn't been wrong.

The bloke who'd drawn the short straw and been left to babysit the equipment greeted his mates with grins and catcalls. At least someone was happy here.

Mr. Bling waved a hand at it all. "You see? We have everything. You think you could do this alone? *Stupido*."

"Rather not do it at all, thanks," I muttered.

He barked a laugh. "You expect me to believe that? After Signor Hills?"

After Wayne what? I didn't bother asking. Presumably he was tarring all us Brits with the same greedy brush.

Phil was directed to a corner well away from the entrance and from anything he might have used as a weapon or to get his hands loose—not that he seemed up for any improvising right now in any case. I took a step towards him and winced as Mr. Bling's gun jabbed into my stomach.

"Can't I even check he's okay?" I demanded.

"First, you tell us where the treasures are." Mr. Bling smirked. "Or he won't stay okay."

Shit. Crunch time. I glanced at Phil, desperately hoping he had some idea how to get us out of this. He opened his mouth—and one of those *bastards* punched him in the gut. He doubled over, wheezing.

I started forward again but was held back by my own personal goons. "You don't have to keep bloody hurting him!"

"Then you do what I say." Mr. Bling rattled off some instructions in Italian to the gits in charge of Phil, who got him to sit down on the ground, his arms behind his back against the hard stone wall of the tunnel.

"Is dangerous, your man. But there is more danger to him now."

Was Mr. Bling's English getting worse or was it just me struggling to think under the crushing fear and panic?

A couple of the heavies sauntered over to the box of tricks, grabbed a pickaxe each and started swinging them about like kids with toy swords. Gruesome visions of impromptu lobotomies danced through my head.

"I'll do it, okay," I said quickly. "But I need quiet. Got to concentrate."

Further quick-fire Italian. The guys playing with the pickaxes stopped swinging them, but didn't put them down.

Low-level thugs, Phil had reckoned. Amateurs. Didn't mean they couldn't be deadly.

I tried to get my brain in gear. "Right. Got a torch? Uh, light?" I added, when all I got were baffled looks.

Someone handed me a battered metal lantern. Could be handy as a blunt instrument if it kicked off down here—but then again, what's the old saying? *Don't bring a lamp to a gunfight*?

We were clustered near the entrance, but when I held up the light I could see the tunnel led back twenty feet or so directly into the hillside and then forked into two. I took a few tentative steps, my footfalls dull on the packed-earth floor, then a few more as nobody tried to stop me.

The walls of the tunnel were rough-hewn stone, and the deeper I went, the damper it got. Chilly, too. I suppressed a shiver. Didn't want them thinking I was scared.

I stopped at the fork, but Mr. Bling yelled at me to "Go *further*," so I picked a branch at random and walked along the few yards it extended. Then I stood still, took a deep breath, and got ready to do my party trick.

I hadn't done this for a while.

Although Phil's always been keen on me trying to stretch the limits, we'd been a bit distracted of late. What with a wedding to plan and all that. Gary's bright idea of making the wedding gifts into an Easter egg hunt for yours truly, guests for the entertainment of, had been vetoed sharpish. So yeah, it'd been a while.

And . . . if I was honest, I was nervous of what I'd find. I pick up on emotions, not objects. It's a fair bet that ancient Romans about to flee from, seemingly, the end of the world wouldn't have had a lot in the way of warm and fluffy feelings. I had enough mortal terror of my own to be getting on with right now, without taking on anyone else's.

Then again, if they'd been hiding stuff, it would have been in hope they'd come back for it, so maybe it wouldn't be so bad? And at the end of the day, it wasn't like I had a choice.

I told myself not to be such a wuss, and *listened*.

The vibes were everywhere. And nowhere. It was like when you're in your car listening to the radio and you go under a motorway bridge or out of range of the station. Fizzing static all over the shop. There was nothing I could separate out. Not a single trail.

Oh Christ. I knew, same as if I was reading a flippin' movie script, what was going to happen if I told them I'd hit a blank.

They wouldn't believe me. So they'd do their bastard best to persuade me to come up with the goods—and no prizes for guessing what form that persuasion would take. Yeah, they'd brought the pickaxes and stuff down to dig, but I didn't like to think how much damage one of them could do to a human body. And it wouldn't be my body either, would it? It'd be Phil's.

I swallowed. *Try harder, Paretski.*

What had Phil reckoned, that time we'd talked about it after the pub fire? *Need,* that was it. Focus and need were the key.

Shouldn't be an issue, should it? I really fucking *needed* to get us out of here alive.

"You find something?" Mr. Bling's voice broke into my thoughts, and I whirled to find he'd followed me down the tunnel.

"*Jesus,* let me concentrate, all right?" The minute I'd said it I tensed for reprisals—but Mr. Bling backed off, hands held up in apology.

I'd have had greater faith in his sincerity if he hadn't still been holding a gun in one of them.

I tried harder.

I stood there in that tunnel and tried to find my focus. The bastard in the bling, the thugs behind me holding the man I loved at gunpoint . . . I pushed them all away, even Phil; let them drain into the cold earth floor.

Then I shoved all my *need,* my desperate yearning to find something to save us, into a tightly-furled ball that hovered behind my eyes, and aimed it into the darkness like an invisible searchlight.

The echo that came back nearly floored me, it was so incandescent.

Not hidden treasure.

Water.

There was water near us—no, above us and to one side. A lot of it.

Hadn't Giulia mentioned something about this on our guided tour way back whenever, before murder, kidnappings, and mortal peril had decided to gatecrash our honeymoon? Something about the theatre being buried and waterlogged?

Huh. That's why the world will always need plumbers. Even being dead for two thousand years doesn't stop you having problems with the drains.

It wasn't buried treasure... but maybe it was better than nothing? In the absence of untold Roman riches, the only way me and Phil would stand a chance of getting out of here in one piece would be to give these goons bigger problems than us to worry about.

A shit-ton of water cascading down on them and flooding the tunnels might do the trick. If nothing else, it ought to clue them in that they weren't onto an easy earner here.

I shivered. It was crazy—it was practically bloody suicidal—but what choice did I have?

"Up there." I gestured to a point near the roof of the tunnel. "It's pretty big."

Mr. Bling's eyes lit up. "What is it?"

Shit. "I don't know," I ad-libbed desperately, wondering even as I spoke if I should have out and out lied. "It doesn't work like that. I don't get HDTV or a bloody survey report. But the vibes are strong, which means it's important."

He smiled. It held three parts avarice and a hefty dollop of menace. "I hope you are right. For your sake, and for the sake of your husband."

Christ.

Chapter Thirty-Three

Apparently even these guys had more sense than to just swing a pick into the roof of a tunnel we were standing in. There was a lot of argument about how to handle the excavation—or at any rate that was how I interpreted the raised voices and angry gestures.

I took a chance and picked my way back to the antechamber, where Phil was being watched over by a weedy guy who'd probably been chosen for his skill with a gun rather than a shovel. He gave me a dirty look but didn't shoot me, and I eased myself down to sit on the cold, hard ground with my battered husband. "You okay?" I murmured.

"Peachy," he rasped, then gave me a twitch of a smile. "I'd feel better if I knew which of the two of you said that."

Thank God. He was back to himself. I had a weird urge to cry. "Concussion?" I asked instead.

"Haven't thrown up yet."

Situations like this, you have to find your positives where you can. "Should bloody well hope not. It'd be terrible to think all those prawns gave their little lives in vain."

It was hard to tell in the dimly lit tunnel, but I think his complexion took on a greenish hue. "Probably best if we don't talk about food, then. You found something?"

I glanced at the guard, then back at Phil. "Yeah. Something."

Chances were this guy's English wasn't any better than his excavation skills. But I couldn't risk saying any more.

Phil nodded, like he'd read my mind anyway, then winced.

I took a deep breath. "I'm sorry about all this."

"*You're* sorry?" Phil's voice was louder, and the guard grunted menacingly.

He didn't tell me to sling my hook, though, and after a moment Phil spoke again, softer this time. "You've got nothing to be sorry for. I should have realised what was going on in that alley. Should have known they'd escalate after we brushed them off."

"Oi, there's only room for one psychic in this marriage."

He smiled. I wanted to hold him, to kiss him—for fuck's sake, it could be the last time—but not here. Not in front of these bastards.

"Hey," the guard said. He gestured with his gun and mimed zipping his lips.

I zipped. *Shit.*

All we could do now was wait.

It was taking a lot longer than I'd expected. From the body language and strident voices of the Italian mob, it was taking a lot longer than they'd expected too.

Then again, hadn't I read in the guidebook that Herculaneum had been harder to excavate than Pompeii because all the stuff burying it was much more solid? Come to think of it, it would have to be, wouldn't it? Otherwise modern-day Ercolano would've disappeared into a giant sinkhole by now.

I tried not to think of all those multistorey buildings directly above our heads, separated from us by sixty feet of not-entirely-solid rock. Which I'd told these goons to dig into. But hey, maybe it was a good thing? Maybe they'd get fed up with getting nowhere and give up?

Maybe they'd drop us back off at our hotel with a pat on the head and a Cornetto, too.

One of the guys stomped off to the crate with all the warning stickers. I had to stifle a nervous laugh when he returned waggling a long, sausage-like package of white powder, like a not-quite-stiff-enough dildo.

It wasn't funny, really. That almost certainly wasn't how you were supposed to handle high explosives. I was beginning to think we *all* might die down here.

There was a loud, handwavy argument between him and Mr. Bling. I couldn't tell who won, but the explosives guy stomped back to the crate with his lethal sausage. I breathed a sigh of relief.

Then he stomped back again, this time carrying an electric drill with an industrial-sized bit, a handful of coloured wires, *and* the dynamite dildo.

I had to fight down a slight case of the hysterical giggles—we were all about to get well and truly shafted.

Did the guy with the drill know what he was doing? He seemed workmanlike enough as he made the hole for the charge, as far as I could tell from a distance and with my teeth on edge from the ear-splitting noise like a convention of psycho dentists. I was braced for the water to break through at any minute, but apparently it hadn't been as close as I'd thought.

Had my so-called gift finally stopped giving?

As the guy put down the drill, I glanced away to see Mr. Bling staring at me, narrow-eyed.

Oh, shit. Did he suspect I'd steered them wrong?

He came swaggering down the tunnel towards us, a couple of henchmen in tow. "Signor Paretski, you come with me."

Shit, shit, shit. He *did* suspect something. What the hell were we going to do now?

"Why?" I demanded, as me and Phil scrambled to our feet. With Phil not being able to use his hands, I had to help him, which didn't make me feel any better. "Where are we going?"

Instead of answering, Mr. Bling jerked his head at one of the minions, who stepped forward to motion Phil away from me with his gun.

I sent Phil a helpless look. "It'll be okay," he murmured, before heading off as directed.

The second henchman grabbed my arm and shoved his gun in my stomach. He reeked of sweat and cheap cigarettes.

Oh Christ.

Phil turned to fix me in the eye. And I know I joke about him reading my mind, but right then, it was like we really could hear each other's thoughts. I could see, clear as an Italian summer's day, what he was thinking. It was, *I'm guessing when they break through there, shit's going to hit the fan*. And . . . *When it does, get out of here. Save yourself.*

Leave me.

"No," I rasped out, ignoring the gun in my side to take a step forward before a rough hand yanked me back.

"Signor Paretski," Mr. Bling said smoothly. "Come this way."

He led me and my own personal henchman right out of the tunnel, and I blinked up at the night sky. Would me and Phil ever look at it together again? The air was warm and a lot fresher—particularly after Mr. Bling sent the minion back into the tunnel. He obviously didn't think I was much of a threat. With Phil still in the tunnels with the rest of them, he was right.

My Phil. Stuck underground with the madman with the dynamite dildo. But he'd be safe, wouldn't he? The Italian mob wouldn't still be in there if it wasn't safe. Would they?

"You can't—the explosives. Someone will hear." My voice came out hoarse, and I coughed to clear it.

Mr. Bling gave me a gentle smile. "Don't worry." Then he took out his phone and made a brief call in Italian.

He had no trouble getting a signal. Bastard.

Who the hell was he talking to? A quick reminder to the chief of the local police that he'd paid them off too? How much profit did they think there was going to be left at this rate, even if I came up with the goods?

Then a terrific *bang* split the air and almost made me crap myself as the sky lit up in a blaze of light and colour.

How do you hide the sound of an explosion? Pretty obvious, when you think about it. In the middle of a shedload of other explosions.

As further bangs echoed off the ruins, I stared at the fireworks, seeing in my head the display me and Phil had watched the first night we'd been here, and my heart ached with a fierce, soul-twisting pain.

"Pretty, no?" Mr. Bling beamed up at the sky.

Was this my moment? He was distracted—should I tackle him? If I got his gun, I could use him as a bargaining chip to free Phil. I drew in a shaky breath. But before I could steel myself to make a move, there was a deeper boom, much closer this time. I spun—and the mouth of the tunnel exploded in a torrent of water, mud, and rock.

Oh Christ. *Phil.*

Chapter Thirty-Four

Debris stung my arms and my face. I pushed past an open-mouthed, gesticulating Mr. Bling, and ran towards the tunnel. A couple of guys staggered out—but not the one I wanted to see. Chaos. I scrambled against the flow, desperate to get to Phil. Jesus. If he'd been hurt . . . If he'd *died* . . .

I shut that line of thought down hard and stumbled into the darkness—what the fuck had happened to the lanterns? Shifting debris made the footing uneven, and the rushing water dragged at my legs. It was up to my knees, but no further, thank God. Some bloke slammed into me, his shoulders too low and his arms too free for it to be Phil. I shoved him away and carried on blindly, bashing my elbow against the tunnel wall as I did so. Everything was weirdly quiet and pitch-black. I found myself holding my breath, irrationally convinced I was underwater.

Christ, where was Phil? There was too much water here for my so-called gift to work but sod it all sideways, I *needed* to find him. Needed it more than air.

I could do this, right? I'd done it before, although God alone knew how. In the Dyke fire. I'd sensed a person. Not hidden, just . . . there. Why the hell hadn't I done what Phil had suggested? Tried to explore the possibilities of this bloody gift?

Too late now. But I could find him.

I *had* to find him. I rolled up my desperation into a tight ball and *listened* with everything I had.

Then I saw him. Not with my eyes. Inside my head, somehow. My stomach lurched like I'd stepped off a cliff. He was burning bright white, a good ninety degrees away from the direction I'd been heading.

But not far. I didn't consciously decide to head towards him—but I found myself slip-sliding on the tunnel floor and stumbling against his chest a moment later. I gripped him hard, and his light went out, smothered by a gut-churning wrench of relief.

"Tom?" It seemed like he was shouting, but I could barely hear him.

"It's me. Got to get out."

"Tom?" he shouted again, the sound still muffled. "Take my arm. This way."

I shoved my arm through his, glad one of us had kept his sense of direction. The flooding water was slowing now, and it was only at my ankles. We were following the flow, which when my rattled brain managed to think about it, made a lot of sense. I guessed Phil was keeping his far shoulder against the wall of the tunnel—at least, I didn't bump into the wall like I had on the way in.

Shapes started to resolve in the darkness, and my heady relief was swiftly followed by crushing fear. What was going to happen when we got out? Best-case scenario, the Bling boys would have scarpered.

Worst-case— Shit. I bashed my knee on a wooden box and stumbled, almost falling into the water and taking Phil with me, which cut off that line of thought but strangely failed to make me feel better.

"Tom?" Phil shouted again as he fought to steady us both.

I wanted to tell him to keep it down so as not to bring the guys with guns running back in, but he likely wouldn't hear me unless I yelled it, which would defeat the purpose. I squeezed his arm and took a tentative step.

The knee held, and for once my bastard hip hadn't decided to crash the party.

Small mercies. That wouldn't mean a thing if I ended up with a bullet in me.

Or, God forbid, in my husband.

We'd halted a few yards from the mouth of the tunnel, and enough light seeped in from the ruins that I could finally make out his face. I cupped it in one filthy, wet hand and kissed him.

Just in case.

Phil kissed back with a determination that told me he was right there with me on the *this-isn't-over-yet* front. We stood there in the filthy water, me with my arms around his still-bound form, the box of explosives trying to hump my still-throbbing leg, and I couldn't help thinking that if this was all we were going to get, it'd been worth it.

What with the communications barrier, we couldn't make any kind of plan to deal with the seriously pissed-off Mafiosi who might be waiting for us outside. But we couldn't stay in the tunnel forever either—the water was still flowing, and who knew when it might decide to bring down further debris on our unprotected heads?

If my number was up, I'd rather die out in the open than buried alive in the dark. And I was pretty sure Phil agreed. So after one last kiss, we linked arms again and walked—all right, staggered—out of the tunnel to face the mob.

Chapter Thirty-Five

The first things I saw when we emerged from the tunnel were gun barrels pointing in our direction. My heart seized like a scaled-up pump—until I realised the guys holding them were wearing badges and natty blue trousers with stripes down the legs. Apparently Mr. Bling hadn't, in fact, paid off the *polizia*. And damn, these guys had a light-speed response time. *Must be those go-faster stripes*, I thought, and had to stifle a giggle.

It was just possible I might have been a little bit in shock, here.

Before I could get out the words, *Don't shoot, please, we're British!* The guns lowered, and one set of trousers came walking towards us. "Signor Paretski and Signor Morrison?" their owner asked politely.

"Uh, yeah." How did he know?

"You are injured?"

I glanced at Phil and winced at the state of him. There was blood all down his face from a cut on his forehead, and all that mud near an open wound couldn't be hygienic.

Smiling reassuringly, the policeman put a steadying hand on his shoulder. "Come this way, please."

I'd never been so glad to see a copper in my life. And I could have kissed the paramedics who turned up to take care of Phil. And me, but I'd have been fine whatever—all I had were cuts, bruises, and a shedload of water drying out and leaving gritty deposits on my hair, clothes, and skin. Phil . . . he'd been through much worse. I had to elbow my way into the ambulance they'd packed him into, and I didn't back down when they tried to fob me off.

I wasn't letting him out of my sight. Not tonight, and possibly not ever again.

Times like this, I wished I'd tried harder to learn some of the local lingo. "*Mario*," I repeated, clutching my shock blanket around me like a superhero cape, while they frowned at me in obvious bemusement. I tried sign language, pointing at Phil and then me, and finally holding up my left hand with its wedding ring. "*Mario*."

The penny visibly dropped. "*Marito*," the blonde one corrected me kindly. "Your husband?" She waved me into the back of the ambulance while her colleague rolled his eyes and went around to the front of the van.

Huh. Apparently instead of making my status as Phil's lawfully wedded spouse clear, I'd been insisting I was a vertically-challenged plumber from an eighties video game. Well, two out of three ain't bad.

One. I mean *one* out of three. Obviously.

Once we'd made it to hospital, we were seen fairly quickly. I guessed the *polizia* who'd accompanied us were keen on getting home for the night. They weren't the only ones.

The diagnosis on Phil was concussion—yeah, who'd have thought it?—but no skull fracture, which was a relief. A young doctor who spoke English better than I did explained it all to us patiently, and gave me an English-language sheet of instructions on how to care for a head injury. They were probably used to tourists coming a cropper around here.

Here being, as it turned out, Sorrento, which was a relief as if I'd had to guess, I would've expected to end up in Naples. I was starting to seriously want my bed, and it was good to know it was only ten minutes or so away, rather than over an hour by road.

I was less glad to see the coppers when they came to take our statements just as I hit the adrenaline crash, although what with Phil being tied up, I'd been fairly confident they hadn't thought we were in league with the dynamite crew. As it turned out, they'd had an anonymous tip-off about two English tourists being kidnapped in Sorrento. Said unknown informant had also hinted there might be a raid on the ruins at Pompeii forthcoming. Luckily for me and Phil, someone on the force had put two and two together after they drew a blank at Pompeii, and asked the local plod in Ercolano to check out the site there.

At which point, the unlicensed firework display over the ruins had started. They'd got there as the real explosion went off. Having expected a hostage situation, they had been over the moon to find our kidnappers soggy and disorientated, and had managed to nab the lot of them without anyone getting shot.

Thank God. The nabbing the lot of them, that is. After what they'd done to Phil, I wouldn't have been that fussed about any of the Bling boys ending up with a bullet in them.

It'll be nice not to have them dogging our footsteps for the rest of the honeymoon, I mused—and then goggled at how bizarre it seemed to be thinking about sightseeing after everything that had happened.

The police didn't give us any information on the informant. Could it have been Martin, on the side of the angels after all? He'd been on the spot—*if* it'd really been him I'd seen.

Of course, it could have been a disgruntled gang member who'd turned traitor. Who else could have (a) spotted us being grabbed, (b) known who we were, and (c) been in the know about Wayne's treasure-hunting plans? That last one was the stumbling block with Martin. Siri hadn't been in on the plan, so how could she have told him? And if he'd been in on the plan all along, why scupper it now, when he'd got us where he wanted us?

The lad and lady interviewing me got all interested when I told them the Bling Boys must have been responsible for Wayne's death—which made it embarrassing to have to admit I didn't have a shred of evidence, apart from my other half having recognised some of them in the hotel that night. Specially as they hadn't even been with Wayne at the time, and at no point had Mr. Bling admitted to offing the guy. My "If they didn't do it, who did?" was met with a patient, if somewhat dismissive, "We'll look into it."

It was into the early hours before I was finally able to take delivery of one Phil Morrison, condition slightly foxed.

All right, moderately beared and significantly badgered as well. But not broken.

Not broken, thank God.

My eyes went worryingly blurry. Hoping to avoid blubbing like a baby, I gave a manly gulp and tried to think of other things. Like home, friends and family, and the cats.

God, I missed my cats. I blinked rapidly.

"You okay?" Phil rasped.

"Course," I told him overbrightly. "Too much disinfectant in the air. And dust. From the tunnels. And probably some water too."

Phil rolled his eyes, then winced.

"Headache?"

"Yeah."

"Let's get you back to the hotel."

I'd expected to have to call a taxi, but we managed to catch a ride from the local plod, which was reassuring on several levels. Not least of which was that they'd be able to make sure we got back into our hotel if it turned out management had locked up for the night.

I needn't have worried. There was even a bleary-eyed guy on duty in the lobby, who woke up noticeably when we staggered in with our police escort. Old Enrique would likely be getting one hell of a report tomorrow, but right then I didn't give a monkey's.

Back in our room, we showered in turn and fell into bed. I'd like to report some vigorous, life-affirming sex was had, but to be honest, neither of us had the energy.

"At least it's all over now," I muttered into my pillow.

There was a moment's silence, and I thought Phil was asleep already until he grunted, "Is it?"

I levered open one eye. "What? You don't reckon there's more of those goons out there waiting to grab us for a second time, do you?"

"No, but what about Wayne's killer?"

I blinked. "They're locked up. You know that." Even if their jailors weren't totally convinced.

"Do I?" Phil huffed. "Talk about it tomorrow. Let's get some sleep."

Just as I was thinking that after that bombshell, I'd never fall asleep, I did.

Chapter Thirty-Six

You'd think we'd have slept till noon, after all that.

You'd be wrong. What with my phone alarm going off at regular intervals during what was left of the night to remind me to prod Phil awake—head injuries are a bastard that way—it seemed like we might as well get up once the clock ticked round to a sensible hour.

Also, I was ravenous.

Seriously. It was like I hadn't eaten for a week.

Our appearance as walking wounded caused a bit of a stir as we went to breakfast. And yeah, we could have ordered room service. But I was buggered if I was going to hide in my room like I was scared of the outside world.

We only just made it before the staff started clearing away the buffet, but there were still a few stragglers finishing off their coffee when we limped into the dining room. One of them, I was surprised to see, was Siri—on her own. Not a pair of braces or stripy shirt in sight.

Had the scales fallen from her eyes where Martin was concerned? While it'd save us the thankless task of revealing he'd been lying, I didn't like the idea of her being disillusioned. She was too young and bubbly for that.

Or rather, she was usually. Now, though, she was sitting slumped in her seat, a half-eaten plate of fruit in front of her, staring out over the bay as her coffee went cold.

I nodded to Phil, and we made our way over to her table to cheer her up.

It got off to a rocky start.

"Oh my God!" Siri clutched both hands to her mouth, her eyes wide. "What happened to you?" She stood up so fast her chair almost fell, and grabbed me with both hands.

I winced. "Uh, bruises?"

She let go like I'd given her an electric shock. "Oh God, it wasn't Martin, was it?"

I blinked. "Um . . ."

"I'm so sorry." Her little fists were clenched against her chest. "I tried to tell him, I really did, but he wouldn't listen."

Phil frowned. "What did you try to tell him?"

"That it wasn't you what killed Wayne! He was saying loads of crazy stuff last night at dinner—like I couldn't trust you and it wasn't safe to stay here." She broke off with a choked sob. "I told him, I *said* it wasn't you, but he went on and on. He wanted me to go back to England with him."

I was still trying to process this. "Why the hell would we kill Wayne?"

"'Cos Phil and him had that row, yeah, about this thing Wayne wanted you to do? Martin reckoned you wanted to keep it all for yourselves and not give Wayne a share, and I told him you'd never do that, but he wouldn't believe me. He kept saying Phil had, like, a history of violence . . ." She darted a guilty glance at the man in question.

This time my wince wasn't due to bruises. I guessed Martin must have his own source on the force, and had found out about Phil's suspension for beating the crap out of a domestic abuser. "For fuck's sake, that was years ago," I protested.

Siri drew back in her seat.

"Martin knew about the antiquities deal?" Phil asked sharply.

Huh. Good point.

Siri blinked. "I thought it was some property thing."

I stared at her. "What, that Wayne wanted my help with?"

"They never told me what it was all about. But I thought . . . you're a plumber, aren't you? And buildings have pipes and stuff."

Couldn't argue with that one.

"Where's Martin now?" Phil's expression was stony.

"I don't know. I told him to get stuffed, and I haven't seen him since dinner last night." Her chin wobbled. "It was him what hurt you, wasn't it? I should've warned you, but I was so upset."

"It wasn't him," I reassured her. "It was some other blokes. Martin had nothing to do with it. Probably. But thanks for telling us." Movement off to the side caught my eye. "Uh, I don't want to be rude, but I think they're about to take all the food away."

Siri's hand went to her mouth once more. "Oh God—I'm so sorry. You go and get your breakfast. I'll leave you to it, and we'll talk when you've eaten, yeah? Unless you want me to carry stuff over for you?"

Having assured her we weren't quite so decrepit we couldn't carry our own meals, we went straight to the buffet and piled a couple of plates high with the least tired-looking pastries, plus a large milky coffee apiece. It was a comfort-food sort of morning.

At the last minute I grabbed a load of sliced meats and cheese. Hey, protein's important too. Phil raised an eyebrow, like he wouldn't be nabbing half of it anyway.

"What the hell was that all about?" I asked in a low voice. True to her word, Siri had disappeared, so we made for a table at the far end of the terrace and sat down gingerly so as not to provoke any of our aches and pains. "Smokescreen? He tells her we killed Wayne 'cos it was him all along?"

"Could be. Especially since we now know he was lying to us yesterday when he claimed not to know anything about the local deal." Phil paused. "Why would he want to kill Wayne, though? If he was getting paid to investigate the man—even managed to wangle a free holiday out of it—"

"Then Wayne was his own personal golden goose," I cut in, purely for the sake of the warm-and-fuzzies I got when Phil glared at me for the mangled metaphor. "Unless that was a lie too? Him investigating Wayne, I mean."

"If we accept that he's here on business and not just getting away from the wife and kids, who else could he be investigating? Latching on to Siri only makes sense if it was Wayne."

"Unless he's only after a leg-over." Cynical, moi? I took a bite of a sticky Danish-type thing with a custard cream filling. *Come to me, sweet calories.*

"Which he's unlikely to get now." Phil hesitated. "Of course, it could have been Siri he was interested in all along. Professionally speaking."

I sent him a steady look, the impact of which might have been lessened by the crumbs of flaky pastry clinging to my chin. "You're not going to convince me that girl's got skeletons in her closet. The only reason I can think of for siccing a PI on her is if you're a jealous boyfriend with a nasty suspicious mind, and if Martin was working for Wayne, why carry on after he'd died?"

Phil half smiled. "Just because you like her doesn't mean she hasn't got a dark past. But no, I don't think it's likely." He grabbed one of my salami slices, rolled it up, and shoved it in his gob.

"Oi, manners." I did likewise with the next one before he could snaffle the lot. "Think she's dashed off to see Martin? Or did he manage to put her off him last night?"

"We should probably check in on her after breakfast." Phil's expression turned grim. "She needs to know the truth about him."

"Does she? Long as he leaves her alone from now on, maybe she's happier not knowing how much he lied to her?"

Phil's face softened, and he put his hand on my arm. "She's a grown woman. She needs to know. You're not going to be around to save her from the next bastard, are you?"

"We could keep in touch?" I sighed. "I guess you're right. Bastards."

On our way back past the reception desk after refuelling, our old friend Enrique Udinese hailed us. I tensed, wondering what he was going to complain about now—were we lowering the tone of the place with our bruised faces?

He gave us a startled glance, then converted it seamlessly into a polite smile. "Signor Paretski? I have a message for you." He handed me a slip of paper.

"Huh," I said, looking at it. *Call DCI Dave Southgate*, it read. Possibly he'd left the job title on there so they wouldn't forget to pass the message on, but my money was on the shine not having worn off his promotion yet.

Enrique coughed, managing to sound disapproving. "I trust you are not in difficulties with the English police?"

"No—Dave's an old mate," I assured him.

His eyes narrowed a smidge. "And with our local police?"

"Not at all," Phil said firmly.

"Because I hear that you returned very late last night, in a police car."

I flashed him a smile. "Yep. Good of them to give us a lift. Right, got to go—got a mate to call."

Phil huffed as we strode off. "You know it's not actually a state secret that we were attacked last night."

"So? If he's going to have a nasty suspicious mind about us, he doesn't deserve an explanation."

"You do realise having a nasty suspicious mind is basically my job description, don't you?"

"That's different. You only suspect people who deserve it. Well, mostly. And it's all in a good cause. Generally. Okay, I'm shutting up about it now."

Phil laughed. "Come on. Let's find out from Dave if any of my nasty suspicions have turned out to be true."

It seemed a little indiscreet to give Dave a bell from the public area of the hotel—especially with the way people couldn't seem to stop staring at us like they'd never seen facial abrasions before—so we went back to the room to make the call.

Dave answered on the second ring.

"About bleedin' time. I was trying to get hold of you all last night. Ever think about leaving your flippin' phone switched on now and then?"

I could have given him chapter and verse about why I hadn't been answering calls last night, but I felt exhausted at the thought of going through all that right now. Not to mention the lecture that was bound to follow. I glanced at Phil. He looked pretty much how I felt. Yeah, it could wait until we weren't still reeling from having lived it.

"Wouldn't have helped," I said. "Trust me on that. So what's the urgency? Junior take his first steps today?" I could just about cope with some heartwarming tales of childhood milestones passed.

"What? No, but it'll be any day now. He's a proper little tiger, you'd never guess what he— Christ, stop distracting me. This is important."

More important than Dave's son, heir, and apple of his jaundiced eye? "What is?"

"That little old lady of yours. Cassandra Austin."

"Yeah, that's one of 'em."

"Formerly married to one Brian Carrie."

"No wonder she never took his name. Cass and Carrie?" I gave a tired laugh.

"Focus, Paretski. The late Brian Carrie met his end nineteen years ago." Dave's voice had taken on a portentous tone. "*When*, I might add, he went for a walk. A long one. Off a short clifftop."

Chapter Thirty-Seven

You could have heard a pin drop, and it wouldn't have had to be from any great height either. I stared at Phil, my eyes wide. Then I remembered he couldn't have heard what Dave had said. "You're saying Cassie's former husband fell to his death?"

Phil froze.

"Got it in one," Dave was saying. "Now, what does that remind me of?"

"Wayne," I said weakly. "But that's crazy. Why would Cassie want to kill him? Was she a suspect when her husband died?"

Phil was making urgent gestures. Belatedly, I realised what he was after and put the phone on speaker. Why hadn't I thought of that to start with?

"It was ruled an accident. There was some suggestion he might have topped himself, but the grieving widow"—you could almost taste the sarcasm in Dave's tone—"shut that one down. Reckoned he was far too fond of himself."

"So . . . she never made a secret of there not being much love lost there?" I blurted out, my mind supplying an image of Cassie cheerfully calling her dead husband *a shit*. "And they still didn't haul her in for questioning? I thought you lot always assumed it was the significant other what dunnit."

"No evidence of foul play. Apparently. And the SIO was a useless twat who couldn't tell his arse from an elephant. Or so I'm inferring. So watch your back. That goes for you too, Morrison. You're listening, right?"

"I'm here," Phil confirmed, his tone sombre.

"So no cosy clifftop walks with Cassandra Austin. Don't even pass her on the bleedin' staircase. Morrison, if that husband of yours comes home in a coffin, you'd better measure yourself up for a matching one, you got that?"

"Got it," Phil said grimly.

"Oi, I'm not the only one who could be in danger here," I protested.

"No, but out of the two of you, you're the only one not built like a brick shithouse. It'd take a bloody coachload of old ladies to shove Morrison off a balcony."

"I'm pretty sure it's all to do with leverage—"

"Jesus. I do *not* need a physics lesson right now. Just stay safe, all right? Can you manage that? Christ, who am I even asking? Of course you bloody can't."

He had me bang to rights there.

Dave was speaking again. "Morrison? It's on you."

"Got it," Phil said again.

"Good," said Dave, and hung up.

I sat down heavily on the bed. "I don't believe it. Cassie, a murderer? I could get her, I dunno, throwing a punch at a bloke. Or throwing something else. But sneaking up behind him and shoving him off a cliff? Doesn't seem her style."

Phil stared into the middle distance for a mo. "If he was abusive, maybe . . ."

"She did say he was a shit." I frowned. "But it has to be a coincidence—them both falling, I mean. It was the local mafia who topped Wayne."

"Was it, though?"

Hadn't he mumbled something about this last night? "Uh . . . what are you saying, here?"

"One of the taunts the gang threw at me in the back of that van." Phil's face hardened. "You know the sort of thing—'Not so tough now, are you?' And all that. But one of them called me a killer. 'Mr. Big-Shot Killer,' if you want the exact words."

"Why would they think you'd killed someone?" I asked stupidly.

"Maybe if they knew they hadn't? Even while they were taunting me, there was a kind of . . ." His brow furrowed. "Respect, maybe. Wariness."

"Mr. Bling said something too," I remembered. "About you being a dangerous man. Bloody hell, is that why they were on us like a ton of bricks—they thought *we* were the ruthless killers?"

"One of us, anyhow." Phil gave a weak smile.

"Oi, I could be a ruthless killer if I wanted to be. Which I don't," I added, in case he was in any doubt.

Phil patted my hand. "Course you could."

"Oi, don't patronise me. Christ. Could it really have been Cassie? Why would she want to kill Wayne?"

"Maybe he reminded her of her husband? I don't—" Phil didn't get to finish that thought, as there was a knock on the door.

I looked at him. "Housekeeping?"

"Only one way to find out." He strode over and opened the door.

It was Martin.

He stood in our open doorway, looking . . . different. He hadn't bothered with the braces, and his shirt was one I wouldn't have been totally ashamed to be seen in. His hair was less slicked-back and oily too.

He gave us a tight little smile. "You survived, then?"

"Sorry to hear that?" I asked, mindful of what Siri had told us.

"No, God, no. Can I come in?"

Phil and me exchanged glances, then stood aside to let him enter the room.

There were two of us and only one of him. Even in our current state, we could take him if he turned out to be as miffed with us as Siri reckoned.

I hoped.

"What do you want?" I asked more abruptly than I meant to. I'd had a bad night, all right?

Martin shoved his hands in his pockets and hunched his shoulders. "I, ah, I thought we ought to have things out. As it were." Then he clammed up.

Phil gave him a penetrating stare. "Was it you who tipped off the police about us getting snatched last night?"

Huh. Great minds, and all that.

Martin nodded jerkily. "Look, cards on the table here. Wayne offered to cut me in on the deal. That's why I came to Italy."

I blinked. "Why would he do that?" Not known for being the generous sort, our late, unlamented Wayne.

"Because . . ." Martin took a deep breath. "I was investigating him on behalf of a client he defrauded back home."

"And this was his way of paying you to keep quiet about what you found?" Phil's tone was a lot more neutral than I would have managed.

Martin ran a hand through his hair, which further emphasised the lack of oily product in it. "I'm not proud of it. But have you any idea how *expensive* kids are? I've got four of the little bleeders. All of them wanting new computers and designer sportswear and hot-and-cold running bloody ponies." He gazed at us earnestly. "Wayne talked a good talk. Bigged up the whole buried-treasure idea. And then he died and I didn't know what to do. I honestly thought you'd killed him."

How come everyone was so ready to suspect us? Did we look like killers?

"What changed your mind?" Phil asked.

"Last night. I, ah, happened to be passing—"

I gave an incredulous snort, and he broke off to glare at me.

"—and I saw what happened in that alley. Bit of an eye-opener as to the sort of fellows Wayne had been dealing with, in all honesty. *Not* the sort of people I want anything to do with. It made me realise Siri was right, and I'd got rather the wrong end of the stick about you two." He shook his head slowly. "We all should have stayed in Britain. Too many bloody guns all over the place once you cross the English Channel. Couldn't resist the lure of a free holiday, that's my problem."

I goggled at him. "Wayne even paid for your stay?"

Martin cleared his throat. "The, ah, client was persuaded that I could make a breakthrough in the investigation if I observed Mr. Hills in, as it were, his natural habitat."

"Christ, you were screwing them over properly, weren't you?" I blurted out.

He reddened and scowled at me. "Oh, come off it. Everyone fiddles their expenses. It's *expected.* And, as it happens, some of the things Siri's told me will be very helpful in making my client's case against him. Or rather, the corporate entity that has hopefully survived him. It'll all go in the report."

What a shit . . . If Cassie really was on a mission to rid the world of unpleasant men, Martin was lucky she hadn't bumped him off too.

And on the subject of his shittiness . . . "Why did you tell Siri you were gay?"

Martin stared at me. "So she wouldn't get the wrong idea, obviously. I'm a married man."

I gave him a sceptical look. "You're trying to tell us you're not interested in her?"

"Only as a source of information. And all right, for God's sake, I'm not *blind*, but I'm not going to risk my marriage for a bit of how's-your-father with a woman who's young enough for me to *be* her father." He gave a rueful smile. "Siri rather brings out the protective instincts, doesn't she?"

I coughed. Phil glanced at me with the suspicion of a smirk.

"So what was all that bollocks about thinking we were investigating her?" I asked, trying to match up what he'd told us last night with today's story.

"As you say. Bollocks." Martin shrugged. "For all I knew, admitting I was in on Wayne's little scheme would be as good as hopping up on the balcony railings with a notice on my back saying *Shove here.* I had to tell you something."

"Did you have to be such a smug bastard about it?" I muttered.

Martin glared at me. "I think you'll find it was a masterful performance of breezy nonchalance in the face of a couple of—as I firmly believed at the time—cold-blooded killers. And there's no need to be insulting. I *did* save your lives last night, if you'll recall."

He had a point. A bit of a point, anyhow. He hadn't exactly rushed in to rescue us, guns blazing, but who knew how it might have turned out if not for his tip-off to *il plod*?

"We appreciate you calling the police," Phil ground out, clearly having come to the same conclusion.

"Yeah, cheers, mate," I forced myself to say. "Buy you a drink tonight?"

Hey, it didn't mean I'd have to stay and watch him drink it.

"Thanks, but to be blunt, bugger that. I'm flying home today. Back to sensible temperatures, nice boring infidelity cases, and a total lack of mafia murderers."

"And the little bleeders," I said.

"God, don't remind me." He grimaced, but I was fairly sure there was a twinkle of fondness there. "Right, I'll leave you two to lick your wounds. Or each other's. *Chacun à son goût.* Take care of Siri, won't you?"

He swept out of the room with a distinct air of shaking the dust off his shoes.

"Do you think he was telling the truth?" I asked after the door had closed behind him.

"Not sure. More of it than before, at any rate."

"He seemed to think the local mob killed Wayne."

Phil nodded. "Or he wants us to think he thinks that."

"Because it was actually him? Course, that could also apply to Mr. Bling and his merry men."

"Except for the fact they were holding us at gunpoint to force you to work for them. Why would they want to convince us they *weren't* ruthless killers?"

"Huh." I thought about it. "Call me naïve, but I'm not sure I buy Martin as the killer. He was in this for easy money, right? So why make things harder for himself by killing the bloke who was doing the work?"

"You've got a point. I'm not sure he fits the profile, either."

"So where does that leave us?"

Phil took a deep breath. "Back with Cassie. We need to follow up on Dave's information. See where that gets us."

"As long as it's not splatted on the tarmac from a sixty-foot fall," I said with a grim attempt at humour.

Phil didn't smile.

"What?" I asked. "You don't seriously think we're in danger, do you?" We'd survived the local mob. Surely we could handle one not-so-little old lady?

"Wayne wasn't dragged to that balcony, was he?" Phil said slowly. "Whoever he walked over there with . . . he didn't think he was in danger."

I swallowed. And now I wasn't smiling any more, either.

Chapter Thirty-Eight

Of course, the next problem was finding the lady in question to, well, question.

We decided to check out the hotel terrace first, possibly influenced by subconscious killer-always-returns vibes. There was no sign of Cassie, but Siri was there, sitting on her lonesome nursing a bottle of mineral water. I wondered if she'd been there since breakfast. Did she even know Martin had gone home? Did she care?

"Siri might have spoken to Jane and Cassie about their plans for today," I suggested.

Phil huffed. "You mean you want to check she's okay."

"Oi, she *might* know something."

"Did I say she didn't? Come on, then."

We made our way over, and I slipped into the chair next to Siri, while Phil wandered off to order coffee.

"All right, love?" I said cheerily.

"Tom." Her greeting was on the subdued side, but she gave me a smile. "You feeling better since breakfast?"

"Yeah, there's not much a good meal can't cure." She kindly didn't call me on my bollocks. I leaned forward and added with a casual air, "Any idea what Cassie and Jane are up to today?"

Siri frowned. "I think they were going to take it easy. Maybe have a swim. You and Phil ought to do that too. Get yourselves better."

"Might take your advice on that," I said, feeling vindicated.

Siri looked happier. "Holidays aren't all about seeing stuff. They're about being together too." Now she looked sad again.

"There's all kinds of togetherness, aren't there?" I babbled inadequately in the face of her grief. "I mean, we're together now, aren't we? And when you go home, you'll have your family, right?"

"Yeah. Family's important," Siri said with a doubtful air. Then she brightened. "They're sweet, aren't they? That family." She nodded to the earwig clan from our first breakfast, who were sitting at a nearby table playing cards for sweeties. I caught Dad stealthily helping the youngest to win and gave him a mental fist bump.

When I turned back to Siri, she wore a soppy expression. "You and Phil, you think you're gonna have kids?"

I couldn't help smiling. "Yeah. We've been talking about it recently. It's gonna take a while to get it sorted, but yeah."

"Did I miss something?" Phil asked, sitting down with us.

Only the whereabouts of our quarry, I didn't say. Although I might have looked a bit smug about it.

Siri gave a sad little smile. "We was talking about you and Tom having kids. Would you want to adopt? Or, like, have a surrogate?"

"Uh, we hadn't got that far yet." I turned to Phil. "What do you reckon? Your DNA or mine? Or neither?"

"Would *neither* bother you?"

"Speaking as someone whose dad's not actually his father . . . No, it wouldn't. Blood's not what makes a family. But, you know, if you want to pass on the Morrison genes . . ." There was a lot to be said for them, in my humble opinion.

Phil's answer was firm. "I want to adopt. There's too many kids in the world already who need families."

"Aw, that's so sweet." Siri's voice startled me. I'd kind of forgotten we had an audience. She beamed. "I think you're going to be a great dad. Between you."

I wasn't sure if I should be flattered or not. Did she mean we'd make half a great dad each? "Have you got a big family?" I asked, because asking if she planned to *have* one seemed tactless in the circs.

She shook her head. "Just me and mum. And my nan, but she lives in Swindon. I think it's why me and Wayne got on so well," she added unexpectedly.

I frowned. "What, has he got family in Swindon too?"

"No, silly." She gave me a playful nudge, but it was clear her heart wasn't in it. It wouldn't even leave a bruise. "'Cos we both haven't got much family. He was really close to his mum, but then she died. I wish he could've made things up with his dad, though."

"Maybe he didn't want to," Phil's tone was harsh, and I blinked in shock.

The waiter, who'd turned up with a couple of lattes, jumped as he was putting them down and slopped half the contents onto the saucers. I sent him a *never mind* smile and he scurried off.

"You mean whatever happened between them, he couldn't forgive his dad for it?" I suggested, trying to pour oil on the troubled waters I could see welling up in Siri's eyes.

"Or he just didn't care." Phil glared at his latte, as if to intimidate the spilled coffee into pouring itself back into the cup.

I went the easier route and poured mine back myself, while Siri rounded on him. "That's not fair! People always assumed he didn't care about stuff, or have feelings or anything, but he did. Like when you and him had that row in the gallery. It really upset his nerves. He had a terrible headache after that. And then he was mad at me for not bringing any headache pills, but I was worried they'd think we was smuggling drugs at the airport."

I took a sip of my latte and frowned. "Hang on, I thought it was a dicky tum that made him miss dinner that evening."

"Oh, yeah—but that was later, you know?" She sniffled. "That was probably 'cos he got so upset and all."

"Was that why he was drinking?" I asked. "Dull the pain with alcohol?"

Siri bit her lip. "Not sure. I mean, I got him some headache pills in the end."

"From Cassie?" Phil asked sharply.

"Yeah—well, her or Jane. They were both there when I asked, but it was Jane who came back with them. She said Cassie was having a lie down." Siri smiled. "I thought old ladies would have all kinds of pills, and I was right."

Me and Phil exchanged glances.

"What were these pills?" Phil asked.

"Dunno. Jane just said to take two. Does it matter?"

"Maybe," I admitted.

Her eyes opened wide. "Oh God, do you think it was that what made him fall? 'Cos he was drinking after he'd had them pills? She never said he wasn't supposed to drink!"

"I've had the odd beer after a paracetamol," I said to reassure her.

Siri still had a stricken expression. "Do you think I ought to ask her what they were?"

"No, that's fine," Phil said firmly. But I was willing to bet my last Euro he was planning to ask her himself.

Siri turned to me, clearly uncertain, and I patted her arm. "Nah, don't worry. I'm sure it's not important." My mind was racing. What if it *had* been the pills—and they hadn't been painkillers. What if they'd been, say, Cassie's meds that shouldn't be mixed with alcohol?

What happened if you *did* mix them with alcohol? I thought back to Capri. Cassie had been pretty unsteady on her feet on the way back to the boat, hadn't she? And someone of her size should never have got that drunk on a single Spritz.

Why the hell hadn't I seen it at the time?

"Are you sure it's got nothing to do with it?" Siri took a deep breath. "'Cos I've been thinking . . . Maybe I should let all this investigating business go, yeah? Stop trying to find someone to blame for Wayne's death?"

"You can't give up now," I said without thinking. My mind was too busy running on *Did Jane know what the pills were she'd handed over? Were they in on it together?*

"But maybe it really was just one of them things? Like, an accident? He wasn't well, was he? He could have got dizzy, like the police said. And I'm not happy about what's gone on. Like Martin, trying to make me think you two might have done it? And then worrying it was him what beat you up? That was horrible. I hate thinking people I like would be violent like that."

"Sometimes you have to turn up unpleasant things to get at the truth," Phil said in a low voice.

"But what if the truth's what the police thought all along? Then you've dug up all this horrible stuff for nothing. And this is your honeymoon. It ought to be all about you two being together, not having me playing gooseberry and making Phil work on his holidays. 'Specially now you've both got hurt and all." She pressed her lips together, then stood. "Think I'll have a go at changing my flight. You two have some nice couple time, yeah?"

I watched her go with a grimace. Me, that is, not her. "Just when it feels like we're getting somewhere . . . But maybe she's right. Let sleeping dogs lie, and all that? Let's face it, if it turns out it was the pills that made him dizzy, it's going to make her feel guilty for the rest of her life."

"This isn't only about Siri, though." There was something in Phil's tone I couldn't make out. "Wayne was . . . what he was. But did he deserve to die for it?"

White-collar crime, fraud . . . it was all about money, not physically hurting people, but losing money could destroy lives, couldn't it? And then there was the antiquities-stealing plan too. Not to mention, Wayne's greed almost got Phil killed.

Okay. Maybe I wasn't thinking totally objectively about it. "So you think we should carry on? Solve the case even if no one wants us to?"

"People . . . can't take justice into their own hands." Phil didn't sound as certain as he usually did, while he stared straight out at the bay.

He was going to miss that view when we got back home. Maybe I should buy him a calendar. "Is this about what happened when you left the force?" I tried to keep my tone light. "You giving that wife-beater a taste of his own medicine?"

Phil turned to fix me in the eye. "Do you think I'm a violent man?"

I didn't even have to think about it. "No. Any time I've seen you use force, it's been necessary, and you've kept it to a minimum. Maybe you lost your temper when you were younger . . . but that's not who you are now. Think I'd be here if you were?" I took a deep breath and reached out to grasp his hand. "That's the difference between you and Wayne. You changed. He didn't."

Phil's hand squeezed mine back, and there was a long and slightly mushy silence. Then he broke it: "If Wayne was murdered, I can't let the killer walk free."

"*If* Jane gave Siri the wrong pills, and if she did it on purpose."

"If Cassie's on something like beta blockers, those wouldn't mix well with alcohol. Which we already know from seeing her reaction to having a drink. It could have been the—" he broke off, his face pained.

I grimaced in sympathy. "You were about to say 'tipping point,' weren't you? But how could either of them have known Wayne would want some pain pills? As murderous schemes go, it's leaving a hell of a lot to chance."

Phil's face was stony. "Maybe it wasn't premeditated."

"You think it was a spur-of-the-moment decision? I'm not sure that doesn't make it worse."

"Worse than cold-bloodedly planning to kill someone?"

I grimaced. "I guess not. But . . . murder shouldn't be like drunk-buying crap on Amazon. If you're going to kill someone, at least think about it a bit first."

"Preferably don't do it at all." Phil huffed. "But say there was someone you thought the world would be better off without, and you were given the chance to hand them some drugs that might do the trick . . ."

"It'd be rude not to?" Bloody hell. "So . . . you reckon she gave him the pills just to see what would happen? Is that still murder? Manslaughter? Gross negligence aforethought?"

"Maybe the drugs made him dizzy, but that doesn't mean she didn't give him a helping hand over those railings too." Phil's tone was dark, as well it might be.

"Which 'she' are we talking about? Jane or Cassie?" I swallowed. "Or both?"

I really hoped we weren't dealing with a geriatric murder sisterhood here.

"It's all conjecture, though Cassie's the one who may have previous, from what Dave dug up," Phil said. "We don't know the wrong pills were given, and even if they were, it could have been a mistake. We don't have any reason to suppose Jane or Cassie would have wanted to kill Wayne."

"Yeah, I guess you're right . . . It's all questions, innit? What do you reckon Cassie warning Siri off Martin was about? Maybe she spotted him in town with a *signorina*?"

"Or she saw him poking his nose in where he shouldn't?"

"Maybe she simply got the wrong end of the stick about him. She was barking up the wrong tree about Wayne topping his repressed gay self, wasn't she?" I grimaced. "Or just generally barking."

Phil nodded. "Worth asking, though."

"Siri thought they'd be at the pool. Wanna go grab our towels and cossies?"

"Let's head straight up." Phil downed the rest of his coffee and stood. "I don't think there's going to be a lot of rest and relaxation in our immediate future."

Chapter Thirty-Nine

The first thing I saw when we got up to the roof was Mr. & Mrs. Snipe, occupying a couple of pushed-together loungers. They seemed all loved-up today, judging from the amount of canoodling that was going on. They glanced at us, smirked, and then returned to ignoring us completely.

"New theory," I muttered. "Those two wanted a three-way with Siri, and shoved Wayne over the balcony 'cos the thought of him joining in was too horrifying to contemplate."

Phil huffed. "Then how come they haven't propositioned her since he died?"

"Maybe they did, and she was too innocent to understand what they were on about?"

"Face me," Phil said, and when I turned, he stared me in the eye.

"What?"

"Just checking your sunglasses for rose-tinted lenses." He smirked.

I glared. Probably pointlessly, given said sunglasses.

On the other side of the pool, there was a tanned old bloke in Speedos sprawled out asleep on a lounger—and Jane, in a chair, reading an English newspaper.

"Think Cassie's gone off on her own somewhere? Possibly to claim another victim?" I murmured to Phil. There was a slight itch between my shoulder blades, but I manfully resisted the urge to look behind me for anyone sneaking up with murderous intent.

"She's not gone far. Her cardigan's on the chair there.

So it was: a salmon-pink affair of far too ample dimensions to belong to Jane. God bless the ability of old ladies to feel a draught even at pavement-melting temperatures.

"Don't often see them apart, do we?" I said meaningfully . . .

"No. We don't." Phil was clearly on my wavelength. "I'll hang around to catch Cassie when she comes back. How about you distract Jane? Regale her with interesting snippets from your guidebook. Lay on a bit of the old Paretski charm, whatever."

"You want me to flirt with a pensioner. A female pensioner. *Not* what I envisaged doing on my honeymoon, just so's you know. But . . . are you sure about this? From what Dave said, Cassie could be a ruthless murderer. Murderess. Whatever. And, well, not to put too fine a point on it, you're not exactly on top form right now."

Phil didn't quite roll his eyes, but it was obviously a close-run thing. "I'm fine. And forewarned, forearmed, remember? If you think I *need* an advantage when going up against a little old lady with health issues."

"Oi, overconfidence is what leads to a fall, you know."

"No, allowing yourself to be manoeuvred close to high balconies is what leads to a fall. I'll be careful. Cross my heart."

"Do not complete that phrase." I glared at him. He gave me half a smile, and a gentle shove in the direction of the pool. Not without misgivings, I went.

Jane looked horrified when I approached her, which I chose to interpret as concern for my slightly battered state rather than a fervent desire to avoid my company.

"All right there?" I said cheerily, pulling up a chair beside her. "Had a good day?"

"Better than you have, from the sight of you." She sent a steely glance over to where Phil was loitering with intent, and her eyes narrowed. "I hope you and that husband of yours haven't been fighting. Never stay with a man who raises a hand to you. He won't change, you can guarantee it."

I was taken aback by her vehemence. "What, me and Phil? Never. No, we, uh, we got mugged last night." It was quicker than saying *We were kidnapped at gunpoint and forced to desecrate a priceless archaeological site.* And less likely to lead to questions, which I for one had had a belly full of from the *polizia* last night.

She pressed her narrow lips into a thin line for a moment. "I can't say I agree with the way things are nowadays. But people like that are the lowest of the low."

"Muggers?"

"*Gay-bashers*, I believe the term is." Her lip curled in distaste. "They should bring back corporal punishment, in my view."

Huh. Who'd have thought Jane would be so down on homophobes? I found myself warming to her, suspected serial-killing sisterhood notwithstanding. "Oh, nah, seriously. That had nothing to do with it. Just ordinary criminals."

"I trust you reported them to the police."

I nodded. "Oh yes. At length. Listen—daft question, probably—but do you know if Cassie ever met Wayne before he came here?"

"Why on earth would she have?" Jane snapped, her colour heightened. "I don't know why you'd ask such a question."

Oops. And we'd been getting on so chummily. "Well, you know we're kind of looking into his death—"

"I understood his death was an accident." Jane's tone could have been used to cool down a bathtub full of Spritzes. "Certainly, the police don't appear to have taken an interest. I had hoped you'd put an end to stirring up all this unpleasantness. This whole thing has been trying enough."

Yeah, I was sure old Wayne kicking the bucket had completely ruined her hols. "Uh, yeah, not what you want to happen."

"It isn't fair to his young lady, either," she went on. "Of course, for all I know she's cut from the same cloth he was, but one has to be charitable and give her the benefit of the doubt. Stop trying to humour her grief-stricken fantasies and let her mourn him—misguided though she may be—in peace." Jane fixed me with a dagger glare. "Those who upset apple carts are rarely popular."

That told me. But hang about, what did she mean by *cut from the same cloth*?

I was about to ask when I was interrupted by the loud arrival of Cassie and Phil. Or rather, she was loud; he was just hovering, looking frustrated. "Have you seen what's happened to young Phil?" Cassie barked. "I've been telling him he needs to contact his travel insurers and make a claim. Personal injury, emotional distress—not to mention, their honeymoon photos will be ruined."

Me and young Phil exchanged a glance. "Nah, gives 'em character," I said fondly, gazing at that beloved, battered face.

"You must sit down at once," Cassie commanded, chivvying my Phil onto a lounger like a mother hen with a baby eagle for a foster child. "Do you need anything? A drink? Some pain pills?"

I winced, as Phil said a curt, "I'm fine."

I hastened to change the subject. "We were talking to Siri earlier, and she's planning to head home soon."

Cassie nodded, settling herself down in her chair. "Good thing too. She needs to move on with her life."

That was a bit callous, since as far as I knew Wayne hadn't even been laid to rest yet. Still, she wasn't wrong in principle. "Yeah. And she'll have her mum at home. Did you know Martin's flown back already?"

"I hope *that* has nothing to do with her decision. Still, if her mother has any sense, she'll keep the girl out of his clutches."

There was the faintest suspicion of a sniff from Jane. Since Cassie had given me a good lead in, I ignored it. "Siri said you warned her off Martin. What made you do that?"

Cassie laughed. "It was nothing personal. Actually, sod that. He's a con man and a liar—I could tell his type a mile off. Particularly when I found out he's a member of *that* profession."

"Meaning?" Phil put in.

"Oh, didn't you know? He's one of those dreadful people who smarm their way up to you and try to get you to buy a property in some tourist trap."

Ah. *That* profession. I could feel Phil relaxing beside me at the news she hadn't seen through Martin any better than he had. "So what have you got against people selling you a place in the sun? Got done by a dodgy timeshare dealer, did you?"

Cassie snorted. "Not me. Can't see the point of owning a flat abroad. Give me a hotel any day—I don't go on holiday to do my own cooking. And you wouldn't catch me letting anyone browbeat me into signing a contract."

That sounded suspiciously specific. "But you know someone who did?"

"Jane did—back when her husband was still alive. Of course, he always was a wet blanket. About as useful as a chocolate teapot at standing up for himself." She turned to her sister and raised her voice. "Jane, tell Tom about you and Ralph getting ripped off."

Jane's cheeks, already flushed, went pinker still, and she fanned herself with her *Daily Mail.* "I hardly think it's appropriate to be airing family laundry in public."

"Oh, nonsense. Tom's a chum."

I suffered a pang of guilt at her putting it that way, but I nodded anyway. "You can trust me. And Phil, obviously," I added belatedly.

Cassie rolled her eyes. "Oh, we know *that.* Straight as a die, your Phil. You can tell by looking at him." She made sure to prove the point by giving him a thorough going-over.

He coloured faintly. "Thanks for the vote of confidence. So, Jane . . . ?"

"I'm sure you don't really want to hear my tale of woe."

I nodded sincerely. "Yes, we do. Problem shared is a problem halved."

"I hardly think in this case—"

"Oh, get on with it, Jane," Cassie said impatiently. "If you don't tell them, I will. And then you'll complain I got all the details wrong."

"If I must . . ." Jane folded her newspaper with quick, neat movements. Then she took a deep breath and let it out slowly. "I suppose you'll say we were naïve, but it seemed such a good deal. Too good to turn down."

Too good to be true, I thought, but didn't say it. "Go on."

"It was a few years ago now, of course. This company—FarAway they called themselves—were offering a free weekend in Stratford-Upon-Avon, all for spending an hour listening to a presentation. And I'd never been to Stratford, and with the Shakespeare connection . . . I've always been a fan of the Bard, you know."

"So you went to Stratford?" Phil prompted, before she could go off on a tangent of Productions I Have Seen and Loved. "What happened then?"

"The hotel they put us up in was perfectly adequate. Not luxury, you understand, rather a corporate one, where they have conferences and so on. We'd had breakfast the first morning, and we were wondering what to do first, when a young person from FarAway came to meet us." Her mouth turned down. "She said she'd come to take us to the presentation. Naturally we'd assumed it would be in the hotel, but she said she was going to drive us there."

"Did she take you far?" Phil asked.

"*Much* farther than we were expecting. She kept telling us it was only down the road, but we were in that car for a good twenty minutes. She chatted away at us all the time, saying how wonderful the holiday flats were. Finally, she let us out at an office building in another town—quite a pretty little place, but not at all where we'd been planning to spend the day." She pursed her lips. "We were ushered into a meeting room overlooking the high street, and a man was there with a stack of glossy brochures."

"So it was just you and your husband with this bloke and the woman who drove you?" I asked.

"Yes. I'd imagined there would be a room full of potential customers. That's what you expect when someone talks about a presentation, isn't it? We weren't quite prepared to have all the attention on us."

"Yeah, I guess that meant no chance of dozing off in the back row while you waited for it to finish." Which would generally be my way of dealing with an unwanted presentation.

"We would not have *dozed off*. We were not in our dotage, and nor were we possessed of such appallingly bad manners. I simply meant that it exposed us to their hard-selling techniques. Of which there were plenty. They kept us there *seven hours*, with nothing more than a cup of weak tea and a biscuit." She pressed her lips together. "I know what you're thinking, young man. Why didn't we simply walk out?"

Yep, she had me bang to rights there. "Well, I s'pose it's—"

She didn't bother waiting for me to finish. "I asked myself that many times, afterwards. But at the time . . . They wouldn't stop *talking*, and it seemed so rude to cut them off midflow."

Clearly she'd got over *that* little social barrier in the meantime. "And they kept pressuring you into signing up?"

She nodded. "In the end, we were both quite worn down. It seemed easier to give in. Ralph was getting worried because he hadn't had his angina medicine that morning. He didn't like to take pills on an empty stomach, so he'd been planning to have them when we got back to the room. It was all getting to be a terrible strain on him.

And, of course, we were dependent on these people to get back to the hotel. We didn't even know where we were, not properly."

"It must have been quite an ordeal." Phil's tone was sympathetic.

"You can't imagine it! I was in a dreadful state by the time we left—left to make our own way back to Stratford, I might add. We both just wanted to get back to the hotel and forget about it all. It was far too late to go anywhere or do anything, and the whole day had been wasted. But we thought that was the end of it."

I grimaced. "But you'd signed up to this property scheme? If you don't mind me asking, how much did they sting you for?"

She named a figure that had me whistling. "But at least—or so we thought—we'd be getting something for our money. And yes, it had all been a dreadful experience, but we thought, well, we'll keep the property for a few years, have a few holidays there, and then sell it on." She paused. "The young man had been so very optimistic about the property market rising."

"But that didn't happen?" Phil asked.

She sniffed. "Property market! There never *was* a property."

I stared at her. "What, it was a total con? They were selling you stuff they not only didn't own, but that didn't even exist?"

"Oh, they were cleverer than that. It was all in the small print of the contract—we were buying on plans, which was *not* made clear to us at the time, and timescales for completion would be subject to change for practically any reason those swindlers might care to come up with. Later—much later—we found out they hadn't so much as got planning permission, and never would."

Gits. "So did you take them to court? Get Trading Standards involved?"

"We took legal advice. And the advice was that there was little we could do. By that time, the company had ceased trading, although the people concerned simply set straight back up again under another name. Why that's allowed I have no idea." Her lips formed that tight, unhappy line once more. "I've no doubt the stress of it all hastened poor Ralph's passing. Worse than animals, these people are. Simply vermin."

There was a tight knot in my chest. Didn't these bastards know the harm they were causing, all in the name of greed? Or did they just not care?

Phil leaned forward and said gently, "It was Wayne, wasn't it? He was the one who defrauded you and your husband."

I'd guessed it was coming, but it still hit me like a punch in the gut to hear it out loud.

Jane glared at Phil, and for a moment it seemed like she wasn't going to answer—but then all her resentment broke from her in a rush. "And then he had the absolute *nerve* to try to swindle me all over again! Struck up a conversation in the bar with the express purpose of making money. It was quite clear he didn't recognise me as someone he'd already fleeced. As though my husband and I meant *nothing* to him—we were simply another two faceless victims of his greed."

"Jane?" Cassie said sharply. "Is that true? Why didn't you tell me? I'd have shoved the little perisher off the balcony myself."

"Don't be ridiculous," Jane snapped, then clammed up tighter than a thingy's whatsit, looking way more than ten years older than her sister.

Suddenly I wasn't sure I wanted this to go on. Didn't want to be part of pushing an old lady to incriminate herself in the murder of the git who'd hurt her—who'd probably hurt hundreds of other people too. Who'd still been making greedy, selfish plans until the day he died.

But killing him had hurt Siri. Not to mention Wayne's family. And even Phil, on some level. Didn't that count for something too?

"You gave Siri some pills to give to Wayne, didn't you?" Phil asked. "What did you give him?"

"Painkillers," Jane said shortly.

"So if Cassie checked her medications, she wouldn't find she was missing, say, a couple of beta blockers?"

Cassie barked an uncomfortable laugh. "Oh, I'm terrible at remembering my pills. Forget to take them, take them twice . . . Ask anyone."

Jane gave her an oddly gentle frown. "I think you've had enough time in the sun, dear. Why don't you go and lie down? I'll be along soon."

"Bugger that. I'm staying with you."

"No." There was the firmness of the schoolroom in that tone. "Go back to the room, Cassandra. I mean it."

For a moment, I could see the little girl in Cassie, the one who'd looked up to her big sister—had maybe been brought up by her, even. I had the weirdest urge to hug her—but she drew in a deep, ragged breath and stood. "Half an hour, Jane. Then I'm coming back for you."

Phil didn't beat around the bush once Cassie had gone. "How did you get Wayne to go over by the railings?"

Jane's expression didn't alter. "I don't know what you mean. I didn't make him go anywhere."

"Let's assume, hypothetically, that you wanted to. How might you have done it?" There was something hypnotic about Phil's even tones.

Jane took a sip from the glass by her side. I'd assumed it was fizzy water, but I caught an unmistakeable whiff of gin. Her hands didn't tremble, and her gaze didn't waver. "Then I suppose, *hypothetically* . . . there are *some* advantages to being written off as a little old lady. People underestimate one terribly, and they don't like to be rude—not in public, at any rate. So if, say, I had taken his arm and asked him to accompany me over to the balcony to watch the fireworks, as silly me, I was terribly afraid of heights . . . well, it wouldn't be surprising if he simply came."

Phil nodded. "And once you were there?"

"Perhaps I might have drawn his attention to something below. And the elderly can be so unsteady on their feet, can't they? Prone to stumbling. And if one stumbled in the right way, it would be quite easy to push a companion off-balance. Or so I imagine."

"And then—" I broke off. "Did Cassie know what you were doing? With the pills and . . . later? Was it her idea, even?"

Her face paled. "My sister is *not* to blame in any of this, and I'll thank you not to insinuate such things." She picked up her drink but had to steady her glass with both hands before taking a gulp.

It was painful to watch. I felt like I should apologise for suspecting her little sis, but the words caught in my throat.

Jane rested her glass on her lap and stared at it for a moment. "I'm going to join her now. I wouldn't want her to worry. And you will *not* be bothering her with your baseless suggestions in the future." She stood, clutching her drink like a shield in front of her.

We let her go. There wasn't much of an alternative, was there? Not without causing a scene and/or assaulting the elderly.

I sighed. "That . . . was almost a confession, wasn't it? What are we going to do about it?"

Phil looked away and didn't answer.

I tried again. "Do you think Wayne really didn't recognise Jane?"

"What, a few years on, out of context, and without her husband?" Phil's face was grim. "Should think one mug looked a lot like another to him."

Ouch. It had to hurt, even if Wayne was only an ex–best friend, to plumb the full depths of his character like that. "But wouldn't her name ring a bell?"

"Plenty of Janes around. I don't remember anyone using surnames after that first introduction. And Wayne wasn't with us for that."

"But she recognised him."

"I should think he made quite an impression on her. Must have been a big shock to run into him here."

"She hid that well." I gave a twisted smile. "I s'pose when you go around acting pissed off with everyone all the time, it's easier to hide when you're *actually* pissed off with someone."

"Not that we ever saw them together," Phil said.

I frowned. "Didn't we? Huh. But Siri must have, mustn't she?" I sighed. "Seriously, what are we going to do? Do you think we ought to tell the police we reckon Jane dunnit? And Siri?"

Phil frowned. "An autopsy might show if Wayne was drugged. It'd depend how soon whatever she gave him was metabolised. But she could still claim it was a mistake."

I nodded. "Just her having a senior moment. Cassie would back her up, no question. And without any witnesses . . ."

"If anyone had seen anything, it would have come out by now. We'd only be stirring up a can of worms. All to get an elderly widow shoved in jail for having her revenge on the man who robbed her and harassed her husband into an early grave."

I screwed up my face. "But . . . what about people not taking the law into their own hands?"

Phil's face darkened. "I don't know, all right? All I know is, if it'd been us, if I'd lost you because of one of Wayne's stupid schemes . . . I don't know if I could have stopped myself from making him pay."

"No." I cleared my throat. "No, I'm not sure I'd have been any different."

"Anyhow," Phil went on briskly. "The chance a jury would convict her is slim to none. If we start throwing accusations around . . ." He huffed. "I doubt the police would take them seriously in any case."

"I'm not saying you're wrong, but if she did kill Wayne, don't we have, you know, an obligation? Like, morally?"

"Morally? To the man who nearly got you killed?"

"To be fair, he didn't do that on purpose . . ."

"No. He simply did what he wanted without caring what the consequences would be for anyone else." His tone was harsh and unforgiving. "Just like when we were kids."

I opened my mouth and then closed it again. When had I become Wayne's advocate? "At least you've got better taste in mates now," I said weakly.

Phil cupped my face with his hand. "Thank God for that."

I really, *really* hated to ruin the moment, but . . . "What if she kills again?"

Phil let his hand drop, and I regretted my words already. "I don't know," he said, his shoulders slumping. "I don't know."

Chapter Forty

We didn't see either of the sisters at dinner that night, by which time we still hadn't decided what to do.

Next morning, when we went to breakfast, Cassie was at the reception desk talking to the manager, her voice uncharacteristically quiet. As we drew near, he nodded and disappeared through the side door to the office. Cassie turned, and her face hardened at the sight of us. "You should probably know, Jane passed in the night."

I gaped and barely stopped myself from blurting out, *Are you sure?* Cassie wasn't the sort to make a mistake about something like that.

"What happened?" Phil asked gently.

"Heart attack, I think." Cassie had lost her bounce, and her unsmiling face seemed older. Even her curls were flat. "It's not totally unexpected. She would go on and on at me about my health, but the fact is that heart problems run in the family. *Ran*, I suppose I should say. Now there's only me left, as neither of us managed to pop out any sprogs."

"I'm so sorry," I managed. "You must be devastated. You and her being so close. Her always looking out for you."

It seemed to help. "She did, you know. All her life. Oh, she'd scold me terribly for whatever I'd done, but she always did what she could to protect me from the consequences." Cassie huffed a quiet laugh. "I always wondered about her and Brian. She never did like him, which showed far better judgement of character than she had in some other instances, and after he . . . Well, that's all husbands over the cliff, now, isn't it? And then there's Ralph, of course, although it was honestly a mercy when he went so suddenly in the end."

Did she mean . . . A chill ran through my veins. But what would be the point of asking Cassie if she really meant her late and clearly lamented sister was secretly a multiple murderess?

"I'll be taking her back to England as soon as we can arrange it," Cassie went on. "We've got a family burial plot in the village where we grew up. Lovely place, around fifty years behind the times. She'll like that."

"Uh, right. Yeah." What else was there to say?

Phil coughed. "Let us know if there's anything we can do to help."

Oh. Right. That. "Yeah, anything we can do," I echoed hastily.

"Oh, I think you've done enough, don't you?" She fixed us with a shrewd gaze, and guilt squirmed in my stomach. Then she seemed to soften again. "It's not like I've never buried anyone before. Don't worry about the dead—they're well past worrying about you."

With that, she was off, her plump figure trotting off with determination, if maybe a tad more heavily than yesterday.

Me and Phil shared a long look. "Breakfast?" I said at last.

He nodded, and we headed into the dining room.

"Are you thinking what I'm thinking?" I asked as soon as we were out of earshot of the front desk.

"Depends on what you're thinking."

"That it's a tiny bit of a coincidence, Jane's number coming up the very night after she sort of confessed to killing Wayne?"

Phil wasn't smiling. "Not sure any good's going to come of asking questions about it."

"No. Guess not." I frowned. "Unless . . . you don't think Cassie might have, uh, given her sister a helping hand off this mortal coil?"

Phil pursed his lips for a long moment. "No. And if she did, it'll have been because Jane wanted her to."

"So . . . sleeping dogs, don't kick?"

He nodded.

I sighed, and then the waiter was there with coffee, and my stomach reminded me there was a buffet full of food over there that wasn't going to eat itself.

Siri must have been tucked away in a corner having breakfast at the same time as we were, as she caught up with us on the way out.

"Tom, Phil?" She was all businesslike in a dark linen frock. "I wanted to say goodbye. I'm going home today. And, like, thanks for looking into Wayne's death for me? Even though it turned out it was just . . . anyway, you done work on it and all, so you send me a bill, all right?"

"Course," Phil assured her.

Siri beamed sadly and gave us each a hug. "Sorry about taking over your honeymoon for nothing," she murmured into my shell-like.

"No problem. You take care now, okay? Watch out for older blokes in stripy shirts," I added to lighten the tone.

She sniffed, nodded, and left.

"You gonna bill her?" I muttered as we watched her walk away.

"Nope."

"Good."

After all that . . . well, what is there to say? We went on with the honeymoon, of course, but there's no denying recent events had put a bit of a dampener on the mood. Still, we'd have a lifetime of holidays together to make up for it. And it wasn't all doom and gloom, by any means. I let Phil drag me round the museum in Naples, and he consented to a slow boat trip round the Amalfi Coast so I could spend four hours lounging in a deck chair in the sun. My tan got darker. Phil's blond hair got lighter.

Cassie took her sister's body home for burial. I flicked through the photos in my camera that evening before bed, and paused on one taken in the garden on Capri. It showed the two of them, Jane's faded English rose complexion set off by the vivid pink of the bargain-whatsits. "Do you really think she killed three people?" I asked the room in general.

Phil stuck his head out the bathroom, a speck of toothpaste on his cheek. "What?"

I shook my head and gave him a smile. "Never mind. Talking to myself."

He raised an eyebrow. "Sign of madness."

I raised a finger. "Only way round here I won't get insulted by my conversational partner. You coming to bed?"

He grinned. "Try and stop me."

Just to be contrary, I did.

Fun times.

Chapter Forty-One

It always takes longer to get through an airport than you expect. It was getting late by the time we emerged, blinking, into the last throes of Luton daylight, and there was a chill wind in the air. I glanced up at the good old British clouds that more-or-less covered the sky.

Home.

Beside me, Phil huffed a laugh. "What are you smirking about?"

"Oi, I don't smirk. That's your department."

"And in other news, the Pope's a Buddhist and bears use specially built banks of Portaloos."

"They do at Pride." All right, I *did* actually smirk at that point. "I'm glad to be back home, that's all. Think the cats will be there to greet us when we get back to St. Albans?"

As it happened, the cats *were* there, but not to greet us. Merlin took one glance at us coming in the front door and bolted to parts unknown. Arthur, comfortably ensconced on the sofa, didn't walk out when he saw us—but he turned round huffily to present us with a view of his furry behind.

"Told you they'd miss us," I said cheerily.

Life settled back into its usual patterns, as it does.

I soon found out what Gary's cryptic texts had been all about: Julian, Gary's faithful St. Bernard, now had his very own mini-me, Clary, a four-month-old neutered bitch. Yeah, that's right—the tiny footsteps Gary had been so excited about turned out to be those of their new puppy. Apparently Julian, far from resenting the younger model, worshipped the ground she pitter-pattered on.

"Disappointed Gary and Darren aren't sprogging up?" Phil asked me when we found out, clearly making an effort to sound like he was joking.

"Don't be daft." Anyway, who knew how long it'd be before me and Phil ended up as parents? I still wouldn't put it past Gary and Darren somehow stealing a march on us in that. All it would take would be Gary getting an idea into his head and hopping on a plane to somewhere in the world where babies came with a lot less red tape than in dear old Britain. Or, as might be, Darren turning up with another possible consequence of his years doing straight porn, and one of an age to need a bit more parenting than his maybe-daughter Lorelei.

Me and Phil got back to work, and our mixed bag of a honeymoon lived on only in memories, the occasional nightmare, and a shedload of holiday snaps. Until, that was, the visit we got around the start of September.

It was a warm, if overcast, day and we were lazing around at home after a rare Sunday lunch for just the two of us, when there was a knock on the door. I ambled over to open it, and found myself gazing in surprise at Siri.

She was looking a bit soft around the edges—not fat or anything like it, but a little like she might have been finding her comfort in food since getting back from Italy. Mind you, most of her was hidden by the oversized T-shirt she was wearing over her leggings, which didn't seem very *her*, somehow.

Maybe she only dressed to impress when she was with a bloke?

"Hello, love," I said, trying not to act quite as gobsmacked as I actually was. "Fancy seeing you here. Come on in and put your feet up. Cup of tea?"

She smiled and padded inside in her pastel-pink trainers. "Just a glass of water, ta."

I showed her into the living room first. "Phil? Guess who's here?"

Merlin stopped batting his ping-pong ball under the furniture, and even Arthur pricked up his ears from his position on Phil's lap.

Siri broke into a smile. "Aw, you've got kitties! They're so sweet." She crouched down and put out a hand for Merlin to sniff.

Being a contrary animal, i.e. a cat, he bolted out of the room, but she didn't seem too bothered as she stood up again, one hand on the arm of the sofa to help her rise. "She's so funny."

"He. Or, well, it. You know." I made a snip-snip gesture.

Siri giggled. "Aw, poor love!"

"Come and sit down." Phil patted the seat next to him, as though she was a cat herself.

Siri proved her lack of felinity—if that's a word—by doing as she was bid. I nipped out to the kitchen to get that glass of water, and when I came back, found her stroking Arthur, who true to form hadn't been arsed to get out of Phil's lap.

I handed her drink over. "Here you go, love. Now, what can we do you for?"

Siri took a careful sip of water and put her glass down on the coffee table. She paused, bit her lip—and then burst out with, "I'm pregnant!"

Me and Phil exchanged startled glances.

"Uh . . . Congratulations?" She didn't look like she was exactly jumping for joy over it. "So, um, is this a new bloke you've got, or . . .?"

She patted her tummy. "It's Wayne's."

Well, bugger. Poor kid, having those genes to live down.

"When did you find out?" Phil asked.

"It was a while after I got back home. I thought it was just stress at first, what with everything that'd happened, but then Mum made me go and buy a test."

"And you're certain?" I couldn't help asking.

She nodded solemnly. "Did two more tests after that. Bit of a shock, I can tell you."

"So you're what—three months gone?"

"Four. I've had a scan and everything. It's due seventeenth March next year."

"That's . . . wow. Going to be a big change in your life." Tom Paretski: stating the obvious like a champ.

Siri's lip quivered. "I don't even know what to do with a baby."

"You'll be fine," I said reassuringly. "You'll make a great mum. And you've got your mum to help, haven't you?"

"Mum went right off on one when she found out. She says she's too young to be a granny at forty-five. She says having a kid takes over *everything*, and she's only just got her life back after having me." Siri gazed down at her hands, which were making invisible origami in her lap. "I've made an appointment to get rid of it. Mum said she'd go with me."

Something twisted inside me.

Phil said gently, "But you're not sure it's the right decision?"

Siri made a loud noise, a cross between a sob and a sniff. "It's . . . It's the last bit of Wayne, innit? Once it's gone, that's it."

Personally, my lunch wasn't sitting too easy at the thought of having a bit of Wayne inside me, but obviously she felt differently. And it wasn't the kid's fault who its dad was. "You shouldn't let your mum make the decision for you. If you want to keep it, I'm sure you can manage."

"But what if I'm a rubbish mum? And . . . I don't want to be, like, this is my life? With a kid and no bloke. I'm too young. There's all this stuff I want to do. And I don't want to do it on my own, like, single, you know? I'm not strong like that."

"You could be," Phil said gently.

She looked him right in the eye. "That's just something people say. It doesn't mean anything."

I couldn't help thinking she had him bang to rights there. All the platitudes in the world weren't going to help when it came to changing nappies and bringing the kid up right. But why was she even here talking about it if she'd made up her mind to have an abortion? If she wanted to be talked into it, I didn't reckon I could do that. Not when I thought she might spend the rest of her life regretting it.

"Have you considered adoption?" I asked cautiously.

Siri jumped up and hugged my unprepared self. "Oh, that's so sweet of you, Tom! I know you'd be great with kids, and Wayne would be so pleased, what with you being mates of his."

Uh, what?

And once more with feeling, *what*?

Did she actually mean . . . Any thought of argument died on my lips. I couldn't meet Phil's eyes. I'd promised him *sooner*, hadn't I? How could I justify looking a gift kid in the mouth just 'cos *sooner* turned out to be less than six months from now, rather than a couple of years down the road?

I'd have to be ready for it, that was all. Even if I wasn't. I swallowed.

Phil cleared his throat. "Siri, what are you saying?"

"I'm saying it's so kind of Tom to offer—"

I managed not to blurt out, *I didn't!*

"—and it's kind of made me see straight, you know? Made me see there's other people what care about this kid apart from me. 'Cos you cared about his dad, right?"

"Oi, we care about its mum too," I said awkwardly.

"That's so sweet of you. So I've made up my mind."

She paused, and I braced myself to look delighted.

"I'm going to keep him."

"That's— What?"

"I'm sorry, Tom. I know you and Phil want a family. But I'm his mum, and I reckon that's important. But it means everything that you and Phil would've taken him in, and I know you'll want to be involved. It means a lot, it really does."

"Don't mention it. And, uh, no worries."

"I'd better be off now. Think I'll go and see Wayne's dad—he still lives round here. I haven't seen him since the funeral, and I want to tell him he's going to have a grandson."

We'd missed the funeral, having still been in Italy when Wayne had gone to his eternal rest. He'd been cremated, which had also put to rest any lingering ideas of finding out if he really had been doped up when he'd died.

"It's a boy, then?" Phil asked mildly.

"Yeah. They said at the scan. They weren't going to, but I kept asking."

And who did that if they were seriously thinking about an abortion? I was beginning to think Siri had made up her mind long before she'd come to see us.

We waved her off, and then trooped back to the living room. Phil smirked at me. "Wish I'd had a camera to record your face when you thought she was going to hand us her baby."

"Oi, you know I want kids. It was just a bit sudden, that's all."

He huffed a laugh. "Just a bit."

"So . . . you're not, well, upset we're not getting Wayne's kid?"

"Believe it or not, even I wasn't planning on *that* soon." He paused. "It wouldn't have happened, anyhow. There's laws against private adoption in this country."

"Huh. I didn't know that. Me and Siri both, I'm guessing." I put my arm around him. "So, back to plan A, then? Start looking into how many official hoops we have to jump through to get approved for adoption?"

"Sounds good to me."

"Me too." And you know what?

It really did.

Explore more of The Plumber's Mate Mysteries: riptidepublishing.com/collections/plumbers-mate-mysteries

Dear Reader,

Thank you for reading JL Merrow's *Stop Cock*!

We know your time is precious and you have many, many entertainment options, so it means a lot that you've chosen to spend your time reading. We really hope you enjoyed it.

We'd be honored if you'd consider posting a review—good or bad—on sites like **Amazon, Barnes & Noble, Kobo, Goodreads, Twitter, Facebook, Tumblr,** and your blog or website. We'd also be honored if you told your friends and family about this book. Word of mouth is a book's lifeblood!

For more information on upcoming releases, author interviews, blog tours, contests, giveaways, and more, please sign up for our weekly, spam-free newsletter and visit us around the web:

Newsletter: riptidepublishing.com/newsletter
Twitter: twitter.com/RiptideBooks
Facebook: facebook.com/RiptidePublishing
Goodreads: tinyurl.com/RiptideOnGoodreads
Tumblr: riptidepublishing.tumblr.com

Thank you so much for Reading the Rainbow!

RiptidePublishing.com

ACKNOWLEDGEMENTS

With thanks to Larissa, Elin Gregory, and Kristin Matherly.

Also By
JL Merrow

The Plumber's Mate Mysteries
Pressure Head
Relief Valve
Heat Trap
Blow Down
Lock Nut

Porthkennack
Wake Up Call
One Under
Love at First Hate

The Shamwell Tales
Caught!
Played!
Out!
Spun!

The Midwinter Manor Series
Poacher's Fall
Keeper's Pledge

Southampton Stories
Pricks and Pragmatism
Hard Tail

Counter Culture
Lovers Leap
It's All Geek to Me
Damned If You Do
Alpaca My Bags
Camwolf
Muscling Through
Wight Mischief
Midnight in Berlin
Slam!
Fall Hard
Raising the Rent
To Love a Traitor
Trick of Time
Snared
A Flirty Dozen

About THE AUTHOR

JL Merrow is that rare beast, an English person who refuses to drink tea. She read Natural Sciences at Cambridge, where she learned many things, chief amongst which was that she never wanted to see the inside of a lab ever again. Her one regret is that she never mastered the ability of punting one-handed whilst holding a glass of champagne.

She writes across genres, with a preference for contemporary gay romance and mysteries, and is frequently accused of humour. Her novel *Slam!* Won the 2013 Rainbow Award for Best LGBT Romantic Comedy, and her novella *Muscling Through* and novel *Relief Valve* were both EPIC Awards finalists.

JL Merrow is a member of the Romantic Novelists' Association, Crime Writers Association, International Thriller Writers, Verulam Writers and the UK GLBTQ Fiction Meet organising team.

Find JL Merrow on Twitter as @jlmerrow, and on Facebook at facebook.com/jl.merrow

For a full list of books available, see: jlmerrow.com or JL Merrow's Amazon author page: viewauthor.at/JLMerrow

Enjoy more stories like

Stop Cock

at RiptidePublishing.com!

The Best Corpse for the Job

Tea and sympathy have never been so deadly.

ISBN: 978-1-62649-192-2

Marry Him

It was meant to be a one-night stand, not "I do."

ISBN: 978-1-62649-935-5

www.ingramcontent.com/pod-product-compliance
Lightning Source LLC
LaVergne TN
LVHW091107080826
845145LV00008B/1839